also by judy budnitz

flying leap

if i told you once

nice big american baby

nice big american baby

stories

judy budnitz

  alfred a. knopf · new york · 2005

This Is a Borzoi Book Published by Alfred A. Knopf

Copyright © 2005 by Judy Budnitz

All rights reserved under International and Pan-American Copyright Conventions.
Published in the United States by Alfred A. Knopf, a division of Random
House, Inc., New York, and simultaneously in Canada by Random House
of Canada Limited, Toronto. Distributed by Random House, Inc., New York.

www.aaknopf.com

Knopf, Borzoi Books, and the colophon are registered trademarks of Random House, Inc.

Some of the stories in this collection were previously published in the following:
  "Visitors" in *The Black Warrior Review*
  "Motherland" in *The Cincinnati Review*
  "Sales" in *McSweeney's*
  "Miracle" in *The New Yorker*
  "Nadia" in *One Story*
  "The Kindest Cut" in *The Oxford American*
  "Flush" in *McSweeney's* and *Prize Stories 2000: The O'Henry Awards* (Anchor Books, New York)

Library of Congress Cataloging-in-Publication Data
Budnitz, Judy.
Nice big American baby / Judy Budnitz.—1st ed.
p.   cm.
ISBN 0-375-41242-5 (alk. paper)
I. Title.
PS3552.U3479N53 2005
813'.54—dc22   200404857

Manufactured in the United States of America
First Edition

for amanda davis

contents

nice big american baby

I. before

There was a woman who had seven sons and was happy. Then she had a daughter.

She loved her sons with a furious devotion. But she did not want the daughter, even before she knew it was a daughter. She could feel the baby sitting low in her belly and did not want it.

Another burden on my back, the woman thought, another mouth to feed.

From the moment the girl was born she was frail and sickly; she greeted the world with a sneeze. The mother heard the sneeze and felt a heaviness descend upon her heart. Even with the best coddling and foreign medicine, the girl would probably die within the month. Three years at the most. A waste. It would be better, she thought, if the girl died now and got it over with. There were many ways a baby could die. Infant death was common in that part of the world; no one would notice one baby more or less.

Then she looked at the tiny wrinkled face and felt ashamed. She resolved to love her daughter as she did her sons.

She named the girl Precious, to remind herself.

She made a promise to her daughter, but her seven sons were a delight and a distraction and if she did not break that promise she did bend it to its limits, like a young tree in a windstorm. Precious learned to make no demands on her mother. She took the food from the bottom of the bowl at meals and kept her feet clean so she would not leave footprints behind her.

The woman was happy. Her sons grew tall. People told her how lucky she was: eight children, all of them still living.

But I have seven children, she would say. And then: Oh. Yes.

One year the rains came doubly hard, the roads became rivers of mud, and the fruit rotted on the vine. The next year the rains did not come at all. Surely, people said, the third year will be a good year. But they were wrong.

It had never happened before—two years without rain. Even those people who considered themselves modern began to pray again and to hang charms at their doors.

The underground stream that fed the electric pump in the village dried up. The woman's sons went searching for water. They were tall and thin and knew how to travel in the heat of day. They ran and rested, ran and rested. Each time they paused they arranged themselves in a descending line so that all but the oldest could rest in a brother's shadow.

They had taken buckets and jars to carry water back to their mother. And to Precious. Precious: always remembered, but always as an afterthought.

They found a wire fence. The top of the fence was lined with prickly wire like a thornbush. They tore their hands on it, climbing over. Far in the distance they could see a dark smudge bleeding into the sky. They ran closer. It was the largest building they had ever seen, massive and gray and faceless, with three tall chimneys like fingers pointing to the sky. The black smoke that poured from them was like nothing they had ever seen before. It hung in the sky without dissipating, it was dense and heavy, like rain clouds about to burst.

The oldest said it was a rain factory. He said he remembered hearing people talk about it. He was sure.

Yes, said another, I heard that too. It's true.

Beyond the building they saw a pool, almost a lake. It was perfectly shaped and perfectly still, and the water was the strangest color they had ever seen—bright, bright blue and iridescent, with pearly rainbows on its surface. They agreed that the color must mean it was very pure.

The first one to taste the water became very sick. His brothers watched him twisting and retching, his arms folded in on themselves like wings. A thick white gravy came out of his mouth and nose. They heard a roaring in the stillness and looked up to see two trucks speeding toward them trailing clouds of dust. They lifted their brother and ran.

They knew their brother could not climb the fence, so they hid among the rocks where they knew the trucks could not follow, and they waited for dark. They dug beneath the fence with their hands. It took them most of the night. They knotted their shirts into a sling and headed home, carrying their brother between them.

The woman was waiting on her doorstep for her sons to return. In the red light of dawn she saw their silhouettes approaching. She counted only six bobbing heads and began to keen in her throat.

Her son did not die. Eventually his hands uncoiled and he was able to walk again. But he was not the same as he was before. His face had hardened into a new expression that made him look like a suspicious stranger.

She knew that was not the end of it. The poisoned water was the beginning, a portent of what was to come. She was not surprised when, soon after, her sons began to disappear one by one.

The rains still did not fall. Everyone was hungry. The earth was cracked and barren. There was no work to be done, and anger and discontent began to ferment in the hearts of the people. Some complained against the government, though many had never seen the slightest evidence of any government and did not believe it existed. There was talk of electing leaders, building an army, an army for the people. The woman listened but did not understand how an army could bring the rains.

The woman's eldest son came to her and said he was going to become a soldier.

But you're just a child, she said.

The army has a whole division just for children, he said. I'm already too old for it. I will have to join the men.

She saw his thin chest surge with pride as he said this, and her heart ached.

So he left and she knew she would not see him again. Soon another son left to join his brother. It was the one who had drunk the tainted water; he waved as he walked up the dusty road and she could see he was trying to smile for her, but his facial muscles were frozen in a sneer.

One of the younger boys announced that he was going to join the children's army. She forbade it. He ran away in the night.

She heard rumors of fighting, the people's army fighting the government's, factions of the people's army fighting each other. There was an outbreak of fever in the village and many people died, including her youngest son.

So she had three sons left. Then two more went off to fight. They went together; that, at least, was a comfort.

Don't become a soldier, she told her last remaining son.

I don't want to, he said, but they will force me to if I stay.

She knew. She had seen boys being dragged down the street, people averting their eyes. But she did not want him to leave.

He told her he wanted to go to the capital. He asked for money to get there. She would not give it to him, but he stole it and left while she slept. He was a hundred miles from home when the bus skidded off the road and rolled over.

Now the daughter she didn't want was all she had. The woman was not so much bitter as resigned to her fate; she suspected she was being punished for her thoughts at the girl's birth. All the furious love the woman had lavished on her sons she now poured on her daughter, and for the first time Precious's name seemed justified.

The daughter cowered under the assault, after the years in her brothers' shadows. She had been accustomed to being invisible. Her mother's attention now seemed like a burden; she missed the airy feeling of being disposable, inconsequential.

The woman did not speak of her sons at home. To the others in the village she bemoaned her losses. But you are lucky, people said. You still have a child. Still alive. Many of us have none left. You are one of the lucky ones.

Yes, she said, I suppose I am.

The woman who had never been afraid now began to fear that her one last child would be taken from her. She tried to hide her daughter, disguise her value, shield her from anyone who might take her away.

She stopped calling her daughter by her name and instead used "Sister."

Precious did not mind. Her mother seemed determined to name her exactly what she was not.

The woman closed her doors and kept her happiness close and hidden, a miser with her hoard.

. . .

The soldier appeared at the door, and before Precious could say a word he cried out how he'd missed her and hugged her to him. He smelled like a week's worth of sweat, and when he smiled his cheeks stretched into taut creases that looked like they might split at any moment. Don't you remember me? he said. Of course she didn't. She'd never seen him before.

He did the same to her mother, embracing her before she could resist. Precious saw her mother's face, propped on the man's shoulder, the eyes closed, and for just a moment her mother looked blissful. Then the eyes opened and her mother's face hardened again.

It's good to be home, he said.

He's lying, Precious said sullenly.

Her mother knew it too. And yet she cooked him a meal and allowed him to stay the night. She kept closing her eyes for a few seconds at a time; Precious knew she was imagining that it was true, that one of her sons really had come home.

In the dark of early morning Precious heard a creak and felt a breath on her shoulder. A finger found its way beneath her blanket, it pointed and beckoned. She turned over. And then everything happened fast, before she could say a word, like a gourd cracked open and the pulp scooped out, to be replaced by something else.

In the morning the woman arose to find her imposter son gone and her daughter too. One of them had taken all the money she had.

This is the story the daughter tells to her unseen audience, the listener swaying in a travel hammock made of her own flesh. She tells the story over and over, the rhythm of her voice matching the rocking rhythm of her legs, hoping he will understand.

2. during

"If you're an illegal," the man says, "the only absolutely sure-fire way to get into America is to stow away inside a woman's belly."

She asks him what he means. He tells her that anyone born on American soil is automatically a citizen. "Doesn't matter who or what the parents are."

"But what happens to the baby's mother? She's the mother of a citizen now."

"Doesn't matter," he says. "Anyone without papers, if they catch you they'll deport you. And they *will* catch you. Probably take your baby away."

Her hands slide down the front of her dress.

He narrows his eyes. "You seem determined." She nods. "Do you know how to swim? Ever been chased by dogs? Can you run fast on those pretty legs?" She nods; she has never done the first two, but surely they are instinctive. Surely, under duress, her body will know what to do.

"Will you still be able to run fast in a month? Two?" he says and with a sudden brisk movement cups his hand against her stomach.

"Yes," she says, trying not to flinch.

"I might just be able to help you," he says. "How much money do you have?"

.   .   .

She wants to go to America. She's heard they give you a free dishwasher the minute you cross the border. In American stores there is always a hundred of everything, food as far as the eye can see, more food than you could eat in a lifetime. There is plenty of work for anyone who wants it, because the

Americans are the laziest people on earth and will do nothing they can pay someone else to do for them.

Once you get there, everyone agrees, the rest is easy. Soon you'll be a lazy American yourself, having fat children and buying furniture. Furniture? Yes, a woman tells her, in America if you want furniture, a refrigerator, even a car, you can pay a tenth of the price and take the things home; the Americans will trust you to pay the rest later. They are as trusting and gullible as children.

The visions of abundance keep her up at night. It's not for herself that she wants these things. It's for her baby. She knows he is a son, riding high inside her; with every breath she feels his heels crowding against her lungs.

Months earlier, when she told her cousin she was pregnant, her cousin hugged her and said, "Don't worry. We'll take care of it. I know two good ways. One hurts less but takes longer. The other hurts a lot but is over quick. Which do you want?"

"No!" she cried. "Neither," she said, pushing her cousin away.

She cannot even contemplate getting rid of the baby. She loves him already, has begun crooning to him and addressing conversations to her belly long before she starts to show. But as her son pushes out the front of her dress farther and farther, she begins to wonder. Does she want to raise her son in a country where half the babies die before they are a year old? A country where a woman could have eight children and consider herself lucky if one survives to adulthood?

She begins collecting stories of America. She builds a house in her mind, furnishes it, plants trees outside. She imagines her son, fat and white, playing on a vast expanse of immaculate carpet. She sees him as a boy, big and healthy and strong, wearing stiff brand-new clothes, pushing the other boys so they fall down. She pictures him when he's her age—

by American standards, still a child, he'll be going to school, playing with his friends, whistling at girls, and trying to put his hand up their short American skirts.

For some reason, whenever she pictures her son he is bald, his head white and oversized and glowing slightly, like an enormous lightbulb. She puts a baseball cap on him. Better.

"You're crazy," her cousin says. "They'll take your baby away and give him to some American parents. They'll snatch him away the minute you get there and send you back. Americans love foreign babies."

"Love to *eat* them," the cousin's friend says. "At least that's what I've heard."

"Do you want your baby taken away and raised by foreigners?" her cousin says.

Of course not, she says, and suddenly realizes she does.

· · ·

She sees the strange man again and asks if he can help her.

"You want to cross over," he says. She gives him half a nod.

"You're in luck. It's a side business of mine, arranging these things."

She looks around to see if anyone is listening.

"Just remember," he says, "there are no guarantees. If they catch you and deport you, I don't give you your money back. If they catch you, I don't know you. I've never seen you before in my life."

She nods. The first time she met him he was wearing a flowered shirt and a baseball cap like the one her son wears in her daydreams. Today he is wearing a cowboy hat and a nice-looking suit. When he turns to go she sees that it is all crumpled in the back, riding up into his armpits.

She tries, and fails, to remember his eyes. She thinks he has a mustache.

. . .

They meet again so she can give him the money, and he asks for her name.

"Precious," she says, and looks away. She does not like to reveal her name; she senses it is dangerous for anyone to know her true worth. Precious is the name of someone treasured, adored. It means there are people somewhere who would gladly pay ransom for her, rescue her from a tower, lay down their lives for her. This is not true, but it is what people assume. She's afraid he'll raise his price.

But he grins a wide face-creasing grin. He thinks they're playing a game, giving themselves nicknames. "Then call me Hopper," he says. "First name Border. And what about"—he nods at the front of her dress—"what about Junior there?"

She stares back at him stonily refusing to acknowledge anything.

"You know," he says softly, "they don't like it. They don't like this kind of thing."

"What thing?"

"What you're trying to do. They see it as an abuse of the system. They'll try to stop you."

"I don't care."

"Good!" he says, breaking into a smile again. Today he is wearing grease-stained coveralls such as a car mechanic would wear and, beneath it, incongruously, a spotless white dress shirt. In a brisk businesslike voice, he says, "We here at Hopper and Associates have many options to offer the busy traveler. Would you prefer plane, train, boat, or automobile? Business class or coach? Smoking or nonsmoking?"

She turns the choices over in her mind. "I've never been on a boat."

"I'm joking, sweetie."

"Yes," she says. "I knew that."

. . .

She sees the border in her dreams: an orange stripe, wide as a road, dividing a desert from horizon to horizon. The border is hot; people run across it screaming in pain, their shoes smoking. The border guards are lined up in pairs on the other side, each pair with a swatch of black rubbery webbing stretched between them. The moment someone reaches their side of the border, two guards snag him and slingshot him back to the other side. The guards are neat and precise; nobody gets through. The people pick themselves up and try again, running across the scalding line. Again and again they are repulsed. Some are flung through the air; some are sent skidding across the border on their faces. The people tire, they are staggering, crawling, propping each other up. The guards continue their work mechanically, occasionally pausing to take a man's wallet or fondle a woman's breast before sending them back over. There is something about the guards' alert, smooth movements that seems familiar, as if she's seen all this before.

. . .

She must work out the timing of the crossing as precisely as possible. If she goes too soon, it will mean spending more time, pregnant and waiting, on the other side. The longer she's there, the greater the chances the deportation people will catch her and send her back before her son is even born.

But if she waits too long he'll be born outside the border, on un-American soil, and will never get his baseball cap, his citizenship.

She has told her son about America, told him about her plans. Told him the story of a woman and her seven stolen sons. That's what you can look forward to, she told him, if we stay. She hopes she can count on his cooperation.

. . .

The man, Hopper, doesn't care about her plans. "You'll go when I tell you to go," he says. "You can't control these things. You have to seize opportunities as they arise."

She waits and waits. Apparently the opportunities are slow to bubble up. She's in her ninth month when the time comes. She rides a bus to a border town, arrives at the meeting place.

She and six others cram into a secret space behind a false panel in the back of a delivery truck. There are a few nail holes for air. They are afraid to talk; when one makes the slightest noise the others pinch him, roll their eyes. They are all strangers to one another. Their initial excessive courtesy dissipates with the rising heat. The metal walls are like an oven. One man insists on smoking. The two people on either side of Precious accuse her of taking up too much room.

There are delays; the truck stops and starts, the back door opens and closes. At first they all freeze expectantly every time this happens. But the stops continue. Precious begins to wonder if the driver has forgotten about them and is going about his usual deliveries.

Night falls, they know this when dots of light in the nail holes go out and they are in total blackness. No one lets them out.

The second day is more of the same. One man wants to bang on the walls; they've forgotten us, he says. The others restrain him. The heat rises and they squabble silently over the last plastic jug of water.

On the third day they all fall into a stupor, frozen in positions of cramped despair. The only one stirring is Precious's son, kicking impatiently. On the evening of the third day they cross the border without knowing it.

It is dark again when the truck stops, footsteps approach,

the metal door is wrenched back. They blink in the glare of a flashlight as the driver helps them out. He tries to make them hurry but they cannot unfold themselves. He carries them out one by one, like statues in tortured poses, and places them on the ground, where they lie unmoving for a long time and then begin to uncurl as slowly as new leaves unfurling.

They lie on hard earth surrounded by trees. The truck disappears down a dirt track leading back to the highway. They begin to groan and creak and stretch themselves—small things first, fingers and toes. Precious stands up and leans against a tree. She tries walking a few steps. The movement makes something shift within her, then shift again, sinking lower, like the tumblers of a lock falling into place. Good, she thinks. Right on time.

She heads down the track toward the highway. The others call after her, warnings, halfhearted offers of help. She knows they're glad to be rid of her. She's a burden, a liability.

She walks along the highway. So far America is a disappointment, bare and empty. It'll get better, she tells herself. Americans, she knows, are optimistic. She thinks of big white gleaming American hospitals.

She waves at the occasional cars zooming past. She can't see the drivers' faces. If she were in their place she wouldn't stop either, she thinks. Who wants a strange woman having a baby all over your nice clean American car?

But within minutes a car pulls over to the shoulder ahead of her. She clutches her son, tries to walk more quickly. Americans really are friendly after all.

The car is a dull gray, dirty, unremarkable, and she's close before she notices the heavy wire mesh separating the backseat from the front. The driver has already stepped out of the car and has his hand on her arm before she can think of running.

He helps her into the backseat and drives on. He doesn't

seem surprised to see her, seems to know exactly who she is and what she's doing. He's driving in the same direction she'd been heading. At first she thinks he's going to help her after all; then she realizes that they are heading back to the border, that she'd been pointed in the wrong direction.

She's still hopeful. Everyone says even when you get caught, they make you stay in a detention center for weeks while they ask you questions and write words on pieces of paper. She'll have her baby and then go home.

But that's not allowed to happen. She's rushed through a series of gates and hallways and waiting rooms, and people ask her questions and eye her belly and hustle her along. Before she knows it she's sitting in a van with other defeated-looking people who don't meet her eyes. She recognizes two of the people who shared her secret place in the delivery truck but pretends not to.

This time she can see the border as they cross it. It's not how she pictured it. Just a fence, a checkpoint on the road. She holds her belly. Her son is shifting around. Not yet, she thinks fiercely. Not yet.

. . .

She looks for the Hopper man. She assumes he would have disappeared by now, but no, there he is. "Don't be mad, little mama," he says. "I told you there were no guarantees."

She stamps her foot. The pressure inside her is unbelievable. But she wills her body to hold itself together.

"Tell you what," he says. "How about I set up another trip for you? Free of charge? Because I'm such a nice guy?"

"Not the truck. The driver was bad. I think he told the border police where to find us."

"That's terrible," the man says. "You just can't trust anyone, can you? I won't use him again."

. . .

The second time is on a boat, a huge boat, a cargo ship. She doesn't know what it's carrying; the cargo could be anything; it's packed into truck-sized metal rectangles, stacked up in anonymous piles.

She and twelve others hide in the hold. It's dank, dark, cramped, but the gentle motion of the boat soothes her; this is what it must feel like for her son, she thinks.

Her son is very still. She worries that he is dead, but she tells herself that it's only because he's grown too big, has no room to move. Just a little longer, she thinks, and then you can come out and begin your new life. Some people told her America's territory extends from its coastline, fifty miles into the ocean. Others have said five miles. She wants to wait for solid land to be absolutely sure.

But they're stopped almost immediately. She and the others are sought out with flashlights, led up to the deck, and lowered into a smaller boat that speeds them back to the harbor. She would have tried to run, to hide, if not for her son. Any violent motion, she fears, will bring him tumbling out. If she jumped in the water, he might swim right out of her to play in the familiar element.

. . .

"My goodness," the Hopper man says when he sees her. "Are you having twins?"

"Your boat people are bad," she says furiously. "They told the border people we were there."

"You don't say! I certainly won't be using their services anymore."

"I think the border people pay them money to turn us in. A price for each person."

"What makes you think that?"

She has heard people arguing, pointing at her and arguing over whether she should bring the price of one or two.

"We'll get you over there," the man says. "I give you my promise. Three's the charm."

. . .

The next time, she rides in a hiding place built between the backseat and trunk of a small car. They have trouble shutting her in; her belly gets in the way. It seems luxurious, after the first two trips. She has the space to herself. A man and woman sit in the front. On the backseat, inches from her, a baby coos in a car seat. She doesn't know if it's their baby or someone else's, a borrowed prop. Her son shifts irritably, probably sensing the other baby, probably thinking, Now *that's* the way to travel.

At the border they're stopped, the trunk is opened. The panel is ripped away, and for the third time she's blinking in bright light. She imagines her son beating his fists against the sides of her womb.

Not yet, she thinks, not yet, my son. Just a little longer.

. . .

She's now nearing the end of her tenth month. Her belly is strained to the breaking point, her back aches, her knees buckle. But she's more determined than ever. And her son seems to be as stubborn as she is.

"Now it looks like quadruplets," Hopper says.

"He's going to be an American baby," she says, through gritted teeth. "Babies are bigger there. A nice big healthy American baby."

"Is that what he told you?"

"He's not going to come out until we get there," she says. "I'll do what I can," he says. "No guarantees."

She's been told there are places where you can climb over the fence. There are places where there is no fence, only guards in towers who sometimes look the other way. She's going to take her chances on her own. Enough of his gambles.

"I wish you the best," he says, tipping his fishing hat.

. . .

She can barely walk; she stumbles, lurching and weaving. Other people look at her and say, "There's no way. It's impossible." She ignores them.

She walks, through scrub brush and rocks and burning sand and stagnant, stinking water. She walks and walks, thinking: American baby. Nice big American baby.

She hears a sound echoing from far away: dogs yelping, frenzied. She can almost hear them calling to one another: *There she is, there she is, get her.*

They burst over a rise and she can see them, a mob of dark insects growing rapidly bigger, a man with a gun trailing far behind. Has she crossed the border already? It's impossible to tell.

The first dog runs straight at her. She stands still and waits. It seems nearly as big as she is, a small horse. At the last minute it veers away and circles. All the dogs swarm around her. But they do not touch her. They keep their heads lowered abjectly to the ground. They seem in awe of her big belly.

The fat sweating guard who comes puffing up behind them is not impressed. Soon she's sitting in a familiar van, heading back.

. . .

She's been carrying her son for over a year now, with no intention of letting him go.

"Now, that can't possibly be good for him, little mama," Hopper says. "You should let the little feller out."

"He's going to be an *American* baby," she says, slowly, as if talking to a child.

"Let me help you," he says. "I know a man—"

"No," she says.

"We'll try another way. I can get you a fake passport."

"No," she says. She hobbles back to the border, is stopped by a fence, and begins tunneling under it, clawing the dirt with her fingernails. She's crawling through, nearly breaking the surface on the other side, when her son shifts, or perhaps instantaneously grows a fraction of an inch, and suddenly she's stuck. Border guards come and drag her out by her heels. They don't seem surprised, they seem as if they've been expecting her. They look bored, almost disappointed, as if they'd expected her to have a little more originality.

.   .   .

"Why won't you let me help you?" Hopper says.

She doesn't answer.

"Free of charge."

"Why are you being so generous?"

"I don't know. Out of the goodness of my heart?"

Today he's wearing a bolo tie, a snakeskin vest. He is wearing rings on every finger, like a king, like a pirate. Like a pirate king.

"Please," he says. "I *want* to. I insist."

She realizes something she should have seen months ago. He's been tipping off the border guards. He takes money from people for helping them cross; then he takes money from the guards for telling them when and where to expect visitors. She's been making money for him with each of her trips.

"You are a bad man," she says.

"Oh, come now," he says. "You can't blame me. It's a game of chance."

"An evil man. When my son gets big he'll come back and kill you."

"Your son's already big," he says. "And I don't see him doing anything."

.   .   .

She is determined. She flings herself at the border again and again. She travels in cars, trucks, buses. She walks on blistered feet. She travels in a fishing boat, an inflatable raft. She wears disguises, buys false papers. Each time the border repulses her, spits her back.

Big American baby, she tells herself. She sees his size as proof of his American-ness. Only American babies could be so big, so healthy. She has convinced herself that he has always been American, that she is merely a vehicle, a shell, a seed casing meant to protect him until he can be planted in his rightful home.

She carries him for two years. She constructs a sort of sling for herself, with shoulder straps and a strip of webbing, to balance the weight. She uses a cane. She looks like a spider, round fat body, limbs like sticks.

Her son is alive; she can feel the pulse of his heartbeat, feel the pressure as he strains to stretch a finger, an eyelid.

She thinks she can see a dark shadow through the taut translucent skin of her belly. She can see his hair growing long and black.

Her body is adaptable. Her skin stretches, her bones shift, her blood feeds him. When people see her they are amazed, but she is not; she has seen it before, the lengths the body will go to to preserve itself, to cling to life.

Big American baby, she thinks. Nice big American baby. It is her mantra.

She carries him for three years. Three and a half. She becomes a legend, then a joke, with the border guards. They wave to her as she creeps past, cheer her on, drag her back at the last minute.

Don't you think he wants to come out by now? people at home say to her.

He's safer living in my belly than in this wretched country, she says, though she has been so single-mindedly set on her mission that she has taken no notice of external events. War, famine, peace, prosperity: it is all the same to her. America is the only option, the only ray of hope.

She carries him for four years.

Big American baby. Nice big American baby.

She has in her mind pictures of hot-air balloons attached to bicycles, fanciful flying machines. Some days she imagines she will simply lift off the ground and float over, suspended by the power of her will alone. Hers and her son's. Or she imagines that she is invisible, intangible; she breezes across the border. The air, it seems, is the only thing that crosses freely.

Her son is so big, she imagines he fills her completely, his arms fill her arms, his legs fill her legs. She is a mere skin covering him, like an insect's carapace, soon to be flaked off and shucked away.

She's too tired to speak now, just pants and whistles through her teeth. The words rattle in her head.

Nice big American baby, someone chants. Not her. Him. The voice of her son gurgling up from her belly. Muffled and airless but undeniable.

My son's first words, she thinks, smiling proudly at a shriveled bush. You hear that? No baby-talk preliminaries, no babbling or lisping. My son: so precocious, so American.

One day, as she is panting out her mantra and picking her way across the sand, a border guard appears: suddenly, as if he sprang up out of the ground. He carries the usual gun, wears the usual impenetrable sunglasses, has the regulation sweat stains blooming from his armpits. He takes her arm. She obediently turns around and begins walking back. She does not want him to start pushing her, getting rough; the baby might come out.

But to her surprise she finds him pulling her forward, forward across the magic invisible line. Forward, toward the magnificent city that hovers like a mirage in the distance.

"Come on, little mama," he says. "You've had enough."

. . .

When she closes her eyes she sees the hospital of her dreams, a white sparkling grand hotel. When she opens them she sees speckled ceiling tiles, masked alien faces. She can't feel a thing; she's a floating head. It's finally happened, then: her stubborn impatient head has taken off and left the slow body behind somewhere to gestate, egg and nest all in one.

"My son," she says.

"He's coming," they tell her. They have to operate. "There's no way he's fitting through the usual door," they tell her.

She sees a foot kicking. It's as long as her hand. She hears a stupendous, deafening roar. The foot catches one of the masked doctors on the chin and sends him flying backward into the spattered arms of another masked figure.

Her balloon head is bobbing near the ceiling now, borne on the baby's howls, but she'd swear she can hear, interspersed with the empty cries, bellowed words. I want, the baby demands. Give me, I want, I need, I deserve, I have earned. . . .

She sees rising up out of her tired body a sodden mop of long black hair. She sees grasping fists.

She hears—and surely she must be dreaming now—she hears the scrape of a rubber-gloved hand rubbing a sore chin and a doctor's voice saying, "Now *that's* what I call a nice big American baby."

.   .   .

Empty, deflated, she sits alone in the back of the van. She hears weeping somewhere, mingled with the sounds of tires on asphalt. It must be the driver. It can't be her. Can it? Impossible. There's nothing inside her to come out, not a drop. She's hollow, she's still floating, they forgot to reattach her head to those rags and remnants that were her body.

"But it's what you wanted, isn't it? Wasn't that the whole plan, give birth and leave him here with a new set of folks?"

"I never even got a chance to hold him."

"He's too big for holding already. He could hold you."

"I had things to say. Stories to tell him."

"He heard them. He was listening, all those years when you talked to him. He'll remember."

It's the voice of the Hopper man; she's not sure if he's the man driving the van or if the voice is inside her head. It doesn't matter.

"I want to stay," she whispers. "He's mine."

"You can always have another."

3 . after

The prospective parents had applied for a newborn baby, so they did not know what to make of the walking, talking child they visited at the temporary foster home. The adoption agent assured them he had been born only a few days earlier. "I have his birth certificate right here," she said.

Maybe children these days grow up faster than they used to, the hopeful parents told themselves. We should have studied the child development book more carefully, they thought.

They did not voice their doubts, fearing they'd reveal their inexperience, their ignorance. One slip of the tongue and their application would be rejected.

They felt intimidated by the adoption agent, who handled babies as carelessly as basketballs, and also by the foster mother, who had eight children in her charge.

The prospective mother had been looking forward to the cuddling, burping, nurturing years; she'd been gearing herself up for sleepless nights of colic and lullabies and martyrdom. The child before them, calmly regarding them with large brown eyes, was already far beyond that stage. Yet there was something so appealing, so desirable, so eminently *wantable* about him that both prospective parents found themselves smitten. They *had* to have him. He sat on the carpet knocking one block against another, seemingly bored, covertly watchful. They both felt a quickening in their hearts: the anxiety of bargain hunting—the sensation that if they did not get him immediately, someone else would come along, perceive his value, and snatch him up.

When they brought him home he ran through the house pointing at things, wanting to learn their names. "Microwave," they said. "Piano." "Baby monitor." "Treadmill." "Shoe tree." "Television."

They were charmed by his curiosity. Privately they fretted over the way he stiffened whenever they touched him. He was remote, as patiently tolerant as a teenager suffering the whims of unhip parents.

He just needs time, they thought, to get used to us.

What does bonding mean, *exactly*? the new mother wondered. She thought of the unknown woman, the biological mother who'd carried the boy inside her body for nine whole months, and realized she was jealous.

The boy was too well-behaved, too precocious, too perfect. It made them nervous. His perfection made him seem vulnerable, ripe for spoiling. Doesn't it seem like the perfect, angelic little boys are always the ones to get cancer, get hit by cars? the mother thought.

He never made any mistakes. If there were mistakes to be made, they'd be made by the parents. So they washed everything twice, planned educational vacations. The pressure was excruciating.

He'd been their son for over a year when he told them about the face.

He appeared at their bedside in the middle of the night, white and glowing in his astronaut pajamas. "Can I come in?" he said.

They relished the moment, kissing him, tickling him, tucking him in between them.

"Did you have a bad dream?" the mother said.

"There was a face in the window," the boy said, and described glittering eyes and shining teeth and a wiry net of hair, long fingers scrabbling at the sill and warm breath that seeped into the room. A sad face. It watched him for a long time, he said, not moving.

"It isn't real," the father said. "It's only a dream."

The mother thought of goblins, gypsies, pirates, a hundred fairy tales of stolen children. She tightened her grip. "We'll protect you," she whispered fervently. "We'll never let anyone take you away."

"Take me away?" the boy said. The father groaned softly.

She realized she'd made a blunder, planting a new fear in his head that had not been there before.

The next day the father made a great show of testing the

locks on the boy's bedroom window. He pointed out the tree branches that moved in the wind like hair. He talked about the damp smells rising up from the basement, the stink and scrabbling of skunks digging through the garbage cans. The boy listened impassively.

For the next few nights the boy slept peacefully. The parents did not.

And then he was back, glowing in the dark, his feet padding across the floor. "It's back," he said calmly. They lifted their covers for him, pleased that he was finally having the normal problems of a normal child.

The face came back periodically. Not often, but every few weeks. The parents tried to dispel the son's fears, but with less and less enthusiasm as time went on. They worried that if the nightmares stopped, the tenuous intimacy with their son would be gone forever. The mother, in her heart of hearts, secretly made contingency plans—if his nightmares stopped, she'd simulate them (a Halloween mask dangled from the roof, say).

If she left the imprint of a finger in his sandwich, her son would eat around it and leave the little island on his plate. He continued to flinch at the touch of her hand. Still, she sometimes wondered if he was secretly starved for affection, if he'd fabricated the face story as an excuse.

Or maybe, she thought, he'd invented the face as a way of comforting *them*. She wouldn't put it past him, her wise little son.

In the night she stroked her son's shoulders and kissed the top of his head. She wrapped her arms around him and pretended he was inside her.

The next morning she went into his room to make the bed and found the window open and the curtains frothing in the wind. She felt a momentary panic—danger! falling baby!—but the window guard was still in place. She closed the window and locked it. As she was turning away she noticed finger-prints spotting the glass. She must have done that herself, just now. How careless. I'll clean it later, she thought, and bent to the bed, brushing away a few of her son's long black hairs.

To her surprise, she found the bottom sheet damp. Never before had her son wet the bed. She dipped her fingers in the wet spot, feeling fascinated, amazed, intensely maternal. My son, she thought proudly, wets the bed. She imagined telling a friend about it. *Oh, yes, like any normal child, he wets the bed occasionally. When he has a nightmare. What can you do? No, of course we're not worried about it. He'll outgrow it eventually.*

But still there was something strange about it. . . . The stain was perfectly clear; it looked like water. And rather than one spot it was composed of many, a string of drops.

She glanced around furtively to make sure she was alone, then raised her wet fingers to her nose. She smelled nothing. She put her fingers to her tongue. The wetness tasted like tears.

I called my sister and said, What does a miscarriage look like?

What? she said. Oh. It looks like when you're having your period, I guess. You have cramps, and then there's blood.

What do people do with it? I asked.

With what?

The blood and stuff.

I don't know, she said impatiently. I don't know these things, I'm not a doctor. All I can tell you about anything is who you should sue.

Sorry, I said.

Why are you asking me this? she said.

I'm just having an argument with someone, that's all. Just thought you could help settle it.

Well, I hope you win, she said.

. . .

I went home because my sister told me to.

She called me and said, It's your turn.

No, it can't be, I feel like I was just there, I said.

No, I went the last time. I've been keeping track, I have incontestable proof, she said. She was in law school.

But Mitch, I said. Her name was Michelle but everyone called her Mitch except our mother, who thought it sounded obscene.

Lisa, said Mitch, don't whine.

I could hear her chewing on something, a ballpoint pen, probably. I pictured her with blue marks on her lips, another pen stuck in her hair.

It's close to Thanksgiving, I said. Why don't we wait and both go home then?

You forget—they're going down to Florida to be with Nana.

I don't have time to go right now. I have a job, you know. I do have a life.

I don't have time to argue about it, I'm studying, Mitch said. I knew she was sitting on the floor with her papers scattered around her, the stacks of casebooks sprouting yellow Post-its from all sides, like lichen, Mitch in the middle with her legs spread, doing ballet stretches.

I heard a background cough.

You're not studying, I said. Neil's there.

Neil isn't doing anything, she said. He's sitting quietly in the corner waiting for me to finish. Aren't you, sweetheart?

Meek noises from Neil.

You call him sweetheart? I said.

Are you going home or not?

Do I have to?

I can't come over there and *make* you go, Mitch said.

The thing was, we had both decided, some time ago, to take turns going home every now and then to check up on them. Our parents did not need checking up, but Mitch thought we should get in the habit of doing it anyway. To get in practice for the future.

After a minute Mitch said, They'll think we don't care.
Sometimes I think they'd rather we left them alone.
Fine. Fine. Do what you want.
Oh, all right. I'll go.

.　.　.

I flew home on a Thursday night, and though I'd told them not
to meet me at the airport, there they were, both of them,
when I stepped off the ramp. They were the only still figures
in the terminal; around them people dashed with garment
bags, stewardesses hustled in pairs wheeling tiny suitcases.

My mother wore a brown coat the color of her hair. She
looked anxious. My father stood tall, swaying slightly. The
lights bounced off the lenses of his glasses; he wore jeans that
were probably twenty years old. I would have liked to be the
one to see them first, to compose my face and walk up to them
unsuspected, like a stranger. But that never happened. They
always spotted me before I saw them and had their faces
ready and their hands out.

Is that all you brought? Just the one bag?

Here, I'll take it.

Lisa, honey, you don't look so good. How are you?

Yes, how are you? You look terrible.

Thanks, Dad.

How are you? they said, over and over, as they wrestled
the suitcase from my hand.

.　.　.

Back at the house, my mother stirred something on the stove
and my father leaned in the doorway to the dining room and
looked out the window at the backyard. He's always leaned in
that doorway to talk to my mother.

I made that soup for you, my mother said. The one where I have to peel the tomatoes and pick all the seeds out by hand.

Mother. I wish you wouldn't do that.

You mean you don't like it? I thought you liked it.

I like it, I like it. But I wish you wouldn't bother.

It's no bother. I wanted to.

She was up until two in the morning pulling skin off tomatoes, my father said. I could hear them screaming in agony.

How would you know? You were asleep, my mother said.

I get up at five-thirty every morning to do work in the yard before I go in to the office, he said.

I looked out at the brown yard.

I've been pruning the rosebushes. They're going to be beautiful next summer.

Yes, they will.

Lisa, he said, I want you to do something for me tomorrow, since you're here.

Sure. Anything.

I want you to go with your mother to her doctor's appointment. Make sure she goes.

OK.

She doesn't have to come, my mother said. That's silly, she'll just be bored.

She's supposed to get a mammogram every six months, my father said, but she's been putting it off and putting it off.

I've been busy. You know that's all it is.

She's afraid to go. She's been avoiding it for a year now.

Oh, stop it, that's not it at all.

She always finds a way to get out of it. Your mother, the escape artist.

My mother crossed her arms over her chest. There was a history. Both her mother and an aunt had had to have things removed.

It's the same with all her doctors, my father said. Remember the contact lenses?

That was different. I didn't need new contacts.

She stopped going to her eye doctor for fifteen years. For fifteen years she was wearing the same contacts. When she finally went in, the doctor was amazed, he said he'd never seen anything like it, they don't even make contact lenses like that anymore. He thought she was wearing dessert dishes in her eyes.

You're exaggerating, my mother said.

Mitch—I mean Lise, my father said.

He'd always gotten our names confused; sometimes, to be safe, he just said all three.

She's afraid to go because of the last time, he said.

What happened last time? I said.

I had the mammogram pictures done, she said, and then a few days later they called and said the pictures were inconclusive and they needed to take a second set. So they did that and then they kept me waiting for the results, for weeks, without telling me anything, weeks where I couldn't sleep at night, and I kept your father up too, trying to imagine what it looked like, the growth. Like the streaks in bleu cheese, I thought. I kept feeling these little pains and kept checking my pulse all night. And then finally they called and said everything was fine after all, there was just some kind of blur on the first X-rays, like I must have moved right when they took them or something.

You were probably talking the whole time, my father said. Telling them how to do their job.

I was probably shivering. They keep that office at about forty degrees and leave you sitting around in the cold in a paper robe. The people there don't talk to you or smile; and when they do the pictures they mash your breast between these two cold glass plates like a pancake.

My father looked away. He had a kind of modesty about some things.

My mother said to me, All those nights I kept thinking

about my mother having her surgery. I kept feeling for lumps, waking up your father and asking him to feel for lumps.

Leah, my father said.

He didn't mind that. I think he might have enjoyed it a little.

Please.

Didn't you?

Promise me you'll go, he said.

She's not coming, she said.

.   .   .

The next day we drove to the clinic an hour early. My mother had the seat drawn as close to the steering wheel as she could get it; she gripped the wheel with her hands close together at twelve o'clock. She looked over at me as often as she looked out at the road.

There were squirrels and possums sprawled on the pavement, their heads red smears.

It's something about the weather, my mother said, makes them come out at night.

Oh.

We're so early, my mother said, and we're right near Randy's salon. Why don't we stop in and see if he can give you a haircut and a blowout?

Not now.

He wouldn't mind, I don't think. I talk about you whenever I have my hair done. He'd like to meet you.

No.

If you just got it angled on the sides, here, and got a few bangs in the front—

Just like yours, you mean.

You know, I feel so bad for Randy, he looks terrible, circles under his eyes all the time; he says his boyfriend is back in the hospital. Now whenever I go to get my hair cut, I bake something to give him, banana bread or something. But I think the shampoo girls usually eat it all before he can get it home.

That's nice of you.

I worry about him. He doesn't take care of himself.

Yes.

Why are you still getting pimples? You're twenty-seven years old; why are you still getting pimples like a teenager?

Not everyone has perfect skin like you, I said. Green light. Go.

I do *not* have perfect skin, she said, bringing her hands to her face.

Both hands on the wheel, please. Do you want me to drive?

No, I don't. You must be tired.

I touched my forehead. Small hard bumps like Braille.

She drove. I looked at the side of her face, the smooth taut skin. I wondered when she would start to get wrinkles. I already had wrinkles. On my neck. I could see them.

So, how is it going with this Piotr?

He's all right.

Still playing the—what was it? Guitar?

Bass guitar.

She turned on the radio and started flipping through stations. Maybe we'll hear one of his songs, she said brightly.

I told you he was in a band. I didn't say they were good enough to be on the radio, I said.

Oh. I see. So the band's just for fun. What else does he do?

Nothing. Yet.

So. What kind of name is Piotr? Am I saying it right?

Polish, I said.

I did not feel like telling her that only his grandmother lived in Poland; his parents were both born in Milwaukee, and he had grown up in Chicago and had never been to Poland; Piotr was a name he had given himself; he was not really a Piotr at all, he was a Peter with pretensions and long hair. I did not tell her this.

A black car cut into the lane in front of us. My mother braked suddenly and flung her right arm out across my chest.

Mother! Keep your hands on the wheel!

I'm sorry, she said, it's automatic. Ever since you kids were little. . . .

I'm wearing a seat belt.

I know, honey, I can't help it. Did I hurt you?

No, of course not, I said.

When we reached the parking garage my mother rolled down her window but couldn't reach; she had to unfasten her seat belt and open the car door in order to punch the button and get her parking ticket. I looked at her narrow back as she leaned out of the car, its delicate curve, the shoulder blades like folded wings under her sweater, a strand of dark hair caught in the clasp of her gold necklace. I had the urge to slide across the seat and curl around her. It only lasted for a second.

She turned around and settled back into her seat, and the yellow-and-black-striped mechanical bar swung up in front of the car, and I tapped my feet impatiently while she slammed the door shut and rolled up the window. Now she was fiddling with her rearview mirror and straightening her skirt.

Come on, I said, watching the bar, which was still raised but vibrating a little.

Relax, honey, that thing isn't going to come crashing down on us the minute we're under it. I promise you.

I know that, I said, and then closed my eyes until we were through the gate and weaving around the dark oil-stained aisles of the parking garage. I would have liked to tell her about some of the legal cases Mitch had described to me:

freak accidents, threshing machines gone awry, people caught in giant gears or conveyor belts and torn limb from limb, hands in bread slicers, flimsy walkways over vats of acid. Elevator cases, diving-board cases, subway-train cases, drowning-in-the-bathtub cases, electrocution-by-blender cases. And then there were the ones that were just called Acts of God.

I didn't tell her.

Remember where we parked, she said.

OK.

But she did not get out of the car right away. She sat, gripping the wheel.

I don't see why we have to do this, she said. Your father worries—

He'll be more worried if you don't go, I said, and anyway there's nothing to worry about because everything's going to be fine. Right? Right.

If there's something wrong I'd just rather not know, she said to her hands.

We got out; the car shook as we slammed the doors.

She was right about the clinic. It was cold and it was ugly. She signed in with the receptionist and we sat in the waiting room. The room was gray and bare; the chairs were old vinyl that stuck to your thighs. The lights buzzed and seemed to flicker unless you were looking directly at them.

We sat side by side and stared straight ahead as if we were watching a movie.

There was one other woman waiting. She had enormous breasts. I could not help noticing.

I took my mother's hand. It was very cold, but then her hands were always cold, even in summer, cool and smooth with the blue veins arching elegantly over their backs. Her hand lay limply in mine. I had made the gesture thinking it was the right thing to do, but now that I had her hand I didn't know what to do with it. I patted it, turned it over.

My mother looked at me strangely. My hand began to sweat.

There was noise, activity somewhere; we could hear voices and footsteps, the crash and skid of metal, the brisk tones of people telling each other what to do. But we could see nothing but the receptionist in her window and the one woman who looked asleep, sagging in her chair with her breasts cupped in her arms like babies.

I need to use the restroom, my mother said, and pulled her hand away.

The receptionist directed us down the hall and around the corner. We went in, our footsteps echoing on the tiles. It was empty and reeked of ammonia. The tiles glistened damply.

Here, do something with yourself, my mother said, and handed me her comb. She walked down to the big handicapped stall on the end and latched the door.

I combed my hair and washed my hands and waited.

I looked at myself in the mirror. The lights were that harsh relentless kind that reveal every detail of your face, so that you can see all sorts of flaws and pores you didn't even know you had. They made you feel you could see your own thoughts floating darkly just under your skin, like bruises.

Mother, I said. I watched her feet tapping around.

Lisa, she said, there's a fish in the toilet.

Oh, please.

No, I mean it. It's swimming around.

You're making it up.

No, I'm not. Come see for yourself.

Well, it's probably just some pet goldfish someone tried to flush.

It's too big to be a goldfish. More like a carp. It's bright orange. Almost red.

You're seeing things—maybe it's blood or something, I said; then I wished I hadn't. The clinic was attached to the county hospital; all sorts of things were liable to pop up in the toilets: hypodermic needles, appendixes, tonsils.

No, no, it's a fish, it's beautiful really. It's got these gauzy fins, like veils. I wonder how it got in here. It looks too large to have come through the pipes. It's swimming in circles. Poor thing.

Well, then, come out and use a different one, I said. I suddenly started to worry that she was going to miss her appointment. You're just stalling, I said.

Come in and see. We have to save it somehow.

I heard her pulling up her pantyhose, fixing her skirt. Then she unlatched the door to the stall and opened it. She was smiling. Look, she said.

I followed her into the stall.

Come see, she said. Together we leaned over the bowl.

I saw only the toilet's bland white hollow and our two identical silhouettes reflected in the water.

Now where did he go? my mother said. Isn't that the strangest thing?

We looked at the empty water.

How do you think he got out? she said. Look, you can see, the water's still moving from where he was. Look, look—little fish droppings. I swear. Lisa, honey, look.

My mother is going crazy, I thought. Let's go back to the waiting room, I said.

But I still have to use the bathroom, she said.

I stood by the sink and waited. You're going to miss your appointment, I said. I watched her feet. Silence.

I was making her nervous. I'll wait for you in the hall, I said.

So I left, leaned against the wall, and waited. And waited. She was taking a long time. I started to wonder if she had been hallucinating. I wondered if something really was wrong with her, if she was bleeding internally or having a weird allergic reaction. I didn't think she was making it all up; she couldn't lie, she was a terrible, obvious liar.

Mother, I called.

Mom, I said.

I went back into the bathroom.

She was gone.

The stall doors swung loose, creaking. I checked each cubicle, thinking she might be standing on the toilet seat, with her head ducked down the way we did to avoid detection in high school. In the handicapped stall the toilet water was quivering, as if it had just been flushed. I even checked in the cabinets under the sink and stuck my hand down in the garbage pail.

I stood there, thinking. She must have somehow left and darted past me without my noticing. Maybe I had closed my eyes for a minute. She could move fast when she wanted to.

Had she climbed out the window? It was a small one, closed, high up on the wall.

She had escaped.

I walked slowly down the halls, listening, scanning the floor tiles.

I thought of her narrow back, the gaping mouth of the toilet, pictured her slipping down, whirling around and vanishing in the pipes.

I tried to formulate a reasonable question: Have you seen my mother? A woman, about my height, brown hair, green eyes? Nervous-looking? Have you seen her?

Or were her eyes hazel?

I came back to the waiting room with the question on my lips—I was mouthing the words *she's disappeared*—but when I got there the receptionist was leaning through the window calling out in an irritated voice: Ms. Salant? Ms. Salant? They're ready for you, *Ms. Salant.*

The receptionist was opening the door to the examining

rooms; the nurses and technicians were holding out paper gowns and paper forms and urine sample cups. Ms. Salant, Ms. Salant, we're waiting, they called; people were everywhere suddenly, gesturing impatiently and calling out my name.

So I went in.

. . .

Later I wandered up and down the rows of painted white lines in the lot. I had forgotten where she parked the car. When I finally came upon it I saw her there, leaning against the bumper. For a moment I thought she was smoking a cigarette. She didn't smoke.

When I drew closer I saw that she was nibbling on a pen.

We got in the car and drove home.

All of a sudden I thought of something I wanted to pick up for dinner, she said at one point.

Some fish? I said.

We drove the rest of the way without speaking.

So how did it go today, ladies? my father said that evening.

My mother didn't say anything.

Did you go with her? he asked me. Yeah, I said.

So, you'll hear the results in a few days, right? he said, with his hand on my mother's back.

She looked away.

Right, I said.

She looked at me strangely but said nothing.

. . .

I told them not to but they both came to the airport Sunday night when I left.

Call me when you get the news, all right? I said.

All right, she said.

I wanted to ask her about the fish in the toilet, whether it had really been there. Whether she had followed the same route out of the clinic it had. But I couldn't work myself up to it. And the topic never came up by itself.

We said good-bye at the terminal. My hugs were awkward. I patted their backs as if I were burping babies.

I told them to go home but I knew they would wait in the airport until the plane took off safely. They always did. I think my mother liked to be there in case the plane crashed during takeoff so she could dash onto the runway through the flames and explosions to drag her children from the rubble.

Or maybe they just liked airports. That airport smell.

I had a window seat; I pushed my carry-on under the seat in front. A man in a business suit with a fat red face sat down next to me.

I wondered if my mother even knew what I had done for her. I had helped her escape. Although at the time I hadn't thought of it that way; I hadn't really thought at all; I had gone in when I heard my name, automatic schoolgirl obedience, gone in to the bright lights and paper gowns and people who kneaded your breasts like dough. I began to feel beautiful and noble. I felt like I had gone to the guillotine in her place, like Sydney Carton in A Tale of Two Cities.

.   .   .

I called Piotr when I got home. I'm back, I said.

Let me come over, he said, I'll make you breakfast.

It's seven-thirty at night.

I just got up, he said.

My apartment felt too small and smelled musty. I'd been gone three days but it seemed longer. Piotr came and brought eggs and milk and his own spatula—he knew my kitchen was ill-equipped for anything but sandwiches.

He seemed to have grown, since I last saw him, and gotten more hairy; I looked at the hair on the backs of his hands, and the chest hair tufting out of his T-shirt.

He took up too much space. As he talked his nose and hands popped out at me, huge and distorted, as if I were seeing him through a fish-eye lens. He came close to kiss me and I watched his eyes loom larger and larger and blur out of focus and merge into one big eye over the bridge of his nose.

I was embarrassed. My mouth tasted terrible from the plane.

What kind of pancakes do you want? he asked.

The pancake kind, I said.

He broke two eggs with one hand and the yolks slid out between his fingers.

I can do them shaped like snowmen, he said, or rabbits, or flowers.

He was mixing stuff up in a bowl; flour slopped over the edges and sprinkled on the counter and the floor. I'll have to clean that up, I thought.

Round ones, please, I said.

There was butter bubbling and crackling in the frying pan. Was that pan mine? No, he must have brought it with him—it was a big heavy skillet, the kind you could kill someone with.

He poured in the batter—it was thick and pale yellow—and the hissing butter shut up for a while. I looked in the pan. There were two large lumpy mounds there, side by side, bubbling inside as if they were alive, turning brown on the edges.

He turned them over and I saw the crispy undersides with patterns on them like the moon; and then he pressed them down with the spatula, pressed them flat and the butter sputtered and hissed.

There was a burning smell.

I'm not feeling very hungry right now, I said.

But I brought maple syrup, he said. It's from Vermont, I think.

The pan was starting to smoke. Pushing him aside, I took it off the flame and put it in the sink. It was heavy; the two round shapes were now charred and crusted to the bottom.

Well, we don't have to eat them, he said. He held out the bottle of syrup. Aunt Jemima smiled at me. She looked different. They must have updated her image; new hairstyle, outfit. But that same smile.

There's lots of stuff we can do with syrup, he said. It's a very romantic condiment.

He stepped closer and reached out and turned the knob on the halogen lamp. His face looked even more distorted in the dimness.

What? I said. Where did you get such a stupid idea?

Read it somewhere.

I'm sorry, I'm just not feeling very social tonight, I said. *Peter,* I said.

Oh, come on.

I missed my parents very much suddenly. You're so insensitive, I said. Get out.

Hey, I *am* sensitive. I'm *Mr.* Sensitive. I give change to bums. Pachelbel's Canon makes me cry like a baby.

Like a what? I said.

Why are you screaming at me? he said.

Don't let the door hit you in the ass on the way out, I said. I thought I was being smart and cutting. But he took it literally; he went out and closed the door behind him with great care.

.   .   .

My sister called later that night.

So how were they? she asked.

Fine, I said. Same as always.

Your voice sounds funny; what happened? she said.

Nothing.

Something's wrong. Why don't you ever tell me when something's wrong?

There's nothing, Mitch.

You never tell me what's going on. When you think I'll worry about something you keep it to yourself.

I tell you everything.

Well, then, tell me what was wrong with you earlier in the fall.

Nothing . . . I don't know . . . there's nothing to tell.

That was the truth. All that happened was I got tired of people for a while. I didn't like to go out, didn't shower, and didn't pick up the phone except to call my office with elaborate excuses. The smell of my body became comforting, a ripe presence, nasty but familiar. I lay in bed telling myself that it was just a phase, it would pass. Eventually the bulb on my halogen lamp burned out and after two days of darkness I ventured out to buy a new one. The sunlight on the street did something to my brain, or maybe it was the kind bald man who sold me the bulb. I went back to work.

So how are you? How's Neil?

Oh, we broke up, she said. We had a big fight. He couldn't see that I was right and he was wrong. It was high drama, in a restaurant with people watching, us screaming and stuff, and this fat waitress pushing between us using her tray as a shield and telling us to leave. So we finished it outside on the street, I made my points, one-two-three, and did my closing arguments. If we were in court, I would have won.

I'm sorry, I said. Why didn't you tell me right away?

Oh, I didn't want you feeling bad for me. I'm glad, really. Small-minded jerk. Did I ever tell you he had all this hair on his back? Gray hair, like a silver-back gorilla.

Yes, well. I don't know that I'll be seeing Piotr anymore either.

That's too bad.

No, it's not.

. . .

That night as I lay in bed I thought of my mother and felt my body for lumps the way she said she felt hers, and I put two fingers to the side of my throat. And I began to think of her and think of an undetected cancer, spreading through her body unnoticed. It began to dawn on me that I had done a very stupid thing.

I thought of her lying in bed beside my father at that moment, oblivious to the black thing that might be growing and thickening inside her, maybe in tough strands, maybe in little grainy bits, like oatmeal. She would avoid thinking about it for another six months or a year or two years; she'd deny it until her skin turned gray and she had tentacles growing out of her mouth and her breasts slid from her body and plopped on the floor like lumps of wet clay. Only when all that happened would she give in and say, Hmmm, maybe something *is* wrong, maybe I should see a doctor after all.

I lay awake for most of the night.

At one point I got up to use the bathroom, and as I sat on the toilet in the dark I suddenly became convinced that there was something horrible floating in the water below me. I was sure of it. A live rat. Or a length of my own intestines lying coiled and bloody in the bowl. I sat there afraid to turn on the light and look, yet I couldn't leave the bathroom without looking.

I sat there for half an hour, wracked with indecision. I think I fell asleep for a bit.

And when I finally forced myself to turn on the light, turn around, and look—I was so convinced there would be something floating there that I was horribly shocked, my stomach lurched, to see only the empty toilet.

I went back to work on Tuesday.

Did I miss anything? I asked one of the men.

You were gone? he said.

I didn't know his name; all the men who worked there looked alike. They were all too loud and had too much spit in their mouths.

I had a cubicle all my own, but I dreamed of an office with a door I could close.

.   .   .

A few days later, my father called. Your mother heard the results from the clinic, he said. The mammogram was fine.

That's great, I said.

She doesn't seem happy about it, he said. She's acting very strange.

Oh, I said.

What's going on, Lisa? he said. There's something fishy going on here.

Nothing, I said. Ask your wife, I said. Can I talk to her?

She just dashed out for an appointment, told me to call you. She said you'd be relieved.

Yes.

I'm going to call your sister now, she was waiting to hear. Or do you want to call her?

I'll do it, I said.

It seemed strange to me then that I would need to call Mitch. It felt like she was right here with me, living in my skin. Why should I have to pick up a phone?

.   .   .

We both went home for Christmas.

Later Mitch visited them.

Then I visited.

Then it was Mitch's turn again.

When I called home during Mitch's visit, my father said, Your mother was due for another mammogram, so I sent Lisa with her to make sure she goes.

You mean you sent Mitch, I said. I'm Lisa.

Yes, right. You know who I mean.

A few days later my father called. His voice sounded strained. Your mother talked to the mammography clinic today, he said, but she won't tell me anything. She's been in her room, crying. She's been talking on the phone to your sister for an hour. I guess the doctors found something, but I'll let you know when we know for sure.

OK.

I hung up and called Mitch.

Hello, she said. She sounded like she was choking on one of her pens.

Mitch, I said. It's yours, isn't it?

She sighed and said, It's ridiculous, but I thought I was doing her a favor, I thought I was sparing her some worry.

You went in for her, didn't you?

You know, Mitch said, she's more worried about this than if *she* was the one. She feels like it's her lump, like it was meant for her, like she gave it to me somehow.

That's ridiculous, I said. It was like I was talking to myself.

Although, you know, if it were possible, I would, Mitch said. I mean, if there *was* somehow a way to magically take a lump out of her breast and put it in mine, I'd do it in a second.

I wish I could do that for you, I said.

Yeah, we could all share it.

One dessert and three forks, I said.

And later, as I sat alone on the floor in the apartment, I thought about being my mother's daughter and my sister's sister, and I felt my edges start to bleed a little. I remembered standing in a white room with my breast clamped in the jaws of a humming machine. I imagined the mammogram pictures like lunar landscapes, and I could not remember who had the lump anymore, it seemed we all did, and then the phone rang again and I picked it up and heard my father call out as he sometimes did: Leah-Lise-Mitch.

Our friend Joel got one of those mail-order brides. It was all perfectly legitimate: he made some calls, looked through the catalogs, comparison-shopped. He filled out the forms without lying about his income or his height. Where it asked MARITAL STATUS? he wrote *Divorced!* and *When she left me I threw my ring into the sea.* "That's so romantic," we all said when he did it. "No it wasn't, it was stupid," he said. "I could have sold that ring for a lot of money." We insisted, "No, it's very romantic." "Do you think?" "Any woman would want you now," we said, as we put on bathing suits and diving masks and headed down to the beach.

I'll call her Nadia. That was not her name, but I'll call her that to protect her identity. She came from a place where that was necessary. *Nadia* brings up images of Russian gymnasts. Or is it Romanian? Bulgarian? She had the sad ancient eyes, the strained-back hair, the small knotty muscles. The real Nadia, the famous Nadia, I forget what she did exactly; I have vague memories of her winning a gold medal with a grievous wound, a broken bone, a burst appendix. I think she defected.

I picture her running across a no-man's-land between her country and ours, dressed in her leotard and bare feet, sprinting across a barren minefield where tangles of barbed wire roll about like tumbleweeds and bullets rain down and bounce on the ground like hail.

But our Nadia, Joel's Nadia, came wrapped as if to prevent breakage in a puffy quilted coat that covered her head to foot. She kept the hood up, the strings drawn tight so all we could see was her snout poking out. She must have been cold when she first came; she stood in his apartment, and wouldn't take it off, and then went and leaned against the radiator. We were all there to welcome her; we had come bringing beer and wine and flavored vodkas: orange, pepper, vanilla.

It was an old-fashioned radiator and her coat must have been made of some cheap synthetic because it melted to the metal. When she tried to step away and found she couldn't, she moved in a jerky panicked way that was strangely endearing. Joel tried to help her out of the coat but she wouldn't let him, she jerked and flailed until the coat ripped open and the filling spilled out. It wasn't down, it was like some kind of packing material, polystyrene peanuts or shredded paper.

It reminded me—a few months earlier I'd ordered some dishes, and when they came in the mail I found they'd been packed in popcorn, real popcorn. Some companies do this now, I've been told, because it's biodegradable, more environment-friendly. I took out the dishes and wondered if I should eat all that popcorn, but it seemed unsanitary. It might have touched something, I don't know, at the plant: dust, mouse droppings, the dirty hands of some factory worker. So I threw it away, this big box of popcorn. I still think about it. Probably that box could have fed Nadia's whole family for a week.

Joel and Nadia had written to each other, their letters filtered and garbled by interpreters. They described themselves: hair, eyes, height, weight, preferences in food, drink, animals, colors, recreations. She could speak English but not write it; they had a few phone conversations. What could they possibly have talked about? What did she say? It was enough to make him pay the money, buy the tickets, sign the papers to bring her over the ocean.

These days, ever since her arrival, Joel looked happy. He had a sheen. Someone had cleaned the waxy buildup from his ears. We asked if she was different from the women here, if she had a way of walking, an extra flap of skin, a special smell. Did she smell of cigarettes, patchouli, foreign sewers, unbathedness?

"I think she has some extra bones in her spine," he said. "She seems to have a lot of them. Like a string of beads. A rosary."

We'd seen more of her by then, up close, coatless. Her hair was bright red, black at the roots, which gave her head the look of a tarnished penny.

"Tell us *something* about her," we said.

He closed his eyes. "When I take off her shirt," he said, "her breasts jump right into my hands, asking to be touched."

He opened his eyes to see how we took that.

"Her nipples crinkle up," he said, "like dried fruit. Apricots."

"She has orange nipples?"

We'd always insisted that Joel be completely open with us, tell us everything and anything he would tell a male friend. How could we advise him unless he told us the truth? Utter frankness, we told him, was the basis of any mature friendship between men and women. He often seemed to be trying to test this theory, prove us wrong. "Frankness will be the death of any good relationship," he'd say.

Joel was what we called a teddy-bear type, meaning he was large and hairy and gentle. He had a short soft beard all around his mouth so you could not see any lips. Hair grew in

two bristly patches on the back of his neck. His fingertips
were blunt and square, his eyes set far back in his head so that
they were hard to read. His knees were knobby and full of per-
sonality, almost like two pudgy faces. In fact, he sometimes
drew faces on them, to amuse his soccer team or us. Some of
us had been in love with him once, but that was long past.
Friendship was more important than any illusions of romance.

Nadia did not smile much. At first we thought it was
because she was unhappy. Then she began smirking in an
awful closed-lipped way so we thought she didn't like us. It
took us a while to understand that it was her smile. Eventually
we discovered the reason: her teeth were amazing, gray and
almost translucent, evidence of some vitamin deficiency.
When she spoke, air whistled through them, giving her a
charming lisp.

She spoke English well enough, with a singsong lilting
accent that lifted the end of every word, so that each word
sounded as if it ended with a curlicue, a kite tail, a question
mark.

She trilled certain consonants. "Lovely," she said and
trilled the *V*. Trilled the *V*! Have you ever heard that before?
She must have had some extra ridges on her tongue.

She burst into tears at unpredictable times. She needed
her own bedroom, so he cleared out his home office for her.
We saw her bed, a child-sized cot.

We began to suspect that he had done it all purely out of
kindness, that he had wanted to rescue someone and give her
a better home, a new life. He wanted to be a savior, not a husband. "Why didn't he just adopt a child, then?" we asked each
other.

I thought, Maybe *I* should adopt a child. I ought to have
one of my own; people are always looking at me and saying
"childbearing hips" as if it's a compliment. But then I think of
the rabbit my sister had as a pet when we were little girls. I

remember holding him tightly to my chest until he stopped kicking. I was keeping him warm, but when I let go he was limp. We put him back in the cage for our father to find. I still dream of white fur, one sticky pink eye. I worry I might do the same to a baby. I could adopt a bigger one, a toddler. Not too sickly. But what if it doesn't understand English?

Of course you want to help, but what can you do? We did what we could: we gave money to feed overseas orphans, money for artificial limbs and eye operations; we volunteered at local schools; we took meals to housebound invalids once a month; we passed out leaflets on street corners. A friend of mine volunteers to escort women past the protesters into abortion clinics and has invited me to join her, but it's never a good day for me. We recycle. We get angry and self-righteous about what we see on the news. When I see a homeless person on the street I give whatever's in my pocket.

It's not enough. But what can you do? What can you do?

Joel had a friend, Malcolm, he was always promising to introduce us to. Malcolm worked for some global humanitarian organization. We saw him on television occasionally, reporting from some wartorn, decimated, or drought-stricken place, hospital beds in the background, people missing feet with flies clustered on their eyes, potbellied children washing their heads in what looks like a cesspool. Malcolm was balding but handsome in a weather-beaten cowboy way. His earnest face made you want to reach for your wallet. "That guy, he can relief-effort *me* any time," we'd say to Joel. But we hadn't met him yet. We were beginning to suspect he existed only inside the box and was not allowed out.

As for Nadia: "Where's she from, exactly?" we asked Joel.

"A bad place," he said, frowning. "Her village is right in the middle of contested territory, every week a new name. Don't ask her about it. It makes her sad."

"All right," we said, but privately we wondered at his protecting her feelings like that. No one *we* knew had ever stopped talking about something because it made *us* sad. No one. Not even Joel. Was it because we were fat happy Americans, incapable of real sadness? Was it because he thought we had no feelings, or because he thought we were strong enough to bear sadness? Unlike poor delicate Nadia with her pink-rimmed eyes, Nadia who bought her clothes in the children's department because she had no hips. She said she did it because the clothes were sturdier, better quality, would last longer.

Last longer? How much longer will she need green corduroy overalls, or narrow jeans with unicorns embroidered on the back pockets? How much longer before her hips swell and her legs thicken and her collarbone stops sticking out in that unbecoming way?

Her legs are not like American legs; they are pieces of string, flimsy and boneless.

"We'll take her shopping," we told Joel. "We'll show her the ropes."

"She's doing just fine," he said. "I'll take her."

I said, "You should be careful. I've heard, people like her, the first time they go to an American supermarket, they have seizures or pass out."

"Why?" he said.

"They just can't take it," I said. "They're not used to it. The . . . the *abundance* or something. Overstimulation."

"Thanks for the heads-up," he said, but he wasn't looking at me. Nadia stood at the other end of the room, before a window, so that sunlight set her hair afire and shone right through her pink translucent ears. Her ankles were crossed, her arms folded, a cigarette hung from her fingers. The skin on her face, her arms, was so milky-white her ears didn't seem to belong to her. Around her people moved in shadows.

"Do you know," he said, "she lets me hold her hand. In public? Just walking down the street? All the time."

He was beginning to talk like her, question marks in the wrong places.

"I love her," he said, in a stupid way. He was talking like one of his moony students. There was something black floating in his drink, next to the ice cube, and he didn't even notice.

"How do you hold hands?" I said. "Like this?"

"Well . . . no," he said. "Usually. . . . I take her by the wrist. Or grab her thumb. But she doesn't pull away. She lets me. She likes it."

"Like this?" I said. "Or like *this*?"

"Not exactly," he said. "Her wrist is so little, my fingers go right around . . . like this, see, only hers are even smaller. I can hold them both in one hand."

His palm was the same, still warm and damp, fingers long and blunt-tipped, hair on the backs. The hair almost hid the new wedding ring. There were bulgy things in the breast pockets of his shirt. The toe of my shoe was almost touching the toe of his. I wondered if she would look up and see us holding hands like this.

But she didn't. She was absorbed in her cigarette, her halo of sunlight.

Joel was a high school teacher. He loved kids. People always said that about him, first thing: "He loves kids. Such a nice guy." We had always thought it was a wonderful thing about him; it meant he was caring, he was generous, he was nurturing, he was fun. He would be a terrific father. He taught chemistry; he coached the soccer team. He had won the Teacher of the Year plaque three different times. Kids came to him in tears, they trusted him that much, and he'd let them cry through a box of Kleenex and keep his mouth shut and the classroom door open, and then hand them over to the proper counselor or police officer or health-care worker. There had never been a bit of trouble. Not with the girls, not with anyone. He had perfected the art of the friendly distance, the arm's-length intimacy. We had always known his girlfriend or wife would never have reason to worry about cheerleaders or teen temptresses. Joel was better than that.

At least, we had never suspected anything of him until he brought home this child bride, who must have weighed half of what he did, who sometimes wore her hair in two long braids. Then we had to wonder. Before, we liked to hear him talk about his students. Now there was something off about it, a sour note. "My kids," he would say. "I love those kids. Do you know what they did? Stephanie Riser and Ashley Mink? Listen. . . ." And we would listen, but there was something tainting it now, a thin black thread.

"Don't you think she's a little too young?" we said.

"Nadia? No! She's thirty-three."

"No!" we said.

"Yes," he said, looking pleased.

"She must be lying," we said. "She can't be."

"It's right on her papers," he said.

"As if that proves anything," we said. But we said it nicely.

They bought a house together. What does that mean? *He* bought the house. It was his money. She contributed nothing. What did she do with herself all day? "She makes me happy," Joel said. Her?

"She's trained as a doctor," he said. "She has to pass a test before she can practice here."

"What kind of doctor?"

"It's a source of great frustration. She has to relearn things she studied years ago, chemistry, anatomy, in a new language. You should see the size of these books."

"Are you going to have children?" we asked him.

"Of course," he said.

But there was no sign of them. So we kept asking.

"Of course," he said.

"Later.

"Maybe.

"I don't know."

Of course we were really asking something else. We wondered if she had her own bedroom in the new house. But of course we couldn't ask.

"He seems frustrated," we told one another. "Yes, definitely. Bottled up."

One of our old friends was chosen to be on a televised game show. We had a party to watch her and invited Joel and Nadia. We screamed when we saw her, taking her place among flashing lights and boldly punching her buzzer. But by the third question, a sweaty sheen had broken out above her upper lip. She faltered, mumbled, and in seconds she had disappeared forever. It was hard to work up any kind of real feeling; it was just dots on a screen. Only a game.

Joel seemed distracted. Nadia stared at the wall and then got up to use the bathroom.

"You have no idea what she's been through," Joel said, apropos of nothing. "You have no idea."

Which is unfair; we have all known suffering, we have all known loss. Certainly I have, and Joel should have known that better than anyone.

The sun going behind clouds, trees creaking in the wind. The house Joel bought was all windows, making it easier for the weather to force its mood upon them. That's how I explain the gloom. It was a sunless winter. She decorated the house herself, everything backward: hung rugs on the walls, stood dishes on their rims on the shelves, set table lamps on the floor, left the windows bare but hung curtains round the beds. She used a lot of red for someone so lacking in color.

Whenever we visited now she'd be listening to her own music. She'd found a station, way at one end of the AM dial, that played her type of thing. She'd play it for us if we asked her, to be polite. Horns and bells, nasal voices, songs like sobbing. More often, she'd listen to it on the headphones he'd given her, and he'd talk to us. It was easier this way. She sat among us with a blissful look on her face, and we could talk about her without worrying that she'd hear us.

We saw her country on the news sometimes. Shaky camera, people running. Trucks. Shouting. Crowds of people pulling at one another. Are they using black-and-white film, or is everything gray there? She refused to watch.

"Is she afraid she'll see someone she knows? Does she want to block it all out? Does she still have family back there?"

"I don't know," Joel would say. We could no longer tell when he was lying.

"She doesn't talk about her family?"

"No."

"Maybe she's angry at them. Maybe they sold her to the mail-order people and took the money."

"Maybe," he said, in the way that meant he was not listening at all.

We could not get the picture out of our heads: Nadia ripped from the arms of . . . someone. By . . . someone. That part is hazy. We see the hands reaching out, Nadia crying silently. Women with kerchiefs on their heads weeping, men with huge mustaches looking stern, children hugging her knees. Nadia's chin upraised, throat exposed, martyr light in her eyes. Her shabby relations counting the money and raising their hands to the heavens in thanks, the starving children already stuffing their mouths with bread. It would make a nice painting, Nadia standing among shadows and grubby faces with a shaft of light falling on her, the way it always does no matter where she stands.

Then again, maybe we've seen too many movies. "How do we know her family got the money?" I said. "Maybe *she* came here to get rich. Maybe *she's* the gold digger. Maybe she thought high school teachers make a lot of money."

I thought he'd be more willing to talk about it alone, without the others. I left work in the afternoon and went to his high school. I found him grading papers with a student sitting on his desk. She was sucking on a lollipop, swinging her legs, looked like a twenty-five-year-old pretending to be fifteen, her tiny rear just inches from Joel's pen (purple; he said red was too harsh). She knocked her heels against the desk and he looked up.

"To what do I owe this?" he said. He took off his glasses and pinched the inside corners of his eyes. Heavy indentations marked the sides of his nose. His fingers left purply smudges. Ink and exhaustion had bruised his face like a boxer's. The classroom had the sweaty gym-socks-and-hormones smell of all high schools. On top of that there was an aggressively floral smell that was coming off the girl and a stale, musty, old-man sort of smell that, I realized, was coming from Joel.

"Sondra," he said, "go wait for your bus outside."

"Okay, Mr. J," she said, and slowly got up and fixed her skirt and sauntered out. Her bare thighs left two misty marks on the desk.

"I don't think that's appropriate," I said, tracing them with my finger.

"You have to know how to handle these kids," he said. "Sometimes they're just trying to get your goat, and the best thing to do is ignore them." He wrote an **X** on a student's paper, then scribbled over the **X**, then circled it, then wrote *sorry* in the margin.

"I still think—"

"They get bored in five minutes and do something else. Half these kids have ADD. They have the attention span of a fly."

"I wanted to talk to you about—"

"What? What was that?" He'd gone back to his grading.

If you looked at those few square inches of skin on the nape of his neck, the backs of his ears, you could almost imagine little-boy Joel. A vulnerable angle, looking down at his hunched shoulders and thinning hair. On the desk in front of him, next to a jar full of pens and highlighters, was a tiny snapshot of Nadia set in an oval ceramic frame. The picture was too small and blurry to make out her face. A gesture, that's all it was, having that photo there, nothing more. Joel's hands stopped moving. A flush moved along his scalp. He waited.

It's not a good time, I said, or thought, and left.

Clearly, he was upset. I was worried. We were all worried about Joel. His clothes were limp. He drooped. He yawned constantly. "Is it Nadia?" we said. At first he ignored us. We kept asking. Finally he nodded.

Just as we thought. She was abusing him, demanding things, running him ragged. We knew she had it in her. It's the quiet shy ones who are the hardest inside. And Joel was too kind; of course he would give in to her. All she had to do was find his sensitive spots and pinch him there. We knew where they were. She could probably find them. They were not hard to find.

But no, he said. He said it wasn't like that at all. "She's sad," he said, "about something. She won't tell me. It's killing me to see her so miserable."

We worried. Why shouldn't we? He was our friend. We'd known him for a long time, long enough to see changes in him, long enough to still see the face of younger-Joel embedded in the flesh of older-Joel. We had known him when his pores were small, his hair thick, and his body an inverted triangle rather than a pear. Of course we worried. We had a right to.

Joel was lucky to have us. Men need female friends;

they need our clear-sightedness, our intuition. And certainly women need male friends as well. The ideal male friend is one you've slept with at some point in the past—that way there's no curiosity, no wondering to taint the friendship.

Joel would not do it, he was too kind to deal with her. We took it upon ourselves. On a day when we knew he was coaching "his kids" at a soccer match, we went to the house. Nadia let us in, offered to make tea. She seemed no more dejected than usual. She was wearing enormous furry slippers shaped like bunnies, her narrow ankles plunged deep in their bellies. Perhaps she was accustomed to wearing dead animals on her feet. She shuffled across the floor, raising a foot to show us. "Funny, no?" she said.

Funny. No.

We sat her down and gave her a talking-to. She kicked off the slippers and sat cross-legged on the sofa, and we gathered around her, holding her hands, knees, shoulders, and got right to it.

"Why are you making Joel unhappy?" we asked her.

"I don't," she said. "I make him tea, I make him dinner, I make his bed. I don't make him unhappy."

"What's the trouble," we asked her. "Are you homesick?"

The end of her nose was turning pink. It was easier than we'd expected.

"You can tell us," we said. "Tell us anything. Need a shoulder to cry on? A hand to hold? Let it out. Have a good cry." She kept her head still but her eyes darted back and forth.

"What about children?" we asked. "Don't you want children?"

"We want children."

"*Joel* wants children."

"Joel wants children."

"But you don't."

"No. . . ."

"You can't?"

"No!"

"Are you trying?"

"Yes."

"But you don't want to have a child?"

"I *have* child!" she said. She twisted away from us and went to take the teakettle off the stove. We wanted to press further, but we thought she'd said enough. By the time she returned with cups and spoons and the teapot on a tray, we were gathered at the door ready to leave. She carried the tray so easily, she must have had some waitressing experience in her past, we agreed, as we headed up the street. We must have imagined the shatter and skid of china somewhere in the dark house behind us.

Of course we told Joel, and he got it all out of her in his gentle, imploring way. Nadia had a twelve-year-old daughter back in . . . wherever it was. (I looked it up—one of those places with the devious names that sound nothing like they're spelled.) Joel told her over and over, he told us over and over, that she shouldn't have kept it from him, that of course he would welcome her daughter as his own.

Outside of Nadia's hearing, he hissed that he was furious with us, with what he termed our interfering. Interfering! We'd done it for his own good. For the good of both of them. Frankness, we reminded him, was the basis of any good relationship.

We thought he would want to know what kind of woman his wife really was. How could she do such a thing? Leave her own daughter behind?

Joel didn't mention—though we suspected he brooded over—the fact that a daughter meant there was a father. Dead? An ex-husband? A current husband? A boyfriend past or present? All men are jealous, even men like Joel. They don't get jealous the same way women do, but they get jealous all the same.

"We're going to bring her over," he told us.

"Who, you?"

"Nadia can't go; she won't be able to get out again. I'm going."

"By yourself?"

"Malcolm can help, maybe," he said.

"What are you going to do, just go over there and snatch the kid?"

"There must be a legal way to do it," he said. "And if not. . . ."

Joel had never been the type to make threats; we were almost inclined to laugh. But now look at him, pounding his fist into his hand, throwing back his shoulders, glaring as if looking for a fight. She had changed him, she *had* been riding him after all, but in a more insidious way than we'd suspected. She must have sulked and whined and prodded and provoked him into charging back to her backwoods hometown to rescue her brat. Her daughter, whom we imagined as a miniature, even more doll-like version of Nadia.

We still didn't believe it. Out of those girls'-size-twelve hips? Such a tight squeeze. We pictured a blue and dented baby among gray hospital linen.

Her body—too ungenerous to nurture anything; husband, child. Not like ours. Me, I stand in front of the mirror sometimes, squeezing here and there hard enough to leave pink fingerprints. I imagine people taking bites, here and here and here. *I* could feed a family of five for a week.

Perhaps Joel's resoluteness had something to do with the phantom father—perhaps out of jealousy, or out of chivalry, he wanted to track the man down, see him face-to-face. And then what? We liked the idea of it—Joel as hero avenger, toting the twelve-year-old under his arm and facing down a dark-faced stranger—but we couldn't quite make it work. The picture in our heads looked like Joel manhandling one of his students, getting too rough on the kickball field, overstepping the bounds of discipline. Setting himself up for a lawsuit. The "he's such a nice guy" refrain would be replaced with "but he *seemed* like such a nice guy."

We thought Joel was all bluster, but he did it. He made plans; he bought tickets. Had to get special permission, made shady arrangements. Bought six pairs of Nikes, a dozen pairs of blue jeans. "Gifts." How did he know what size to get? Sunglasses and a money pouch that strapped around his waist.

I went by the house when he was packing to lend him my kit of outlet adapters. So many different configurations of prong and hole. Neither of us knew which he would need.

"Take them all," I said. My hands were overflowing. We were alone in the bedroom, suitcase splayed over the bed. I said, "It doesn't bother you that she has a child? That she loved someone else? Maybe she still thinks about him."

"She left, didn't she?" he said. "Everyone deserves a second chance." He was using the voice he used with his students, brightly chiding.

"Second chance?" I said. "Everyone?"

He walked to the other side of the bed and very studiously folded a T-shirt into a perfect square. "You know, what do I need all these plugs for, anyway? A hair dryer? An electric razor?" He tugged at his beard, just in case I didn't get it. "Thanks, but no thanks."

I passed Nadia in the hallway. "Tea?" she said.

"What?" I said. "What? Enunciate, please."

He went. He left Nadia behind, in the drafty house, which seemed colder than ever in the spring chill. We visited her again; we kept her company in twos and threes; we watched television with her while she listened to her earphones. We noticed bruises on her arms—on her ribs once when she was taking off her sweater and her undershirt rode up. Splotches like handprints. We didn't ask; we figured she was anemic. It would make sense; she must have grown up malnutritioned.

I've heard about people like that, they bruise so easily that sitting in a chair leaves them black and blue. You can bruise them by breathing on them.

We didn't know what Joel was doing over there. He probably didn't call Nadia either. She showed us a picture of her daughter, but it was an old Polaroid and too faded for us to make out the features. A bleached ghost, with a cat clearly visible in the darkened doorway beyond. Cat's eyes were red. The ghost's shoes were untied. Surely, if it was her daughter, she would have tied them before taking the picture? Later we heard that Joel had been befriending journalists, bribing locals, sneaking into places he wasn't supposed to be.

Of course we saw it on the news, the ugly things that were happening over there, but we didn't really think that Joel was in the midst of it. There's a small part of me that wonders if what we see on the news isn't real, if it's fabricated, re-enacted. I swear it's the same shabby group of refugees each time, same line of tanks, the same bandaged heads, even the same flies. Same barbed-wire fences, same hand-dug grave and sloppily wrapped corpse. Same corn-fed private telling the camera he can't wait to get home to his baby daughter. Same concluding shot of a child's toy crushed in a soldier's muddy bootprint. It's as if all the TV stations are borrowing the same bunch of actors.

Oh, I don't *really* think that. I know those things are really happening. I mean, I know now.

We might never have known what happened—Joel would never have told us—if a photojournalist hadn't been there and snapped a picture. And so Joel had to explain—we read the quotes in the newspapers—how he (and Malcolm, the mysterious Malcolm) had talked to people who sent them to a particular neighborhood where they'd seen the girl on a deserted street and thought she was the right one. Something about the shape of a hand, the tentative, up-on-the-toes walk, the translucent ears? I don't know. He wasn't thinking, he said, he just rushed out and grabbed her and then the shooting started.

He said he didn't know about the snipers on the rooftops, he said he thought the street was deserted. He didn't realize people were hiding behind locked doors and boarded windows, waiting in their homes, afraid to go out. He didn't know that only children were sent out to do errands, because a child, being smaller, might have a better chance of dodging bullets. They might not shoot a child.

He said that when he ran out into the street he only wanted to bring the girl home, and when the shooting started he only wanted to protect her. He said he was trying to keep her out of the line of fire, trying to block the bullets. But it's clear from the photograph, in which he's looking to one side and gripping to his chest a bundle of hair and dress and dangling legs, that he's using her body to shield his own.

We saw the photograph, read about it. There's a dark wet spot on the little girl's back, you can see Joel's wedding ring, you can see how bushy his beard's grown. He's wearing a hat we'd never seen before, and though the eyes are a smudge you can see his mouth hanging open, slack, completely unmoored.

We wanted to tell Nadia, couldn't tell Nadia. It wasn't really our place, we decided. We lacked the vocabulary. I doubt Joel called her. What would he say? She found out somehow, I suppose there were people she could call, family, friends, I suppose she's not as alone as she seems.

He came back eventually. Returned to the States, that is. He didn't come to see any of us. We heard he came back without the daughter. Was that because he didn't find her? Or was *that* her, the girl in the photograph? It couldn't be. We told each other that, most likely, he had found the girl, and she'd taken one look at this huge foreign-talking man and decided to stay where she was. Probably she's happier with her father, we told each other. Probably she has a whole family of her own. We pictured a father, now, who was a counterpoint to Joel: small, graceful, clean-shaven, stouthearted.

Joel avoided us. Fine. We didn't want to know what he'd brought back with him. Infection. Those diseases they have over there. Odorous invasions of the skin and digestion, diseases of neglect. The ones the travel books warn you about.

I wonder what that's like. There have been times when I'm sure I'm dying: when my heart flutters in the middle of the night for no reason, when a loneliness or craving is so strong it nauseates me—but of course I'm not. I wonder if living close to the edge of desperation like that makes you feel more alive. It's a cliché, I know, but most clichés have a core of truth, don't they? One time I tried to ask Nadia about it—whether she'd felt more alive back there in her homeland with death all around. She didn't seem to understand the question. She didn't see a difference between there and here. As if for her it was all the same: Life was perilous everywhere, a teetering tightrope walk from one minute to the next.

We wondered what would happen to Joel and Nadia. Surely they couldn't go on together? How could he explain it? Even if it wasn't her daughter, how could he have done such a thing? She wouldn't be able to stay with him. How could she? She might even go back. Maybe she'd realize that her kind of people demand a sort of heroism she won't find here.

We felt certain Joel wouldn't have hidden behind the bodies of *our* hypothetical daughters. He would have taken a bullet, rather. We all knew this. Nadia and her kind were different, they counted less. They were one degree closer to being objects, to his mind. He might deny it, but actions speak louder, don't they? In moments of panic, the true self comes to the surface.

And *she* had abandoned her own daughter. How could

they stay together, knowing these ugly truths about each other? So much for frankness.

To be rid of Nadia. Hadn't that been the intent all along? No one wanted to say it outright, but I will. Yes, it was. But now the prospect of a solitary Joel was no longer appetizing. We knew that, despite the avoidance, Joel was in need of our friendship and pity, probably for the first time. But now we didn't feel like giving it to him; we wanted to lavish it on someone more worthy.

Suddenly, we didn't want Nadia to leave.

"Have you seen Nadia?" we asked each other. "He doesn't let her out," we said. "He's holding her hostage in that miserable house."

We organized a rescue mission. "We'll break the door down if we have to," we said. Of course we didn't have to. Joel opened the door with bowed head. "Where is she?" we said, pushing our way in. We were momentarily distracted; Joel looked like he might tolerate, for once might even welcome, a hug or a kiss on the cheek. We steeled ourselves and pressed on.

"Nadia," we said. "Do you want some tea? Tea? Are you warm enough? Can we make you a sandwich?"

She was sitting before the fireplace, orange light warming her face like sunlight. She looked ageless, beautiful and sorrowful, a classical sculpture. I looked at her and thought, Devastating. I will never in my life look like that. It was both a disappointment and a relief.

"I never asked him to go," she said, twisting her hair in her fingers. "I miss her, but my daughter, she is happy with her father and father's new wife. But Joel, he sees I am sad, so he tries to bring her to me anyway. He thinks he can make her come."

Joel had never told us that part of the story.

We surrounded her, we touched her gently. We tried to tell

her our plans for her. How we were ready to embrace her, shield her, take her in. We wanted to give her the sense of security she'd never had since she'd come here. Nadia could not always follow the gist of the conversation. But we knew she was listening, we knew she understood. We wanted to have with her what she had had with women at home. The unspoken female kinship. I could picture it. Women cooking together, sewing together, braiding each other's hair. Napping with their heads on each other's shoulders and laps. Gathered around beds, wiping each other's foreheads, murmuring encouragement. Birth, death, all the same. Gathered around a candlelit bed. Sewing a swaddling cloth, sewing a shroud. I think they go to public bathhouses, dunk in cold pools, then sit in the steam. All the women together, young ones, pregnant ones, old ones with drooping breasts. Sharing the towels, the moist wooden benches. They have no conception of embarrassment. They rub a gray paste into their hair to dye it red. The longer they leave it in, the redder it gets. They beat each other with hazel branches—I hear it's good for the skin.

"You're safe now," I told her, slowly and clearly. "No more tightrope."

We wanted to live with her. At least until our cycles became synchronized, until our secrets were the same.

The more we talked, the more we realized we had nothing to offer, nothing that compared to the female utopia she'd once known. The desire rose in us not to keep her here but to let her go home—and take us along.

"You miss your daughter, don't you?" we said. "You're jealous of her stepmother, aren't you?" For the first time her eyes snapped into focus.

Joel came into the room, then, and shooed us away like chickens.

We came back in shifts, bringing soup, sweaters, flowers,

children's books—to help her learn English, we thought. I
don't know how to cook—I emptied canned soup into a pot—
but it's the thought that counts.

We tried to be like her. We drank her vodka, listened to
her music. We drank more, and danced, and threw our glasses
in the fireplace. She fell asleep while we sang along to the
incomprehensible lyrics and clapped our hands before falling into giddy heaps on the floor.

Nadia took to her bed. We told Joel it was female trouble,
that he should stay away and let us handle it.

"Are you pregnant?" we asked her.

"Maybe," she said carelessly, sucking on a cigarette. The
ashtray beside her bed was overflowing. The skin around her
eyes was creased and crumpled with a hundred tiny wrinkles.
Her hair lay over her shoulders, spread over the pillow. The
hair, I thought, that's what makes her look so young. If she had
a sensible cut she'd look like everybody else.

She seemed to get weaker and weaker, day by day. We
plied her with pills: extra-strength, fast-acting, non-drowsy,
maximum strength, weapons-grade, strongest medicine you
can buy without a prescription. None of it seemed to do any
good. Joel gave her a Chinese checkers game, and she used
the pills as game pieces.

"She *is* a doctor, you know," Joel said one day, materializing
out of a dark hallway as we were leaving. "She knows how to
take care of herself."

"But she's not doing it," we said. "She's letting herself go.
And you're not taking care of her."

His old-man hands fumbled with his sweater. He'd missed
too many classes and had been given an unpaid leave of
absence. We saw him once or twice strolling past the high
school, staring longingly at his former students, trying to
engage them in conversation on their way in or out. You could
see what he'd eventually turn into.

"You shouldn't smoke," we told her, gently but firmly. "It's bad for the baby."

"You would take away the one thing that gives me pleasure?" she said, smiling an ironic smile. She did this sometimes, said something so sarcastic and knowing that she seemed infinitely older and wiser than any of us. We were shocked to see a gap in her smile. One of her teeth—a canine—had fallen out.

I thought, sometimes, that if I could just be alone with her, we might be able to have a real conversation. But the others were always there, chattering, squawking, plumping pillows, humming over her, stroking her forehead, doing their best Florence Nightingale imitations. I wasn't like them. I had never been. I wasn't sure she could see that.

She seemed to be growing hotter, and hotter, more and more translucent, a mere glow; I was sure one day we'd come in to find an invisible shape, a warm vapor humping up the blankets. We had to stop her. We had to save her.

"Take her to the emergency room," one of us said.

"No," I said. "She doesn't want modern medicine. What she needs is an old-fashioned cure."

The others clucked in surprise. But they liked the idea, I could tell. We discussed the various cures and remedies our grandmothers had dosed us with. We talked of slimy poultices, hideous potions, onions and garlic rubbed on the chest, ointments made from fish eyes, immersion in tea, in tomato soup, in ice water.

"When my grandmother had a fever, she'd go swim naked in the river," I said. "Even in the middle of winter. She swore by it."

The others looked at me suspiciously, but they nodded their heads. Something about the plan seemed appropriate, seemed right, like something they had seen in an old yellowed photograph or in a television documentary. The image of Nadia, pink-nosed, sodden, wrapped in an enormous, scratchy gray blanket, shivering in our arms, luminously grateful—this picture appealed to all of us.

There was still snow on the ground. "Good, good," we told each other. "Nice and cold." We bundled Nadia into the car— "I am all right, I am OK," she insisted, shrugging off our helping hands. We were quiet during the cramped drive, our breaths steaming up the windows as if the car were full of frantically necking teenagers.

The riverbank. I was disappointed, it was not as scenic as I remembered. Deserted picnic tables lumped with snow. Cars whizzing past on the nearby overpass. Bare skeletal trees against a low smothering sky. Everything in shades of black and gray. Like Nadia's home, I realized. Perfect.

The river—mucky banks, thick black water with chunks of ice floating in it.

She was tottering from the car on thin unsteady legs. We reached out to help her. She shook us off. We smiled indulgently. She was like a cartoon of endearing gangliness, a human version of Bambi.

"Take in that breeze," we said encouragingly. "Breathe it in. Aaah. Bracing," we said. "Take big cleansing breaths. Like this."

She looked at us quizzically, the sleeves of Joel's shirt pulled down to cover her hands, a cigarette protruding from one of them.

"She needs to feel the water," someone said.

"Just dunk her feet."

"A splash on her face."

"Get her shoes off."

"What you are doing?" Nadia said.

"It's for your own good," we said. "We're only trying to help."

We got her down to the water; she was not cooperating but not really resisting either. We pulled off her flimsy ballet-type shoes, her crocheted socks. Why did she look so confused? Hadn't she done this before or seen it done to others? I could swear I read it in a book, saw it on an educational program, the women in their shawls and kerchiefs dunking a fever-stricken child in ice-cold water in a rhythmic ritual, child in a nightshirt with thin bone-white feet just like Nadia's. There's singing, or chanting, something, old men rubbing their bare chests with snow—

"Here," we said, holding her arms, nudging her forward into the water. She shrieked, lifted her knees to her chest so that she hung suspended in our grip. "Again," we said.

"No," she said, twisting. She struck someone in the nose, there was a curse, a spray of blood. She kicked me and I fell to my hands and knees, covered in muck: my new trousers; the stain would never come out.

"You ungrateful—" someone shouted.

"We're only trying to—"

"Ignorant little—"

"Think you're so special—"

"And *this* is how you thank us?"

Nadia stood knee-deep in water, cigarette held high above her head. The others were crowded on the bank, blocking her path, so she started backing away. She waded slowly, seemingly unaware of the cold, as the others shouted accusations and encouragement.

Then an undercurrent swept her off her feet and carried her downstream. It happened so swiftly, it was like an amusement park ride, Nadia down and then bobbing back up, spinning like a paper doll, trailing streaming hair. Just like that, she was gone.

Once we couldn't see her, it was like it hadn't happened. It was as if I'd closed my eyes and asked myself, I wonder what Nadia would look like spinning down the river; ah, yes, *that's* what it would look like, and then opened my eyes again.

We looked at one another.

"We killed her," someone said. There were nervous giggles. The words sounded absurd.

"We have to call the police," someone said.

"I can't," I said. "I have to get home. Get these clothes off."

"This was all your idea," someone said.

I admit I would have left right then, if I could have. But we'd all come in the same car.

"It was an accident."

"It doesn't look like one."

"I can't be involved in this," I said.

"Why?"

"Well," I said, "you know how Joel and I . . . how we used to. . . . People might think I had a motive. They'd think I *wanted* to get rid of her."

"That's no reason."

I looked at them all and wondered, not for the first time, how many of them had slept with Joel too. We stared at one another, our breaths puffing white in the air.

What happened next is something I'd rather not dwell on. Someone lunged at someone else, hoping to snatch the car keys and make a run for it. Someone pushed someone else, someone tripped, someone kicked someone else in the mouth. Someone's purse got thrown in the river, and soon there were five purses sailing down the current. Someone particularly bloodthirsty tore an earring from someone else's ear. There were punches, kicks, scratching. Someone picked up a broken bottle. It was a brawl, a melee, mayhem. We surprised ourselves, and not in a good way. Surprised by the extent of the viciousness we had all harbored. We had suspected it was there, but never in our worst paranoid nightmares had we expected there to be so much of it.

And I think I was most surprised by pain. I was surprised by how much it *hurts*. There was nothing heroic or dramatic about it. I thought pain is supposed to bring clarity, as if a jolt to the nerve endings should reveal the meaning of life. Instead, all it does is make you more conscious of your body, how rickety it is, how vulnerable. It gave me an appreciation for the padded living I had always despised.

There was the momentary satisfaction of doing something you had longed to do for years—"I could kill her," you think twice a day, listening to her whining on the phone—followed immediately by disappointment, the dirty, undignified, shameful reality.

. . .

They found Nadia, four miles downstream, washed up against a bridge piling. I saw her on the news, the pink nose and gray blanket just as I'd envisioned. They were calling it a miracle; she'd spent minutes submerged, but the coldness of the water slowed down her body's processes, kept her from drowning.

"Clever Nadia," I said.

I wondered what she would tell people, would tell Joel. I felt strangely immune, as if she could not reach me. Now that she'd entered the television world, she'd be trapped there forever.

I say I felt immune, but really I felt more that I was at an impasse. I was waiting, waiting, I had no idea what would happen next.

But as I said, it was oddly satisfying to see Nadia on the television screen, it was as if she were back where she belonged, as if she could change the channel and zap herself home, to the shouting, the running, the bombs falling, the tanks stirring up clouds of dust. Or, alternately, jump into a sunny sitcom, a dazzling toothpaste commercial, a heavy-breathing pornographic movie.

A reporter grasped her shoulder and shook her, holding a

microphone to her face. "What was it like?" he asked. "Did you have a near-death experience?"

"Near-death experience?" she repeated. Her blue lips strained into a smile. "I have been having one of these for years. I am having it right now."

"You have to leave now. They'll be here any minute."

"Why can't I meet them?" he asked. "You're ashamed of me."

"Of course not. If anything, I'm ashamed of *them*."

"Why?" he said. "Are they really fat or something?"

"No! Why do you say that?"

"Well, you're so worried all the time about getting fat, I figured maybe it's a hereditary thing you're trying to outrun."

"My mother's very thin," she said. "And so is my father."

"Great. I can't wait to meet your very thin parents."

"No."

"I know, I know, you don't want me to see what you're going to turn into."

"But I'm not going to turn into my mother."

"That's what you think."

. . .

"Meredith, honey . . ." Whoosh of trucks, bursts of radio static, deep subterranean rumbling.

"Mom, where are you? I thought you'd be here by now."

"We got off to a late start. You know how your father is."

"But how close are you?"

We're just off Ninety-five. Your father needed to find a bathroom. We'll be there soon. I hope you're not fussing; we don't want you to bother."

"How's Dad?"

"Well, this sun. He's getting a sunburn through the windshield, you know? His forehead. This heat. And you know how your father is about the air-conditioning."

"It's exit seventeen, remember. Be ready, it comes up pretty fast. And then a left at the second intersection—"

"Oh, honey, we remember. We've been there so many times. Here comes your father now. We have something we want to tell you."

"What? I can barely hear you."

"I have a tissue over the receiver. These pay phones at the rest stops, they don't seem very sanitary. These people out here. Did you wash your hands?"

"Yes," she said automatically, as she heard her father's answering bark in the background.

. . .

"They're running late but they'll be here any minute."

"Why can't I stay?"

"It's too soon for this. We hardly know each other."

"How can you say that? I know *you*."

She decided she would not answer that. She was stripping the sheets off the bed, sniffing them, her lips pressed tight together.

For her birthday he had given her a set of mixing spoons,

measuring cups, an eggbeater, a double boiler, basters and graters and strainers.

"So you can putter around the kitchen," he'd explained. "I like a woman who putters."

. . .

"Mom! Where are you? What's taking so long?"

"We must have missed the exit. I don't know how. I'm driving, your father wasn't up to it, but now he says it's my fault. I asked him to watch for signs."

"Where are you now?"

"Well, we got off the highway and turned around and came back in the other direction, but still we must have missed it. So we turned around again. Your father is getting very hot but won't put on the air. He says it overheats the engine."

"What exit are you near?"

"Well, we kept going back and forth, circling, till I'm not sure anymore which way we were going, and then at one point we got off the highway and couldn't seem to get back on. So now we're on this nice country road."

"Where. . . . what are you near?"

"We just passed a billboard that said JESUS IS THE ANSWER. So what was the question, I ask you? Now we're at a gas station with those old-fashioned round-headed pumps. I should ask for directions, but . . . you know how your father is about asking directions."

"What's he doing right now?"

"Washing the windshield with one of those sponge-and-scraper things."

"While he's distracted, why don't you run and ask someone?"

"Oh, honey, don't be silly. Besides, I hate to bother the attendant since we're not buying anything. We'll be there soon."

. . .

"What's your father like?"

"Well, he doesn't talk much. The strong silent type."

"I've never seen you like this. . . . Do you always clean before they come?"

"Well, there are things they don't need to see."

"Where should I put this?"

"In the bathroom."

"And what about this? On the dresser here?"

"God, no! You can't leave something like that just lying out in the open! What are you thinking?"

. . .

"We found a roadside stand. We're buying you some tomatoes."

"Mom, I don't want tomatoes."

"And some beautiful fresh corn. I didn't know you could still find stands like these so close to the city. This nice woman is letting your father use the bathroom up in her house. Nice country people. It's a big white house on the edge of the cornfields. You don't find hospitality like this much anymore."

"I don't want any corn. I . . . it's getting later and later. If you could just tell me what road you're on, I could look at a map."

"I want some corn," he said.

"Who said that?"

"No one . . . just a friend."

"Oh. Does your friend have a name?"

"Not really . . . I mean, yes. Parrish. Everybody calls him Pare."

"Here's your father. I should go now. He's not doing so well, this dust is really bothering him. And he . . ."

"He what? What?"

"Has a look on his face. I don't know. As if he saw something up at the house."

"Saw what? Can you see it?"

"What's there to see? A white house on a hill. A tire swing hanging from a branch. A baby's playpen. A pump in the yard. A dog on a chain. He's getting in the car. Have I told you how your father never wears a seat belt now? He says it chokes him."

.   .   .

"Why are you washing those? I just washed them."

"You only rinsed them."

"They're clean."

"They're not."

"You used to think so. You used to be satisfied with the way I washed dishes."

"Things change."

"Here, I'll do it."

She watched him splashing water on the floor. If you didn't know what he was doing, if you just looked at the bowed posture and pumping elbows and concentrated grunting, you'd think he was doing something obscene. There were funny hairy patches on the backs of his elbows and the tops of his shoulders. He was softer around the middle than she liked. She had never noticed these things before. Had they cropped up overnight?

"What was it like growing up in the South?" he'd asked once. "Were you a debutante? Did you have a coming-out party? Cotillion?"

"Oh, sure," she'd said. "Debutante balls, white dresses, full curtsies, sloe gin fizzes. I was lucky, I got spoken for early on. All the debutantes left single at the end of the night were taken out behind the barn and shot."

. . .

"There was a delay, but now we're back on track."

"What happened?"

"A roadblock. The police were stopping cars, looking for someone. Slowed things up a bit."

"Did you ask for directions?"

"We didn't want to hold things up for the people behind. Had to keep the line moving. You know how your father gets with lines. He's taking a restroom break now."

"Is he all right?"

"I don't know what he does in there, I think he's just washing his hands, getting spruced up for you. You know that piece of hair that always sticks up, he's forever wetting it down."

"Who were they looking for?"

"We don't know . . . but, Mare, they looked at our faces so long and hard, shining flashlights in the middle of the day— waste of batteries, if you ask me—and poking their heads in the car and sniffing . . . as if they'd never seen anything like it before. I tell you, these policemen in rural areas, it's like they have nothing better to do than harass people passing through."

"Rural areas? Where are you?"

"Here comes your father."

. . .

"Funny, they don't look like themselves."

"Pictures always lie. But let me see them anyway."

"This is my mom; it's from several years ago. And here's another . . . funny, this one's more recent but she looks younger than she does in the older photos."

He pressed his hands to his face, stretching his eyes to slits and flattening his cheeks. "Surgery?" he said, and waited for her to laugh.

"Never!"

"Look, I have Chinese eyes," he said.

"Ugh. Grow up."

"This photo, this is your dad? Not bad for an old guy."

"He's in better shape than you are, Pare."

She pulled the pictures away. The name echoed strangely in her head. Pare. Pear. Unfortunate nickname. He was not pear-shaped yet but he was getting there.

"They don't look at all the way I remember them."

.   .   .

"Mare, honey, do you think you could give us directions?"

"But where are you? You have to tell me where you are!"

"I'm not sure." Wind, branches scraping, a bad connection, a tremor in the wire that made her mother's voice vibrate.

"Your father—"

"Don't listen to Dad! He's being ridiculous! Stop and ask someone for directions!"

"Your father . . . see, we hit something. I was driving, and . . . I *was* paying attention, but it came out of the bushes so fast, and before I could even think—*thump!*—and then the back tires went over it."

"Went over what?"

"I couldn't see, really. It's getting dark. Brown, black, down on all fours, scurrying. Fairly large. It was a fairly large thump. I saw orange eyes, for a second, I think, just the reflection of the headlights, I guess."

"And Dad . . ."

"Well, you know how your father is, won't even kill a cockroach, traps them in a paper cup and takes them outside. He was looking out the back window and said the animal was still moving, said we should go back and get it off the road or at least put it out of its misery."

"What, run over it again?"

"So I turned around, no other cars on the road, ditches on either side and I almost got stuck, so dry here the earth just falls away, but I drove back. And I stopped, about twenty feet away, and your father got out . . ."

"What did he think he was doing?"

"Honey, I don't know . . . he walked over, it was just a stain in the road, a big lump like an old coat but shiny and wet. And he bent down to look, and then swung his foot, I think he was going to kick it to the side of the road, and then suddenly the coat comes to life and is clinging to his leg and your father is lunging around in the headlights saying terrible things."

"But you should go to the hospital! Call Nine-one-one!"

"It doesn't look too bad. His good pants are ruined. He made it back to the car and as we drove off we could hear it chasing, snapping and scraping at the side of the car . . . there's this funny dark smear on the door here. I saw this pay phone and thought I'd try you and let you know we'll be late."

"Stop wasting time talking! Get help."

"I tried the Nine-one-one, doesn't work for some reason. So we'll just come along to your place."

"I'll come to you, I'll call the police or something."

"Oh, don't bother them, they have enough work to do. I should get back to your father now."

"Is he all right?"

"Well, you know your father. He never complains."

"I want you to get to the nearest hospital."

"Don't tell us what to do, we can take care of ourselves. Can you see the sunset where you are? Bright deep red, with smudges of black, looks like the insides of your lids when you rub your eyes. Almost can't tell if your eyes are open or closed. I can smell . . . there must be a fire somewhere."

"Do you have enough gas?"

"I should have worn better shoes. There's the horn, your

father must be getting impatient. Or tired, he's sort of slouched over, I think his head hit the horn."

"Mother?"

"Mare."

.   .   .

"I don't know what to do."

"There's nothing you *can* do."

"But they . . . my dad. Something *bit* him."

"They're grown-ups. They can take care of themselves."

"I thought you were leaving. Don't touch me."

"You're all sweaty."

"I'm nervous. When I'm nervous, I sweat. I said don't touch me."

"I've never seen you sweat before. It's interesting."

"It's so hot in here."

"But you're shivering. Why don't you take a shower?"

"What if they come? What if the phone rings?"

"I'll get it."

She intended to jump in the shower and out again, quickly, just get wet, but once she got under the water her back unclenched and she closed her eyes and forgot where she was and stood there for a long peaceful white-tiled moment. Spray on her face. Windshield wipers, spinning tires. Her stomach lurched. When she got out her fingertips had pruned; even her palms had wrinkled.

"Did they call?"

"Nope."

"No?"

"I'm sure that means everything's fine."

"Oh, yeah, I'm sure *that's* what it means."

"Here, let me dry your hair for you," he said magnanimously. She gave him the towel and turned and waited for a

brisk massage. But instead he dabbed at her head, rubbed it
cautiously as if it were a newel post he was dusting, as if he
was not sure of what he was doing. What was wrong with
him? How hard could it be? Everybody knows how to dry hair.

"Do you know you have a bald spot back here?" he said.

"What? No! Where?"

He guided her fingers to it. She was reminded of a time
when she had guided his fingers to a particular spot on her
body that he had not been able to find.

"There. Feel it?"

"No. Yes." An irregular hairless space, larger than a silver
dollar, perfectly centered at the back of her head. Surely it was
a mistake.

"Get out. Get out. Don't look at me."

He was cradling the wet towel as if it were a baby, he was
propped against the door frame as if he were too tired to stand
alone. She touched the spot, probed, picked. He watched,
fascinated.

"Don't look at me." She covered her own eyes.

"Where are my glasses?" he said.

"You wear glasses?"

"I just started."

.   .   .

"You two come along right now! This instant! I'm tired of this!"
she said.

"We'll be there soon."

"Are you back on the highway?"

"I was having trouble driving, it's gotten so dark. It's misty,
smoky or something. Your father says they burn the fields, it's
good for the soil. There's a funny smell, I thought there was
something wrong with the engine, with the air vents. But now
I think it's inside the car, the smell. It's not good."

"Where are you?"

"You see, I was getting too tired to drive, and your father is in no shape . . . so I pulled over for a little rest. And then we met someone. This nice man here has offered to drive us—"

"What's his name?"

"Well, he didn't say. He's very nice."

"But—get his name! What does he look like? Short, tall, old, young—what?"

"I don't know. It's dark. I can't see his face."

.   .   .

"They think it's a joke. They're so irresponsible. They shouldn't be allowed to drive."

"Should we go look for them?"

"I wouldn't know where to start. " She looked at the veins rearing up on the backs of her hands. She felt so tired. Her fingers were still wrinkled from the shower. Her breasts felt heavy, dragging earthward, her bra straps digging into her back. She felt herself slumping, her back curving and humping between the shoulder blades. Parrish was buttoning up a cardigan sweater to hide his paunch.

"It's my fault," she said. "I should have given them better directions. I should take better care of them. They shouldn't be out there all alone."

.   .   .

"Honey, we're almost there. He says he's taking us on a special shortcut. He really knows his way around."

"Do you see street signs?"

"He says I won't be able to call anymore. We'll be needing the change."

"Where's Dad? Where's Dad?"

"Charlie? He's right here."

"Put Dad on."

"He can't get out of the car. But maybe if I stretch the cord . . ."

The voice was a low gargling, a ruminative chewing. Wet breath.

Then the breath stopped.

"Dad? That doesn't sound like Dad! Who is that?"

Although she could not recall her father's voice now, could not remember the last time she had talked to him on the phone.

"You know how your father gets," her mother whispered. "He doesn't like to ask for help. His pride."

"Mom, is there something you're not telling me?"

"Honey, have you been listening to the news? Have you heard?"

"That man . . . driving you? Let me talk to him."

"Oh, he's not for you, you can't hog all the boys now. You said you had a 'friend' already. Parrish? Mare and Pare, that's very cute. He thinks it's funny too, he's laughing."

"Mom! Look around you! What do you see?"

"Is this a game? I see the car, of course. Charlie. This pay phone. The fields. The corn as high as an elephant's eye. The moon in a smudgy sky. Gas station, bright lights, grease stains on the concrete. A minimart. I'll get Charlie a Coke, even though he doesn't like Coke. The corn is moving, waving like an ocean. Even makes a sound like waves. Now it's moving, dark things among the stalks, scuttling around like lice . . . it's people! Now there are people coming out of the corn, there's men, there's children running . . . now they see the car. Now they're all running, their faces, funny, so familiar, now they're running right at us. . . ."

She heard the baying of dogs under and over and around her mother's voice.

"Get in the car."

"What?"

"Get in the car. Now."

.   .   .

They waited for the phone to ring. She checked the cord several times to make sure everything was plugged in the way it was supposed to be. Sometimes she thought she heard it ringing and picked it up. Each time she did, a loud belligerent humming bored into her ear. A fuzzy darkness coated the windows. "Do you hear something?" she asked Parrish, and asked again, and each time he cupped his hand to the side of his head and squinted in a way that reminded her of something, something she couldn't recall, but it filled her with tenderness.

The former prime minister, apprehended after seven years spent in hiding and/or living under an assumed name, offers the following testimony:

. . .

Let me tell you a story about a man named Joss Moorkin. That name means nothing to you, I suppose, which would make him sad; it means he has not yet become the world-renowned artist he hoped to be by now. But give him time. It may happen yet.

When, as an ambitious student, he dreamed about fame—worldwide recognition, a college course devoted to his work, his name used adjectivally (which do you like better, he'd say, Moorkinian, or Moorkish?)—I liked to remind him that fame often waited for you to die before it came knocking.

Then maybe I should speed things up, he'd say, timidly jabbing at his throat with the scissors or palette knife at hand. Poor Joss. All around him students were hacking goat carcasses into fetid sculptures, painting portraits with their own blood, filming grisly shrieking performance-art orgies, and getting top grades, while he was sketching with blunt crayons and using plastic children's safety scissors (he had a fear of blades).

You could never go through with it, I always told him.

I'll do what I have to do, he'd say heatedly. If there were a guarantee, I'd do it in a second. Sell my soul, whatever.

Don't talk like that, you're scaring me, I'd say at that point, not because he was, but because it was what he wanted me to say. Really, I was trying not to laugh.

He was like a bridge jumper who lets go of the railing only when the rescue teams are within reach, a small man who dares to pick a fight because he knows his friends will restrain him before a punch gets thrown, a terrier barking at the end of a leash. At least, that's what I thought then.

. . .

Let me back up a bit and tell you about the face. The face that loomed, that peeked over every shoulder, haunted your dreams, coasted among the clouds beaming down like the moon. Huge and devouring, tiny and penetrating. It is as familiar to me as my own palm, with creases like life lines and love lines and head lines. The face that everyone knew; it flashed in the insides of your eyelids when you blinked. Even the blind were given woodcuts to run their fingers over so they could recognize the face in a heartbeat. So familiar that at times you almost ceased to see it, in much the same way that your eyes learn to ignore the nose cutting off a chunk of your vision because it is always there.

But I will describe it if you like. Because times have changed and you seem to have forgotten. A square face, haloed by an upsweep of black hair. The eyes always met yours, caught and held them whatever your viewing angle;

they were heavy-lidded and dark, radiating lines from their corners, lines that spoke of fatigue and wisdom and lack of vanity. The brows were perfectly shaped, but there was the slightest pucker of tension between them, a pinch of worry, compassion, reproach. A sharp chin, a strong jaw, the cords and knots of an aging neck hidden by a scarf or the high collar of a simple, militaristic, yet feminine jacket. Deep lines framing a mouth that was always closed, a mouth that sometimes looked stern, sometimes seemed to be suppressing a laugh. An expression captivating in its elusiveness. You glanced and found yourself looking again and again, trying to puzzle it out. A monumental, otherworldly calm, and at the same time a close, almost maternal intimacy. You could see the tiny hairs above the lip. The pupils held sparks, ambiguous shapes; you felt you could see your own face reflected in them. You never saw the teeth but you knew they were there, long and curved and slightly yellowish behind the coarse red-painted lips. A strong face, yet vulnerable, it made you both want to protect it and be coddled by it. The eyes had a glassy liquid surface, the glitter of unshed tears.

Sometimes you'd catch a glimpse and you'd swear the portrait had winked or breathed. And sometimes it had; the large portraits in public places had mechanical flaps that would shift at random times. Nothing obvious, just a subtle twitch of the face that would nag irritatingly at your brain. And, too, entire portraits were refreshed often: no substantial change, just enough to snag the eye. A different-colored jacket. Fresh clouds or drapery in the background. A badge or brooch on the chest. A roving brown mole that migrated from nose to forehead to chin.

The giant public posters were refreshed at night, so people were spared the unsettling sight of the face torn and devoured and reborn by maggotlike swarms of tiny men in overalls.

You saw the portrait billboard-sized in parks and squares,

along the highways, among neon advertisements, large enough to leap into, lose yourself in. You saw it tiny, on every piece of paper currency, every subway token; it was printed on packs of cigarettes and condom wrappers. It hung in every classroom, in every home. It hung in pubs, where it was bad for business; a glimpse of the reproachful face sent drinkers guiltily home after a glass or two. It hung in public bathrooms, in stalls, above urinals—Joss always said he couldn't go unless he covered those eyes with his hand.

It was mounted on ambulances and fire trucks.

It was in coloring books—a simplified contour version— in a variety of poses: policewoman, doctor, chef, farmer, scientist. It was always hard to color in the eyes, I remember.

There it was, in a mosaic of a million tiny square tiles, on the floor of the practice pool used by the national swimming team.

Some said it hung in hospital delivery rooms, so that it was the first face a child saw upon entering the world.

You often saw people, older people, for no apparent reason, standing still at busy intersections as the buses and bicycles and pedicabs swarmed past, gazing upward at the face for minutes or hours at a time, jostled and oblivious, rain or sweat dripping off them, awe or adoration on their faces.

There were rumors that the portraits hid cameras that recorded *your* face, and if you clocked up enough hours staring you would be rewarded; you would get exemptions on your taxes, your children would be excused from military service, your application for a car or a vacation permit would be pushed to the top of the years-long waiting lists.

There were rumors that if you stared at the portrait long enough a psychedelic three-dimensional image—a spaceship, a naked woman—would appear: one of the government's odd misguided attempts to engage the younger citizens, the teenagers and students.

There was sometimes a line or two of text. Vague exhorta-
tions and encouragements that, like the portrait itself, stuck
in the brain because they did not quite make sense and
begged to be puzzled out. Responses a parent would give to an
exasperating three-year-old.

You know better than that.

Why? Because I said so.

Make your own fun.

Can't is a four-letter word.

Or did I invent those? Maybe. The edges blur, between
what was and what might have been. The face could do that,
make you project things, fantasize; it was a mirror; it was putty
to plug the gaps in your life. It was a chastising mother with
hawklike eyes, all-knowing; it held out steaming mugs of tea
on billboards facing homebound trains; it leaned close to feel
your forehead for a fever; at night after curfew the signs bear-
ing the face were the only ones aglow, solitary lights in a dark
city, watching over all. Waking up at night and seeing that
light, spilling through the window and into your lap, it made
you feel watched over, safe. Or it made you feel guilty—here
was the face, awake and tirelessly working, while everyone
was asleep.

. . .

But about Joss. We met at the day-care center. We were—
I don't know—five, six? We were at the day-care center because our fathers worked long shifts and our mothers had
gone away. Our fathers were always late to fetch us, so each
day ended with just the two of us on a fenced-in playground
populated by stolid concrete animals: camel, giraffe, elephant.
They didn't spin, or slide, or bounce. They just stood there.

I remember that playground. There was a factory nearby
that spewed out sweet chemical-smelling smoke. If you

breathed it in deep it made your mouth water, even if you weren't hungry.

The pavement was marked with painted lines, boundaries for an indecipherable game. It was dotted with wads of gum and mysterious dark spots. I speculated that these spots were places where children had skinned their knees, and the blood made a stain that would never wash away. If you touched a spot, especially if you licked it, you would get a disease and die. Of course the more I mulled over this, the more I wanted to do it—lie down and touch my tongue to one, just to see what would happen.

Of course the portrait hung in the classroom at the day-care center. It hung above the blackboard, next to the clock. From the way our teacher, Marta, looked up and said, *Now it's time for naps . . . now it's time to put on coats,* I assumed the portrait was dictating orders to her. Sometimes she would look up with hope on her face and look away again with a disappointed sigh; the face had not granted her request, whatever it was. And other times she'd look up and—*Oh, thank God!* she'd say to the face. That meant it was almost time to go home.

Once a day we all had to face the portrait, the portrait of our prime minister, and hold our hands in a particular way and recite something that was a bit like a prayer and a bit like a jump-rope rhyme.

Isn't it incredible that I can't recall the exact words of that pledge, after reciting it every day of my childhood? But beginning in my teens, I started hearing so many bastard versions, profane and filthy and eminently catchier, that I lost track of the original.

When we had juice and biscuits, we had to look up and say thank you before eating. If we did something naughty, we had to tell the portrait we were sorry, because the prime minister saw everything. *Pryminister,* we'd say, making it one word.

When it was naptime you had to go get a mat and a blanket from the closet and spread them out on the floor. Some of the mats had gnaw marks on the edges or were strangely damp and greasy. You had to lie quietly until the face, and Marta, decided it was time to get up. Sometimes you slept and had terrible drab dreams. Sometimes you stared at the ceiling tiles until they started to bulge toward you, like a tent roof filling with water, and it took everything in you to lie still and not scream. Marta would single you out if you didn't have your hands outside the blanket.

Giita, dear, show us your hands, she'd say. I got called out more than anyone else. It was because when I fell asleep my hands liked to curl up into claws on my chest, under the blanket. I couldn't help it. I wasn't doing whatever she thought I was doing. The others would whisper that you were a dirty girl, a squirmy germy girl.

I thought maybe those disobedient hands were the reason none of the others would talk to me. Except strange Joss Moorkin, and only when we were alone on the playground.

There was a crack at the base of the concrete kangaroo. We took turns chipping at it with rocks. We thought the kangaroo might be hollow or have a baby kangaroo inside. I tried to trick him into licking a blood spot as an experiment but he looked at me blankly. Lick the *ground*?

What's your dad do? I said.

Designs new and better wings for new and better wing nuts, he said proudly. It sounded like he was repeating something a sarcastic adult had said, minus the sarcasm.

You're a wing nut, I said, and then felt sorry.

You're a bore-hole changer.

What about your mum?

She got taken away.

Mine too, I said.

There was nothing special about that. It happened all

the time. It wasn't as common as losing a tooth, but more in the vicinity of getting one's tonsils out. If you hadn't had it done, you knew someone who did. People disappeared all the time.

Listen, he said, I'll show you mine if you show me yours.

It makes me laugh to think of him saying that. Even at the time—age six, seven, whatever—it made me roll my eyes. Joss was always so *slow*. I had been through that rigmarole—the elaborate negotiations, the brief and anticlimactic revelations—years before, with the monkey-faced children in my apartment block. Joss looked much older than I but acted younger. He always lagged behind what was fashionable, told stale jokes.

I'll go first, he said, and before I could say a word he had unsnapped his corduroy pants, whipped them down to his knees, and then yanked them back up again. I got the briefest glimpse of thin thighs and dangling shirttails covering the parts I didn't really want to see anyway. I didn't even get a chance to register what his underwear looked like. Maybe he wasn't wearing any. Horrors. At that age, that was the worst of crimes, positively barbaric.

Now you, he said.

But I didn't . . .

I already went, so now you *have* to, he said. It's only fair.

I couldn't argue with that sort of incontestable logic. I started to undo my belt reluctantly. I was wearing my brother's hand-me-down underpants, I remember, but that didn't bother me particularly; in those days of shortages you often saw women in men's boots and trousers, men in women's raincoats. But I was afraid Marta might come outside for a cigarette and spot us, and I didn't want her hands-under-the-blanket suspicions about me to be confirmed.

Now it was Joss's turn to roll his eyes. Not that, he said. *That*. And he pointed to my feet.

How did you know about *that?*

Everybody talks about it. Besides, you walk funny. People say it's catching.

It's not catching, I said, though I thought it might be.

Prove it.

So I took off my shoes and socks and showed him—well, you've seen—I don't need to describe them, do I? I don't know why people always react so strongly. They're not the norm, but they're not *so* strange either. It's a template that occurs in nature all the time, it just doesn't usually occur *here.* I think of seagulls, ducks, swans, the clownish platypus. Frogs, of course. I think of the translucent veiny membrane stretched between a bat's long fingers.

Ugly duckling was my father's nickname for me, or, on special occasions, F.S. for future swan. The doctor told us he had to wait for me to stop growing before he could do anything about it. It sounded like an excuse. He was an ancient tortoise of a man who wanted to put us off until he was safely retired.

Joss stared, stared and touched. Does this hurt? he said, stretching a web between his fingers.

No . . . ow!

But it just feels like skin, he said, surprised. He was crouched over my feet, wrists sticking out of his too-small sweater, his long oddly-shaped head bowed. There was a bit of rash, or maybe a strawberry mark, that started on the back of his neck and disappeared beneath his hair. I had a mean thought.

I lied, I told him. It *is* catching. In a few days, you'll see. You'll start to itch, between your toes, and then . . .

Really? he said, looking up, and his eyes were round and either very scared or very excited, it was hard to tell which. Just like you? he said.

For the next several nights, I lay awake thinking of *him*

lying awake in fearful expectation, and sometimes I felt guilty, and sometimes I felt a guilty pleasure.

I am trying to trace it back for you, go back to when it started. It might have been that moment of him stretching out the membrane between my toes and watching it spring back. Or it might have happened months before, or maybe it didn't happen until a few years later. Can you pinpoint the moment of falling in love, or only the moment of realizing it?

It's not working, he'd say accusingly on the playground day after day. I'm resistant, or something. Take off your shoes. We have to try again.

.   .   .

But about our mothers. I remember the day they took mine away. The government inspectors paid an unexpected visit. My mother was printing out pamphlets on a little hand-cranked printing press on the kitchen table. The finished ones were spread all over the floor to dry. I was stationed on a chair with a hair dryer, trying to speed up the process. We looked at each other. They had a way of knocking. You knew it was them. She'd been waiting for that knock. She knew they'd be coming, it was just a question of when.

Yes, yes, it was pretty much the same for me, Joss told me years later.

I had come to see his first exhibition at the student gallery. We were the only people there, unless you counted the faces staring out of the disturbing paintings on the walls that left me speechless. Joss had emptied six bottles of wine into fifty plastic cups, and these stood lined up hopefully on a velvet-draped table next to careful towers of crackers and a boulder of cheese that someone had stuck several small plastic astronauts into. Unwilling to disturb the formation, he took a flask out of a pocket and drank before offering it to me.

Yes, that knock, he said. Do you think they give them special training for that, lessons in ominous knocking? When we heard it I looked at my mother the way you're supposed to when you know you're never going to see someone again, memorizing every detail. It was this moment that seemed to go on forever. . . .

He closed his eyes as he said this; I thought he was being overly dramatic. I doubted he'd really done that, he was painting the scene in retrospect.

But now that I think about it, I seem to recall doing the same thing. Looking at my mother with her hair flaming up all over her head. A smootch of ink on her nose, a pollen dusting of dry skin under her eyes. She had a way of looking at you as if you were in her way, as if she were trying to see around you, or through you, to something more important. Her pupils looked big enough to poke a finger through. You couldn't stand too close to her; she had this force field of nervous energy around her that you could almost see. I was sure I could see it right then, shooting out of her in rays.

The inspectors came right in without knocking a second time. They came down the hallway and stood in the entrance of the kitchen. From the look of their stiff square suits, you expected them to hum and glide with chilly efficiency, but they didn't. They stumbled and bumbled, they huffed and puffed, they smelled bad, their collars where stained with sweat, their cuffs with something else, they smiled apologetically. This was all somehow more menacing than if they had been robotic. They stood looking at the papers all over the floor. Intent to Disseminate, Sedition, Inflammatory Materials, they said, as they wrote in their notebooks. Inflammatory. I thought that had something to do with the hair dryer in my hand.

Joss said, Every evening after day care my dad would sit me down with some paper and crayons and tell me to draw something to send to my mother. I missed her like crazy. But all I could draw were monsters, mutants, houses on fire, car wrecks. I couldn't draw a whole car, I could only draw one in pieces. Flames, pools of blood, I went through the reds quick.

That was all you *could* draw? Or all you *wanted* to?

Couldn't help it, he insisted. My dad would tell me to draw a flower and it would turn into a Venus flytrap chewing on a hand. I'd start a nice happy beach scene, and then—you can imagine the carnage. Sharks. Tidal waves. For Valentine's Day I drew the massacre. I was pretty single-minded back then. Still am. You can see, he said, gesturing around at the walls, how once I get on a track I can't get off.

Those paintings. I couldn't believe he'd brought them up so casually. I'd been shocked when I first walked in and saw them all. I didn't know what to say. I was horrified, just horrified. Perhaps a tiny bit flattered; mostly horrified. But now, the way he waved at them, so easily, so innocuously, made me wonder if my first impression was wrong. Joss was a terrible actor. If he was acting like nothing was odd or amiss, then nothing really *was* amiss.

But I should tell you about the mothers, where the mothers went when they went away: my mother, Joss's mother, the upstarts and the rabble-rousers, the discontented and the malcontent. The ones who defaced billboards, wrote angry poetry, signed petitions, held whispered meetings in their basements. They all got sent to the work reeducation camps out in the countryside. They milked cows, dug holes, assembled electronic gadgets and artificial limbs, stitched army uniforms. I don't know what they did exactly. All I know is that my mother came back four years later very changed. She seemed both heavier and gaunter than before, and moved as if her center of gravity had sunk from her chest to somewhere around her knees. Before, her normal speaking voice was a shout, and she couldn't talk without waving her hands. When she came back her voice was a whisper and she kept asking my permission to do things, as if she were a visitor.

When people came to welcome her home, neighbors, my uncles, her old friends, they all shook their heads sadly and said, Poor Willa, that place took the fight right out of her.

When they said this I tried to imagine the piece that had been torn from her. I saw it as a little knotty mollusk of flesh, thrashing around in a labeled jar, beating the fluid into a froth, trying to chew its way out.

Joss's mother didn't come back at all. I do wonder, sometimes, where she is now and what she thinks of her son.

He could have used a mother's guidance, or a girlfriend's, that night at the art opening. He was wearing a stained tuxedo jacket, a mesh undershirt, jeans, and ugly women's high-heeled boots. His hair stuck up on his head in two pointy tufts, like devil's horns. It would have been clever if it had been deliberate, but I don't think it was. He was wearing odd old-ladyish screw-back earrings—too afraid to get his ears pierced. He looked pale, even paler than usual, and his lips were very red. I wondered if he was wearing makeup. He looked like a corpse ready for viewing.

Poor Joss. I don't know why I keep saying that. He tried so hard to be like the other students, who were strutting and defiant and outrageous and wore tutus and togas and ten-gallon hats to class. It didn't work on him. He tried too hard. It was embarrassing to see.

And you know what I found out a few months ago? Joss continued. I asked my dad if he remembered all that, about the drawings, and he admitted that he'd been *keeping* all the drawings I did, hiding them away, and forging new ones himself to send, birds and happy trees and ponies, to send to Mum. Every day. Can you imagine?

I tried to act amazed, because he wanted me to be, amazed by this extravagant act of love and deception. But to

be honest, I was not all that impressed. I had heard of far
more spectacular acts of love.

I remember, Joss went on, how I used to do drawings of
that—you know—that damn face, but with the eyeballs dangling out and pustules all over and the neck ending in a bloody
stump. I thought Mum would like that. And every time I did
one and gave it to my dad to mail, he would sit me down and
say, You have to stop this. I don't want to lose you too. If you
have to make a revolution, make a small revolution.

He went on and on, his father's words of wisdom, or caution, acquiescence on the surface and rebellion in the heart,
doing small things to loosen the valve on your anger—
squeezing the toothpaste tube in the middle, hoarding cen-
sored books, thumbing your nose at the portrait, those sorts of
things—but I couldn't concentrate. The paintings all around,
the faces, hands, and feet, were clamoring for attention.
When I'd first walked in I felt I was walking into a hall of mir-
rors; every face in every painting looked like mine. What have
you done, how dare you? I thought. But now, when I looked
more carefully, I saw that they didn't really resemble me at all.

A million small rebellions can add up to one big revolution, *bang!* Joss was saying.

The paintings didn't look like anyone in particular, they
were standard art-school fare—staring eyes, hunched bodies,
lots of lovingly painted breasts, tortured trees in the window,
portentous raised hands, a putrid palette of raw-meat pinks
and reds and sickly whites against black backgrounds useful
for obscuring mistakes. Gloppy paint flung on the canvas,
trapped brush bristles. The shiny staring eyes that met yours
out of every painting—maybe this was what had given me the
looking-in-the-mirror sensation.

Getting a bit self-centered, aren't we? I chided myself.
Why would he do thirty paintings all of you, you, you? How
vain, how paranoid can you be?

I was glad I hadn't blurted out something the moment I walked in. If I'd said anything, Joss would have misconstrued it, twisted it around to mean that I was disappointed, that I'd expected it, *wanted* him to paint a gallery's worth of paintings of me.

Now, looking back. . . . maybe they were of me, maybe they weren't. They were so poorly done it was impossible to tell. He was not a very good artist, back then.

.   .   .

To back up a bit—we must have been in sixth grade, and the government inspectors paid an unexpected visit. No, it wasn't unexpected; they came to the school all the time, checking to see that there were portraits in every room, listening to the history lessons to make sure nothing was being added to the version in the textbooks. The time I am thinking of is when five of them came with stopwatches to Fitness Day and watched us walking on balance beams, doing back bends, kicking balls as we raced up and down the field, swimming laps in the grimy pool in the basement. The pool was un-heated, clammy. Many of us were lackadaisical with the other tests, but now we flailed and kicked with all our might, purely to get done and wrapped up in towels as fast as possible.

They told a few of us to stay and swim again and sent the rest to the changing rooms. Joss was dismissed but stubbornly stayed on, his narrow chest heaving. We swam again, our teacher blowing her whistle and shouting for us to change strokes: backstroke, breaststroke, batterstroke, butterfly. Then we were back in our towels and nearly dry and Joss was still thrashing around in the water. He could barely swim at all but was doggedly trying to complete the set. I think it was because he was so bony, not a pinch of flesh on him anywhere, so he just sank. Fat is lighter than bone, helps you float. Finally our teacher hauled him out by the arm. His face was red, his chest glaring white. There were dark marks on his stomach and legs; for some reason he'd drawn big black Frankenstein stitches on himself with Magic Marker. The inspectors gave me and Eva letters to take home to our parents; *Me too, me too!* Joss shrieked gaspingly as the teacher dragged him away.

That was the day I was recruited for the national swimming team. My life changed immediately; I started training twice a day, morning and evening, and had half-days at school. I received a salary equal to my father's, and he was given a car—a car! Nobody owned a car back then!—to drive me to the national pool.

The funny thing was, I was not an exceptional swimmer. I was good but not dazzling, not even the fastest in my class. I liked to swim but didn't love it overwhelmingly. I liked the peace, the blue silence underwater, but I didn't care about going fast. I wasn't competitive, I wasn't an athlete; in my free time I wasn't out playing footie or chase, I was collecting bugs with Joss.

The selling point, obviously, was my webbed toes. How could I not be a champion swimmer, with those flippers? An unfair advantage, you might say. But is it any more unfair than being born unusually tall? Or with exceptionally long arms, or unusually quick reflexes? To be honest, I don't think my feet made a difference either way; the recruiters and coaches obviously thought they might. At least they might make a difference of a few fractions of a second. And in a swimming competition, a fraction of a second can be crucial.

Aside from that, I suppose they thought of the intimidation factor, for what swimmer wouldn't be thrown off her game at the sight of an opponent with webbed feet?

There was no question of my refusing. The car for my father, military exemption for my brother, even a permit for my mother to buy a new typewriter—she could start writing her poetry again, though she no longer wanted to. Besides, it was an order, not an offer. The stern face stamped at the bottom of the letter made that clear.

The pool complex was like nothing I've seen before or since. The building was magnificent, white, columned like a temple, with a glass roof that retracted on warm days. The pool itself was fifty meters long and fourteen lanes wide, with a separate smaller pool for warming up. The water was vibrantly blue, dancing with light, impeccably clear. The enormous room was filled with the murmur and slap of water, the booming echoes of your own voice. The acoustics made you feel like a giant. We were told the prime minister had had it built especially for us; we were told she had chosen us specifically and would be closely monitoring our progress. And there was her face again, fifty feet across and smiling up at us through the water.

Even if you were apathetic toward the prime minister, even if you hated her or doubted her very existence, it was hard not to feel awed and grateful in that place.

They told us we were representing our country. We were role models for children. Exemplary physical specimens. Heroes. Symbols. You know it's all garbage, but if they keep repeating it to you it begins to seep in.

I am not an athlete, it's not in my temperament. You think I'm just making excuses. I live in my mind, not my body. Those years of practice, I felt like I was training a horse, something utterly separate from me. I worked, and I improved. I couldn't help but get better; it was all I did, a little engine chugging along, week after week, month after month. Swimming four or five miles a day, every day. In the beginning I was bored out of my mind, counting tiles on the floor of the pool just as I'd once counted ceiling tiles during naptime. Then I learned tricks to keep my mind off the tedium. I would like to say I entered some kind of athlete's meditative state, but it's more likely I learned how to sleep while swimming.

I saw the muscles rear up in my legs and arms. I was being

groomed for long-distance events, so I was supposed to stay trim and efficient, not like the sprinters who bulked up like bodybuilders, enormous shoulders and thighs. Poor Eva. She was like a dolphin in the water, rearing and diving with her beautiful butterfly stroke, but on land she waddled like an ape, her hands practically dragging on the ground. Nobody was even taking drugs yet; that came later.

I smelled like chlorine all the time. My hair was like straw, palms forever puckered and eyes always bloodshot. I got sudden cramps just from walking, my legs protesting against gravity, this unnatural upright position. At night after a certain point my bed would begin to float, bobbing like a raft. My father said I flutter-kicked in my sleep.

My father was grateful for the car and the perks and pretended to be proud of me. He came to a practice once, but the sight of me wearing the national colors, swimming across the approving face of the prime minister, was too much for him. After that he waited outside in the car.

I swam and ate, swam and slept. My head was empty.

Who's that? Eva said one day, as we floated at the edge of the pool between sets, licking our goggles to make them stick better. He's there every day, she said. Some perv.

I looked up at the vast bleachers that lined one side of the pool. Eva was pointing to the upper benches, high against the wall. That day the roof had been retracted and sunlight sent reflections dancing everywhere. There was a dark figure up there, hunched like a gargoyle, elbows on knees, chin on hands. He saw us looking and slid his fingers over his eyes, as if we couldn't see him as long as he couldn't see us.

Well, of course it was Joss. But I thought he was just jealous; I thought he wanted webbed feet of his own, thought he wanted to be on the swimming team too.

It dawned on me, after a while, why he was there. After weeks of him hovering, sometimes with a sketch pad. I think it was then, not when he was picking at my toes on a grotty playground, that he fell in love. I'm not trying to romanticize things, I'm not saying I took his breath away with my statuesque beauty and skimpy bathing suit. It was the setting, more than anything else. I mean, who *doesn't* fall in love at swimming pools? The smell of chlorine an aphrodisiac, water that is azure and turquoise and aquamarine and blue-green and green-blue—all the best crayons in the box. Everyone covered in a skin of glittery drops. In a landlocked country, this is our day at the beach.

I fell in love myself at least once a week. It could be anyone: one of the scowling bearish coaches, the lank-haired janitor who endlessly scrubbed the grouting with a toothbrush, one of the boys on the team—Derek or Luka or even Dwayne the caveman. I'd notice some detail—an untied shoelace, a weary eye, a lock of hair—and suddenly I'd be flooded with tenderness. I'd look for the person in the breaks between sets, think of him as I swam. You could pretend the water was hands, arms enveloping you. You could imagine he was there in the water with you, under, over, all around, a spiraling chase. The crushes lasted hours or days, not more than that.

It was inevitable that I turn the laser beam of my desire on Joss at some point. Perhaps it was the way he moved that I noticed, a combination of giraffe and ostrich, head bobbing like a puppet's on a string. Maybe I took a fresh look at his face, which was all angles and facets, a cubist face. Even his ears were triangular. Maybe it was his coloring, the greenish circles under his eyes, the indescribable hair-colored hair.

I looked up at the small dark figure in the bleachers. As I swam I imagined my arms around him, putting my tongue on the red rash or strawberry mark on the back of his neck.

By this time my father had started giving Joss rides home after the practices. He's an all-right lad, my dad would say after dropping him off, but he's not prince enough for you, F.S.

We sat in the backseat during those rides, not talking. I put my hand on the seat between us, palm up, and willed Joss to put his hand in mine. I focused all my telepathic energy on him, but it didn't work. He stared out the window the whole ride, drumming his fingers on the sketch pad he never let me see.

A week later the feeling fizzled out of me as quick as it had poured in. He never knew a thing.

. . .

I remember Joss showing me around the art college for the first time, pointing out the painting studios, the photography labs, the Poetree in the courtyard with verses dangling from its branches, the sculpture rooms noisy with the buzzing of electrical saws, the experimental theater where pantomime plays were performed in complete darkness.

You have to use your other senses to figure out what's going on, he explained. It's amazing. Really visceral.

He'd only been there a week and was already talking differently.

A boy on paint-spattered ten-foot stilts stalked past. Joss saw me staring and waved his hand dismissively, saying: Oh, them. They think they're so special. They even have their own club. It's so overripe, the whole circus thing.

I suppose they think they're above everybody else? I said.

Joss rolled his eyes. He kept inhaling deeply and sighing, as if the smells of paint and turpentine were delicious. Students passed us holding portfolio cases and paint-spotted tackle boxes and cameras, looking intent and distracted. The boys wore more makeup than the girls. The girls had long matted hair and seemed full of mystery and sorrow and secret wisdom. They looked Joss up and down or studiously ignored him. One snapped a Polaroid of him, handed it to him solemnly, and passed on.

Bunch of freaks and drama queens, I said.

That was Marlene Mustiq, Joss said in awe. She's supposed to be brilliant.

I took the photograph and shook it, waiting for the image to emerge.

No one's heard her say a word in three years, he said. Everybody says her work is amazing, absolutely . . .

Visceral? I said meanly.

Exactly! he said.

I was a bit jealous, I admit it. I'm a national athlete; I'm better than them, I told myself, but I didn't feel it. My head was a useless hollow gourd. I was sure every student who walked past could see this and was sneering at me. It was not my fault. Members of the swimming team were discouraged (forbidden) from going to college; it was considered too much of a distraction.

I had been training for six years and hadn't been in an international competition yet. My times were mediocre. The coaches were waiting for improvement.

Three years later my times were exactly the same. It was clear what was happening. I had hit a plateau. I had seen it happen to others on the team. You improve and improve and then, at a certain point, you stop improving. Your racing times stick at a certain number, an evil magical number, and you can't shave off even a fraction of a second. You might stall for months or even years. This is the point of desperation, when you start to try different diets, drugs, practice regimens. This is the point where you turn superstitious, or religious, or devious.

So. I hit my plateau. I raced around in circles on my plateau for years without going anywhere. My mother had a very quiet stroke, so quiet we didn't notice for several days. After that she needed constant care. I started dating Dwayne the caveman. He was kind and decent, if uninspiring, and always there. Lying on his big square chest was like lying on a life raft in the middle of the ocean, solid yet buoyant.

And ultimately vulnerable, I suppose. All it takes is one tiny puncture.

I am telling you this to explain what sounds like an abrupt and arbitrary decision. I was called to a meeting with my coaches and their superiors at the governmental sports bureau. They said that my performance had not met expectations and they felt it was time for me to relinquish my place on the team. However, in light of certain special circumstances, and my potential to influence our country's athletic future, they were willing to make me an offer.

What they were saying, in their clinical language, was that if I agreed to marry a teammate and produce offspring that might potentially turn out to be web-footed superathletes, well, then, I would have the prime minister's blessing.

If I didn't, then I would be off the team and expected to begin the military training that was mandatory for ordinary citizens my age.

Exacerbating everything was the fact that my period was three weeks late at the time. I'd thought I was the only one who knew this. But looking at my coaches, who were studiously averting their eyes from my midsection, I had to wonder.

So I agreed to everything: to a new car and babies and an easy sit-down job and live-in help for my mother and two weeks of across-the-border vacation every year, and imported salmon on Sundays, the best hand-picked peaches, a box of the finest cigars, and I don't know what-all other foolishness. It sounds strange to sign your life away without reading the fine print, but that's the only way to do it—cavalierly, with a flourish of the pen. Think too hard, read too close, and you'll never go through with it.

It was only afterward that I had regrets. My body ached. It

missed swimming. I expected it to balloon without all the rigorous training, but instead I watched it shrivel. I couldn't muster up any appetite. My new job was a matter of answering a phone and then pressing one of three buttons to transfer the call to someone else.

I thought of the heavenly floating days when I thought swimming laps was tedious.

Dwayne and I moved into the new apartment, which seemed huge to me when Dwayne wasn't in it. He had a way of taking up space, blocking doorways, sending lamps rocking. I had promised to get married within two months of signing the contract, and as the deadline approached I felt more and more squeezed and breathless. I remembered Joss on the playground all those years ago saying, *You have to, it's only fair,* that feeling of being snared by irrefutable logic.

I couldn't sleep. I started taking long wandering walks at night, after curfew, half hoping I would get caught and sent to a work camp like my mother and not have go through with any of it.

For the first time in a very long time, I looked at that face, the prime minister's face looming bright-lit on billboards. It beamed back at me kindly, encouragingly. I hated it more than I'd ever hated anything. GO ON. YOU CAN DO IT, the caption beneath the face read. Go fuck yourself, you bitch, I said.

When I looked again at the face I could swear it had changed; now it was sad and hurt. And I actually felt bad. That shows you how deeply that face had wormed its way in.

· · ·

Two things happened in the weeks leading up to the wedding.

I got my period.

And I went to see Joss.

I had not seen him for several months, and I'd never been

to his apartment before—he forbade it—but I knew where it was. It's my work space, he said whenever I tried to invite myself over. It's too personal, it's got my soul splattered all over it.

I went there on one of my late-night walks. I saw his light on, and it was only after I rang the buzzer that I thought, What if he has a woman staying over? And then his voice came crackling through the intercom, doing his Marta imitation: *Giita, dear, show us your hands.*

I looked up and saw his head poking out the window, silhouetted against the weird pink light. I couldn't see his face. For a very long moment he said nothing. Then finally: Right, then. I guess you should come in?

His room was a tiny cube, hot and heady with paint fumes. There were canvases stacked against the walls, a half-finished one on an easel. There was some kind of evil fairyland music playing: finger cymbals and xylophones and electronic whippoorwills.

This was maybe a year after his opening at the student gallery. His painting had improved a great deal in the intervening year. There was no doubting, now, whom the face in all the paintings belonged to.

Well, he said. Well, then. Heh. Brilliant.

He was pulling distractedly at the hair above his forehead. It stuck up there like a unicorn horn. He was wearing a shirt and pants the same nondescript color as his hair—beige, tan, taupe, khaki. His hands, I noticed for the first time, were disproportionately large, floppy, with thick knobby veins on the backs.

I looked at one picture, then another and another. Did I really look like that?

Ahem, he said. I know, I know. . . . But, officer, he *seemed* like such a nice boy, he said, in a high-pitched old-lady voice.

At least half of the paintings were nudes. He'd been very imaginative.

Um, I can explain, he said. He threw up his hands. No, forget it, he said. I can't.

And then—well, you can guess what happened after that. Up to the last second, though, as we were pushing aside the easel to make a space on the floor, there was a chance it wouldn't happen at all, there were a thousand tiny crossroads that might have derailed the whole thing. For instance, if I had thought for even a fraction of a second about Dwayne waiting at home perplexed and fretful, I might have stopped. If the word *stalker* had crossed my mind. If it had occurred to me that maybe there was a real model for the voluptuous nude bodies in the paintings, and that it wasn't me, that thought might have given me pause. Or if I had tried to be clever or sarcastic—if I had shaken my breasts at him and said *Hope the real thing doesn't disappoint you* or even *Turn off that pretentious godawful music*—it might have ruined the mood, broken the spell for both of us.

Or if I had said anything about—well, everything that was happening to me in the world outside that room, it would have brought things to a screeching halt.

When I think back now, I am amazed it happened, with those thousand and one mishaps waiting to intrude in the two minutes it took us to come together, teeth crashing, hip bones knocking, like some incredibly complicated docking maneuver between two orbiting spacecrafts—the kind of operation that, seen on television, looks slow and majestic to the untrained eye. You'd never guess all that slow delicate machinery was tumbling through space at thousands of miles per hour.

.   .   .

My wedding to Dwayne was a brief obligatory ceremony in an office. My mother was too ill to come. Dwayne couldn't find a suit to fit his exaggerated swimmer's physique, but he smiled dazzlingly and kissed everyone and cried just a bit. He was not the crying sort, but he had to make up for the bride, who was not crying or smiling or doing much of anything beyond glaring at the portrait of the prime minister hanging above the officiating clerk's head.

This seems bizarre to me, but perhaps other athletes believe it too: Dwayne thought sex weakened him, sapped his potency. He thought he performed better when he'd abstained for a couple of weeks. So if we wanted to make love we had to schedule it around his competition calendar.

Joss—well, you can imagine how he felt when he found out about the wedding. I'd rather not dwell on it. He didn't seem to understand that I had no choice.

What I'm getting to now is the part you'll want to pay attention to. These are things I didn't witness firsthand; they happened to Joss. But he told me about some of it, and—well, I think I can say with confidence that I know him well enough to infer the rest, the bits he thought he was keeping out of the telling but was broadcasting loud and clear through his eyes and hands and flushing ears.

The government inspectors paid an unexpected visit to the art college. Of course they came frequently; the art college was a hotbed of student rebellion, both organized and anarchic. The portraits of the prime minister that hung in the classrooms were artfully and creatively defaced; no mere graffiti here. The students held meetings and rallies, plastered the buildings, and abused the trees with flyers. They made metaphorical antigovernment statements in their artwork.

The prime minister was determined to keep the art college open, as a sign of her generous liberality, but the inspectors tried to keep it from getting out of hand. Students had a way of disappearing, but only a few, now and then. Fortunately for the students, the government inspectors were usually too dense to perceive the subtleties of their artwork, were unable to see the rebellious messages screaming out of, say, a sculpture of a giant rabbit or an oversize painting of a grassy field sprouting dildos.

So the government inspectors came, two of them. They marched into the studio where Joss's class was having a figure-drawing session. At the sound of their steps, the instructor cringed and the model grabbed her robe and the students' eyes swung in unison to the portrait on the wall. Someone had meticulously given the prime minister's face a Vandyke beard and sweeping hat, with a plume in the style of Velázquez, and then filled the background with a swarm of naked bodies undergoing imaginative tortures worthy of Bosch.

Joss said afterward that every student in the room was eager to take credit for the defacement. As a political statement (an irresistible chance to perform—being dragged screaming from the building), but also simply because the painter's skill was undeniable.

I wish I'd done it differently, Joss said later. Bosch is such an obvious choice. A bit overripe.

But the inspectors said nothing about the portrait. They strolled around the room, looking over students' shoulders at their work.

Joss said he had been bored that day and to amuse himself had aged the model about forty years in his drawing. She was still clearly recognizable beneath the wrinkles. Then he drew in her arms a squalling baby with the features of the instructor. Now, still bored, he was adding some large and elaborate wings to the woman's shoulders.

The inspectors stopped behind him.

It wasn't even a good drawing, Joss said later. I ruined it with the wings. Too much clutter.

The inspectors looked from his drawing to the defaced portrait on the wall with narrowed eyes. Joss began to realize they were smarter than they looked.

They tapped his shoulder and told him to come outside. He was so surprised he forgot to raise his fists or make any kind of dramatic protest.

A car was waiting, engine running. They told him to get in.

He thought they were taking him straight to a work camp, right then and there. Or prison. Or worse. He kept hoping for a work camp—maybe he'd at least get to see his mother again.

They took him to a large faceless government building and led him through many passages and meeting rooms where black-suited inspectors scuttled like beetles. Finally they stopped in a bare windowless room no different from the others. They told him to sit on one of the gray metal office chairs circling a small metal table. They sat facing him.

The floor, he noticed, was concrete and sloped to a drain in one corner.

We want to make you an offer, the inspectors said (Joss *swore* they spoke in unison the entire time).

Do you see anything wrong with that picture? the inspectors said, gesturing to the portrait behind him. Joss turned and looked. It was the standard portrait of the prime minister, with the ambiguous expression, red jacket, mauve background.

No? he said.

The prime minister is looking for a new portraitist, they said. We would like to offer you the job.

Me?

She is looking for someone with a little—and here they both cleared their throats—imagination.

She wants to update her image, they added. It's a great honor.

And then, without any fanfare, the prime minister herself walked in.

Joss was shocked to his very core. He, like me, like many people, had begun to suspect that the prime minister didn't exist. The images you saw on billboards and cigarette packs were always paintings, reproductions of paintings, never photographs. The prime minister never made public appearances or even televised appearances. Older people would tell you they'd seen her give a speech, had touched her sleeve, received a blessing, a handshake, but they could not remember when that had happened. Joss had decided that the benign, motherly, Virgin Mary logo-on-a-box-of-cake-mix face was merely an invention of men in suits or military uniforms, an icon, an advertising mascot.

And now here she was. He was on his feet, then on his knees. He said he couldn't help it. It had been pounded into him since birth, the sanctity of this face.

I should know better than to fall for that crap, he said afterward. Conditioning, brainwashing, that's all it is.

But at the time, he was overwhelmed. It was like meeting God.

She was smaller than he might have expected—under five feet in heels. He couldn't guess her age. She might have been forty or seventy; her skin had the tight shiny look of overzealous plastic surgery, the sort of pinched, botched look that makes you imagine a doctor saying, Trust me, you don't want me to do that, and the patient saying, Yes, yes I do.

Her face was like and not like the one in all the portraits. It was unquestionably her, but details had been tampered with. She was more attractive than her portrait, for one thing. The artist had removed any trace of sexuality and replaced it with the weight and wrinkles of reliability and wisdom. Joss figured that the artist must have aged her when he made the first portraits, twenty years before, and now she had caught up to her own image.

It makes sense, doesn't it? A beautiful woman is dangerous, deceptive, untrustworthy. A beautiful woman will put her own beauty above all else. A plain woman will put you first. A plain woman can be relied on to get the job done.

Her eyes flicked over him as she waited for him to get up. Her eyes were cool, flat, distracted, calculating—nothing like the brimming eyes in the portrait that could bring you to sympathetic tears.

Her cabinet of advisors filed into the room. They sat at the table and talked. She had an odd voice or, rather, two voices—one chirping and girlish, the other throaty and deep. It was a disquieting conversation, what with the two inspectors with one voice, the tiny woman with two, the advisors speaking in wordless murmurs of assent. She spoke of wanting a new, fresher, younger image, she needed to endear herself to the younger generation. There was apathy, unrest, outright rebellion among the young people, she said. She wanted to ease them back gently; she didn't want to force them. She spoke of finesse and delicacy. She talked, Joss said, like an ad executive planning a campaign for a new brand of feminine products.

He couldn't tell whether her decision was motivated by political necessity or by vanity. Perhaps she was trying to tamp down an imminent revolution. Perhaps, like any capricious woman, she'd simply glanced in the mirror and decided she needed a new look.

She took him into another room, leaving the suits behind. This one had a wide south-facing window, a comfortable armchair, and an easel. She sat down and told him to show her what he could do.

He took his time, and she waited, her head tilted, utterly still. This was a woman he'd hated for as long as he could remember. He tried to think of his vanished mum, of my shrunken whispering mother, his friends who had gone off to serve in the military and never returned, all the people who were dead or missing or living cramped and loveless lives because of her, the whispered rumors of political prisoners tortured and killed. There's a different version in the schoolbooks, of course, but rumor had it that she initially seized power by poisoning her own husband. She was a murderer and a thief and a master manipulator. An utter monster. But she was just a woman, sitting on a chair with a run in her stocking. He could not connect the two. He hated the portrait but not her.

He thought about refusing, slamming dramatically out of the room, but he didn't. Perhaps he began to realize how enormous was the power being offered him. Here, finally, was his chance to make his grand, dramatic gesture, strut onstage before an audience of millions. It was every artist's dream. Perhaps he thought of his father's advice: When you can't make a big revolution, you make a small revolution, a subtle one.

He finished his portrait and turned the easel with a flourish so the prime minister could see. The face for the new generation, he said, and held his breath. The face on the canvas looked nothing like her own; it was someone else entirely. The prime minister looked and smiled, pleased. Joss felt a tiny thrill at seeing her mysterious teeth for the first time.

.   .   .

It's astonishing to think that they could replace an icon like that without anyone noticing. It's absurd—like changing the color of the sky and expecting people not to react.

And yet that is what happened. There was no confusion, no rebellion, no breaking of the spell. I'm sure there were a thousand tiny moments of vertigo, unrecognition, second glances, but then people would shrug it off. There was the face, looming where it always had been and always would be, and if it seemed different it was the fault of the people's own shoddy memories.

It was subtly done, not all at once. For a period of months, the largest and most prominent portraits were replaced by a series in which the old face gradually metamorphosed into the new. Once this transition was complete, the next stage began: the portraits in schools, bus stations, hospitals. Reproductions of the new face were printed in all the newspapers; people were encouraged to tear down the old portraits in their homes and hang up the new ones.

By the end of the first year the old currency was being phased out, replaced by crisp new bills.

The idea was for people to notice nothing outright but to subconsciously sense the shift, the change, and feel a sense of hope and uplift, fresh starts, new beginnings.

Joss told me all of this afterward. I, like everyone else, didn't see it happening. The one thing they overlooked, he said, was the imprint on the bus tokens. If you can find some of those, look for yourself. You'll see how drastic the change was.

Aside from that one oversight, they were amazingly thorough. Every image of the old face was tracked down and obliterated. Every child's coloring book, postage stamp, any book or scrap of paper that bore the old face was rounded up and destroyed. Picked clean, as if discriminating Amazon ants had swept through the city. They were determined to erase the past completely and make a fresh start.

You'd think I, of all people, would have noticed. But I didn't. How could I have been oblivious? But it happened so gradually. It was one of those things that you notice all at once, even though it's been right there, under your nose, for months. Since when did the neighbors paint their house yellow, you say, though it's been that way for half a year.

It happens every autumn. You never notice the leaves changing, and then one day it's red, amber, sienna, burnt umber!—everywhere you look. These things creep up on you, and then for no particular reason you see them all of a sudden and yet you sense they have been there all along. Like love, I suppose.

So I didn't notice. Dwayne hit a plateau and was miserable, manic, exercising constantly, gorging himself on vitamin supplements. Joss was always busy, too busy to see me; he had some kind of secret government job he couldn't talk about, and also he was still angry. How could I have gone and gotten married to that lumberbus? and *no*, he did *not* want to be friends and would I please stop calling?

As for me, I went along and went along until one day I looked up from the pavement and saw my face everywhere.

There it was on the billboard in the central market square, among the advertisements, beaming beneficently down. Eyes brimming, chin upraised, a golden beatific glow around the head. An expression I've never worn in my life, but unmistakably me.

I looked around. As usual, there were a few old ladies, paused in their shopping, gazing up worshipfully at the picture. They didn't notice anything amiss.

I had a wild impulse that maybe it was just this one particular billboard, some kind of mistake, some kind of joke. Joss, an art student prank, I don't know.

I walked two paces and saw a portrait hanging in a shop window—there I was again, pursing my lips, cradling a child in my arms, looking maternal and nurturing.

And then I walked faster and started to run. They were everywhere—everywhere!—Godlike, gazing down out of the clouds. Staring up out of the gutters on crumpled newspapers and canceled stamps. It was a nightmare, and like a nightmare it had the glow of familiarity, of déjà vu. As if it had happened to me before, or as if deep down I had always known it was going to happen.

I ascribe that feeling to the effect of the old portrait. The old face looked so familiar, so real; she was a normal person, just like you and me. That was the appeal. Even up on a billboard she didn't seem far away. She came into your most intimate places—your home, your bathroom, your hospital cubicle. She was not superior; she could be your mother, your friend; she could be *you*. She made it seem easy, possible, to switch places.

I tried to tell myself I was overreacting, as I had at Joss's art opening. I was losing my mind. I remembered reading somewhere that a common form of psychosis was believing yourself to be God.

Well, I don't need to go on about it. It was a nightmare, but it was my own private nightmare, because no one else seemed to notice. Strangers might look at me twice on the street, sometimes even stop me and say, You look so familiar, do I know you? But no one made the connection.

I remember one of Dwayne's teammates, Derek, saying something about it. But he didn't say: The prime minister all of a sudden looks like you. What he said was: It's funny, Giita, but you're starting to look like the prime minister.

Dwayne cocked his head and studied me too. I don't see it, he said finally.

And one day my friend Eva asked if I was pregnant.

No. Why?

I don't know, she said. You just have some kind of glow on you, I don't know, I look at you and start thinking you look very calm and motherly; you know, that prime-minister kind of look.

But that was as close as anyone came to the truth.

You're wondering, Didn't anyone in the government get suspicious?

The prime minister loved the new face, Joss told me afterward. He said, I think she convinced herself that it really *was* her I was painting. She kept saying I'd captured her younger self, her inner essence, her *true* face, that sort of trash. And all her little advisors—they assumed I was just trying to please her, flatter her. A lot of them figured I was in love with her, that I *had* to have been, to be able to paint her like that.

Joss never talked about how it felt to see his work blanketing the city, his brushstrokes inflated on huge reproductions plastering the sides of buildings, every man, woman, and child constantly bombarded with his lines, his colors, his ideas. People staring at his work, adoring it, worshiping it.

He would never talk about how it felt. But I can imagine.

And of course, there's the other side. There were plenty of people looking at his work and hating it. Back at the art college, students were probably defacing his work, defiling it, blowing their noses on it.

Plenty of people staring at my face and hating it. I hated it myself. It was complicated. I still hated the prime minister, even when she was wearing my face. It was a bit like my feeling as a swimmer, that my body was something separate from me. Now I felt the same about the mask of skin I wore every day.

Even now, Joss doesn't like to talk about those five years he spent as official portraitist to the prime minister. I think he doesn't like to admit how much he enjoyed it.

Even now, I'm not sure why he did it, whether it was a sort of homage or a sort of revenge. I don't know whether he did it out of love or anger.

Maybe it had nothing to do with me. Maybe it was all about the subtle revolution his father talked about.

I don't know. I don't know! Did he think of himself as a secret agent, fomenting rebellion from inside the system, or as a bandit of love, professing it in pictures twenty feet high all over the city, or did he simply enjoy making pictures that many, many people would see?

We saw each other rarely during those five years. He wouldn't tell me what he was doing, only that he was working for the government. He'd gotten taller, lankier, older-looking. He still wore hideous clothes, but now at least they were expensive-looking. He had a car. I thought he'd sold out, given in, resigned himself, surrendered his life even more than I had. And still, whenever we saw each other, it was awkward and it hurt. Of course I always wanted to ask him about my face on the portraits, whether he was responsible for it. But I didn't. I was afraid he would think I was crazy, paranoid, psychotically self-centered.

Or maybe I was afraid it would remind him of the one night we'd spent together, observed by the painted eyes of three dozen painted me's.

.   .   .

So five years passed. I grew accustomed to the new face and learned to ignore it as I'd ignored the old one. We tried to start a family. But all the drugs Dwayne had taken caused difficulties. We'd been getting politely threatening letters from the sports bureau. If we didn't start producing some offspring soon—well, there would be consequences.

I got pregnant, but there were complications. I was spotting. I spent two months in bed, trying to move as little as possible. I was lying on my back, trying to hold a baby in, while outside the revolution was beginning.

It broke out in bursts and patches: rioting in the outer towns, civilian groups assembling and marching toward the city, a rebellion in the armed forces as reluctant conscripts finally turned on their superiors, and, finally, foreign tanks rolling across the borders.

It had all been building for some time. I had no idea. Living in the capital, where the prime minister's grip was tightest, I'd had no inkling of what was happening all around. Change was impossible, inconceivable, a fanciful dream.

The tide was turning, building, and pushing toward the city; people were rioting, surging through the streets shouting; buildings were on fire; there were shots as loyalist soldiers tried to break up the masses of people; but I was oblivious to most of it because I'd started to miscarry.

I'll spare you the details, and skip to a few days later, when I was able to get up and walk outside for the first time. I don't know where Dwayne was. Looking back, I'm surprised he let me go wandering about alone, in my condition. At any rate, he wasn't there. The first thing I saw was our car. It was lying on its back looking helpless as a turtle. I could see all its complicated guts. It was smoking, scorched, teetering as if trying to right itself. There was litter all over the street. It was strangely quiet. I could hear a distant roar, people massed together somewhere out of sight.

I walked toward the center, swinging my arms. There was a spring breeze fighting with the smell of burning. I wonder how the revolution is coming along, I asked myself idly. I wonder if it's over yet; I wonder who won. Thinking of it as if it were a soccer match.

I must have been dazed, out of my head. Otherwise I would have been frightened at how strange the city felt. The very air felt empty; there was something prominently missing.

I turned a corner and walked into the roar—thousands of people crammed into the open square, all facing in the same direction, waving their arms and shouting. They were all watching a billboard, where two grinning young men were pulling great strips off my face and letting them go so that they drifted down into the crowd, where they were torn to shreds and tossed back into the air like confetti.

It really is happening, I thought. It was incredible. I can't tell you how incredible it felt, like an enormous weight lifted off your chest. You thought you might float away. You were breathless with giddiness, you wanted to embrace everyone in sight. I felt my dry lips stretching into a smile for the first time in months. Years, maybe. I made some kind of noise, a rusty laugh.

The two men up on the billboard ripped out my eyes and sent them fluttering down to the crowd.

Then an old woman turned and saw me. I smiled at her. She nudged the man beside her, who stopped shouting and stared. And then someone else cried out, *Look, that's her, there she is, right here!* and the crowd started to boil and seethe like an anthill.

Naturally it was only then that I noticed how many of the young men in the crowd held guns or pieces of wood in their hands.

I don't like to think about what might have happened then. I'd like to believe I could have explained myself, and there would have been enough reasonable people—but I don't know. When that crowd turned and glared at me, they weren't seeing me, they were seeing the face.

I was backing away and wondering if I was even capable of running, when a car rumbled up behind me, and miraculously there was Joss, like some kind of savior, hero, car-pool angel, knight on a white stallion, leaning across the seat and shouting, For God's sake, get in!

Let me tell the rest quickly. I can see I've nearly talked your ears off; they're dangling by a thread. Joss said he'd just been by the apartment to fetch me; he said we had to leave, the city wasn't safe for me anymore. And it was true, I could see, as we drove through the devastated streets, my face everywhere in flames. We saw the black-suited body of a government inspector hanging from a lamppost.

You'll have to go into hiding, Joss told me. It sounded like he was suggesting a game, I felt as if we were children together, all over again.

I'm serious, he said. Anyone who sees your face is going to try to kill you.

· · ·

So that is how we ended up in the little house on the outskirts of a town—a little village, really—in the farthest backwoods reaches of the country, our house with the walled garden and even a little pond for me to swim in, and for our children to swim in. I haven't been away from that house in over seven years—until now.

At first I wanted to call Dwayne and my parents and tell them I was all right. But Joss forbade it. We could tell no one, absolutely no one where we were.

I thought he was overdoing the caution, but I obeyed.

He reminded me constantly of what would happen if I ever left. The prime minister was hated, despised. She was guilty of hideous crimes, a regime of repression and blood-shed, and the new people in power would want to bring her to justice. Everyone will be hunting for her—hunting for you. There's a price on your head, he said.

I'll just *tell* them, I'd say. Obviously I'm not her.

There's no proof, he said. There are no photographs of her, nothing. The portraits are the only thing they have to go on.

Then *you* could tell them the truth. Since you painted them.

There's no proof, he said again. I was never allowed to sign my work.

After days, weeks, months of this, I came around to his way of thinking. I lost any desire to leave the house. I was afraid to leave it. I couldn't sleep at night; every sound made me jump. I was superstitious about stepping an inch over the property line.

Outside, the world was evolving at a hectic rate. I didn't know then, but I see it now. In our little hermitage under the trees, very little changed. Joss began painting again and tried to find a dealer to sell his work. But no one was interested in his paintings. They just don't have popular appeal, the dealers said.

Once he decided I could be trusted with the telephone,

Joss helped me get my job: I sell magazine subscriptions over the phone. I might have even called you, at some point, without your knowing it. I've solicited a fairly large percentage of the phone book by now.

We have two children. Before both births Joss joked about finding a blind midwife to protect my identity, but in the end brought a woman from the village who didn't pay attention to anything above my waist. Fabiana and Charlotte: he chose the names, of course. They are beautiful girls, perfect, with long aristocratic feet. As for their faces, they look nothing like either of us. Joss says they will when they get older; he says he sees dangerous traces of my features in theirs, waiting to bloom, and he tweaks their noses and cheeks, half jokingly but hard enough to hurt, as if he's trying to sculpt them. For their own protection, he says. But I say they won't change, they will keep the faces they were born with; the essential structure is already there.

For years we have managed to keep quite happy. I mean, Joss gets frustrated at times, for he keeps painting relentlessly; the canvases are stacked to the rafters, but no one will buy them. That makes him unhappy.

But I know he is happy to have me all to himself.

Lately I've started to have strange thoughts. I start to wonder if he's glad things have worked out the way they have, if he's glad he has to keep me hidden away. I start to wonder if he is more my jailor than my protector.

And then one of my daughters will scream at me for holding her hand too tightly when she's walking along a fence, and I'll think, Well, aren't they almost the same thing anyway?

Now the girls are getting old enough to get tired of my company; they want to bring friends home. They are old enough to ask why Mummy doesn't get to come when Daddy takes them to the village for ice cream and new dresses.

And lately I've been questioning Joss myself, saying, Don't

you think enough time has passed? No one will recognize me now. I'd like to see some other human beings again. See my parents. Show them the girls.

You don't understand, he said. They're still hunting for you. You're a fugitive. They've offered huge rewards. They want to put you on trial in front of the whole world for crimes against humanity. They want to give you the death penalty.

The way he was talking, it was as if I really *was* the prime minister.

But I don't even look the same, I said, I'm *old,* for God's sake. I've had two children; no one will look twice. And besides, people will have forgotten by now. Without all those portraits everywhere to remind them, they'll have forgotten all about that face.

People haven't forgotten, he said. You haven't been out there, I have. Everything's changed, but nobody's forgotten.

But I didn't believe him anymore. I thought he was inventing stories to tie me down, I thought he was growing paranoid and strange. I thought, No one's going to care if I take a walk down to the village, take a ride on a bus, buy a cup of coffee. No one's going to notice. No one will care. I'm not so important.

I felt as if I were waking from a long dream. I looked at myself, my old hands, my children, and couldn't believe how much time had passed. This is absurd, I thought. There is no reason to stay here.

So this morning, after he'd locked himself in his studio for the day, I took the girls and left, walked down the hill to the village and—well, you know the rest. It turns out Joss was right, after all. You *have* been looking for me all this time.

Yes, that's me in that painting over there. But it's not the prime minister. Haven't you been listening?

That is the whole story. My name is Giita Tullard. It should be Giita Moorkin. I am thirty-two years old. If you would only think for a minute, you'd realize that I'm far too young to be the woman you're looking for. It's absurd—she came to power before I was even born. She'd be an old woman by now. Surely there must be people who remember, who knew her. Ask Joss, bring him in, *he* can tell you what she looks like.

But I know what you are thinking—that people want justice, they want closure, and my head on a stake will be more satisfying for them than that of some unrecognizable old woman.

I wish you would tell me where my daughters are.

I try to untangle love sometimes. It is like a riddle. I ask myself why I love Joss, and the answer is: Because he loves me. He always has, always did. And then I ask, Why does he love me? And the answer is nowhere to be found. What am I? A failed athlete. A woman who married a caveman out of convenience. Intellectually empty, emotionally weak, and physically—I may as well say it—a bit of a freak. What can there possibly be to love?

I remember suggesting to Joss once that I just ought to get plastic surgery; then we could stop worrying and lead normal lives. He looked at me as if I'd suggested eating one of the children. But then I'd never be able to paint your face again, he said.

"Don't be surprised if he's a little blue when he comes out."

"A little . . . blue. All right."

"I mean it," the doctor says. "Before they start breathing properly, before the oxygen gets flowing. I don't mean a bit blue, like a bruise. I mean *blue*-blue, like this." He taps her elastic-waist jeans.

"We're not anticipating any problems, of course," he says. "But it's best to be prepared."

"I won't be surprised," Julia promises. "I'll act bored."

"Atta girl."

.   .   .

When the baby comes out two weeks later, he doesn't make a sound. Not a peep. She thinks he's dead, even though she can see his arms waving. And he's not blue. He's black.

"I mean, like, coal black, ink black," Jonas says in the hospital room afterward.

"I saw," she reminds him, her hands folded on her gigantic tender belly. It's like there's another baby still up in there.

"I mean, pure black, Julia, like a color that doesn't occur naturally, in nature, you know? It reminds me of those poor penguins after the oil spill, all black and greasy with their poor little flippers sticking out."

"Wings. Penguins are birds."

"And he came out with all that white gunk on him. And the cord was all . . . thick."

"What did you expect? Look at your own belly button."

"I thought it would be, like, a thread." He's ashamed because he was invited to cut the cord but hadn't been able to bring himself to do it.

She wants to see her baby, but the doctor whisked him away to check him over, calling back, "Ten fingers and ten toes. He seems fine."

"Maybe it's a mutation, or he's, like, a reverse albino," Jonas says.

"Don't use that word." Mutation makes her think of swamp monsters, nuclear accidents, hands growing out of heads. The doctor hadn't said exactly *where* those ten fingers and toes were.

"Don't get mad, but . . . he *is* mine, right? I don't even need to ask this, right?"

Finally. She's impressed he managed to restrain himself this long.

"Of course."

She thinks, naïvely, that this will be the end of it.

.   .   .

When they finally come and put the baby in her arms she feels tremendous relief. She kisses his head. The hair, plastered down before, is now dry and soft, perfectly straight and downy, and golden. The hair glows metallic, glittery, like tinsel. His eyes are a startling pale blue, the color of ice, of cataracts.

A lactation coach, a nursing nurse, has come along to help her with the first time.

"He doesn't like it!" Julia cries when the baby turns his face from her breast. "I taste bad!"

"He just doesn't know how," the coach says soothingly. "He has to learn."

"I thought it was instinctive. And why is he so quiet?"

"His ears and throat look fine. Later we'll do a CAT scan just to be sure. But it seems that he's just a calm sweet-tempered baby. He doesn't *want* to cry."

"And his color?" Jonas asks.

The nurse glances at Julia. "Well, I think that's something for the two of you to discuss, isn't it?"

After she leaves, Julia says, "He's not *unnatural*. There are plenty of people in the world just this color." But she can't help thinking that he does look unearthly. His skin has the solid, inorganic sheen of obsidian, an iridescence like oil.

.   .   .

Jonas says, "What are we going to name it? Him?"

"But we already decided on Robert."

"I changed my mind. He doesn't look like a Bobby, does he? He looks more like, say, an Alphonse."

"Alphonse? Why Alphonse?"

"What's wrong with Alphonse?"

"It's atrocious."

"The black kid at my high school was named Alphonse."

"*The* black kid. There was only one?"

"What, like it's my fault there was only one? I was friends with the guy. That baby looks a hundred times more like an Alphonse than a Bobby."

"But you insisted. You wanted him to have your father's name."

"I changed my mind."

. . .

They name him Gabriel. Gabe. They're on their way home, Gabe strapped into the new car seat in back, when Jonas explodes.

"This is all your fault!" He sprays *f*'s and *t*'s all over the windshield.

"Why is it my fault?"

"You . . . you . . . that cigarette you smoked two months in! I saw you! The bathroom was full of smoke! Don't deny it!"

"It made me nauseous. I didn't even finish."

"And the weird food, all the chocolate and burnt toast. I kept telling you the burnt part was carcinogenic, but did you listen?"

"I had cravings."

"And the chocolate. I came home and you were, like, *gnawing* on a big hunk of baker's chocolate. The bitter stuff."

"You're being—"

"And the poppyseed bagels? I kept telling you those were the exact same poppy seeds they extract opium from, but did you listen?"

"We can do a paternity test, if you want. If that would make you feel better."

His cheek pulses in and out.

She says, "Maybe we both have some African ancestors, way, way back. It's some combination of recessive genes."

"I don't have any African ancestors."

"We're all mongrels."

"Not me. Maybe you, you've got those swarthy cousins—"

"Maybe I am. Would that make any difference?"

He doesn't answer that. "Maybe they switched babies at the hospital. It happens all the time."

"We saw him come out."

"I'm not so sure. I go color-blind when I panic."

"He looks just like you."

"Quit it. He doesn't look a speck like me."

. . .

They do not have a paternity test.

"I trust you, honey. I trust you completely. This proves it, right? Right?"

She thinks he's afraid, afraid of what he might find out. About her, about himself. He'd rather not know.

"Besides," he says, "I don't want them to have to stick the baby again. That would be cruel, right, to take blood from a baby for a pointless little test? What color do you think his blood is, anyway?"

. . .

Friends and neighbors stop by, bringing gifts and cards with cherubic pink babies on them, saying *wow,* and *hmmm,* and *gee.* "He's a big one," they all say. His size is a safe topic, uncontroversial, undeniable.

"Do you think his eyes will change?" one neighbor, who had four children of her own, says. "They often do."

"I didn't know that," Julia says.

"Oh, yes. They all have blue eyes to start. Later they sometimes turn green or gray or brown."

The vagueness of the pronoun confuses Julia; for a moment she wants to ask where she can find some of these green, gray, or brown children for Gabe to play with.

Her friend Hugo brings over a miniature basketball and backboard. He hands the box over proudly, then snatches it back after he gets a peek at Gabe in his playpen. "I'm sorry," he blurts, "I didn't know. I didn't mean anything by it."

"By what?" she says. Gabe's far too young for it, but she would have liked to play with the toy herself.

"I was planning to get one of those toy doctor kits, I *was.*"

Friends stop by, but only her friends, not Jonas's. His parents don't visit. His mother is ill and can't travel. Julia knows this, but still it rankles.

Her best friend Missy comes bringing gifts for Gabe and also for her. They go up to the nursery where Gabe is napping. "Whoa!" Missy says admiringly. "You bad girl! Is Jonas mad?"

"No. He's not mad at all."

"Wow. He must be totally pussy-whipped then."

Julia cringes. She's always hated that expression. It makes her picture a whip cracking out between her legs like a demonic tail.

"How did you choose Gabriel? Is that the father's name?"

Even Missy doesn't believe her.

It would have been so much easier if there were a fancy, scientific-sounding label for it, So-and-So's syndrome, a catchy set of initials. If only she had some statistics, if only she could say, "Just one child in ten million is born like this every year," then it would sound better, she would seem lucky, a lottery winner. Instead he's just a mistake, like an error in accounting, upsetting the balance, and people would rather erase him than do the math again, reconfigure the equations to make him work out.

.   .   .

The first time she brings Gabe back to bed with her, Jonas sits up. "What are you doing?"

"He can't sleep."

"Nurse him then."

"He's lonely. Where are you going?"

"I'm afraid I'll roll over in my sleep and crush him."

"You won't."

"I can't even see him in the dark. He blends right in." He insists on moving to the couch.

Jonas won't change diapers. He never smiles when Gabe

burps or waves his arms; he simply stares disinterestedly as if his son were a specimen in a lab or an anthropological sample, performing curious local customs. At night she is the one to get up, every time, when they hear Gabe rustling around. "He's just hungry," Jonas insists. "I'm not the milk machine."

She hopes he will come around eventually.

. . .

"He's gone," she says to the empty house.

Panic rising in her throat. She's running downstairs. Running upstairs again. Wet footprints everywhere. Classic nightmare—curtains billowing around an open window. The stark crib—no blankets, no suffocating toys, totally SIDS-proof—empty of Gabe as well. She put him down for just five minutes while she took a shower.

Just five minutes. That's what they all say. An interval plenty wide enough for disaster to come plowing through.

Downstairs again. Cold air on her wet back. Maybe an animal got in the window? Dashes back up to the nursery. There's a crouching, furry shape on the floor—

Her sopping towel.

"Jonas," she says. Jonas isn't here. Did he sneak in and take Gabe away somewhere? She hears stealthy movement downstairs. She takes a step and it stops. She takes another. It's listening, waiting for her.

She goes downstairs, cupping her heavy breasts. They're aching from all the jouncing around. There's a rustle in the living room. A surprise party, friends in paper hats crouching behind chairs? She crosses the threshold choking on dread.

And sees Gabe, sitting in the special vibrating seat he loves. He's panting a little as he bobs his head, trying to make it go. She snatches him up. He's burning hot against her cold, clammy skin.

"You just forgot," Jonas says when he comes home that night. "You're overtired. You thought you put him in the crib, but really you put him in the seat."

"What, I just *misplaced* him?"

Jonas is smiling, smirking, not meeting her eyes. He's trying to provoke her. He did this, somehow. Let him gloat. The one small satisfaction is that if he smuggled Gabe downstairs, he must have touched him to do it, and that's a first.

.   .   .

Jonas turns to his friends; he has a few of them left over from his grad school days who are stretching out their dissertations as long as possible, whom he likes to drink beer and pontificate with. They spend hours arguing movies, politics, debating who would win in death matches. Superman versus Batman? Bear versus shark? The United States versus an alliance of North Korea, Canada, and Vatican City? A sort of men's club. A men's club for men who never hunt, who hate sports, and who are fanatical about their obscure music choices. This becomes his support group.

The house feels more comfortable without him. She watches tennis tournaments, Gabe nestled in her arms. White-clad people grunt, thrust, grow angry, swear daintily. The ball snaps back and forth with satisfying pops. Anxious crouching runners dart out to snare stray balls. There is a pleasing rhythm, as if even the players, despite their outbursts, are following a script. "I could watch this all day," she tells Gabe. Some days she does.

One evening Jonas comes home late, smelling of beer and cigarette smoke. He stands swaying in the bedroom doorway, his shirt unbuttoned one more button than usual. She wonders about his driving. She'll say something about it tomorrow.

"Tell me honestly. Did you have an affair with a black man?"

"No."

"Not with Martin?"

"Martin's gay."

"So you're saying if he wasn't gay, you'd want to—"

"No!"

"Aliens, then. Don't get mad! Just think about it for a minute. It happens all the time."

"Aliens? I'm beginning to think I'm married to one."

. . .

His chubby legs, his downy blond hair like chick fluff, his bottom in his saggy diapers, his perfect ears. The way he watches everything, his pale eyes full of calm inquiry. He smiles, he does it all the time, though she knows everyone would tell her that it's too soon, that it's only a burp, or a twitch, or a trick of the light.

He gets fretful sometimes, screwing up his face and batting himself with his fists. She takes him to the pediatrician, who looks searchingly between his legs and says, "Bad case of diaper rash."

"But I don't see anything."

"With him it's harder to see the redness. There's a cream you should try."

The doctor is a tall woman with a mass of striking mahogany-colored hair that she always wears knotted on the top of her head and held in place with two chopsticks or knitting needles. This arrangement seems dangerous to Julia; she keeps picturing eyeballs poked out, babies impaled. And yet the hair was a major factor in choosing this doctor. Julia longs to see the hair unknotted, trailing on the floor. She hopes, maybe one day when they are more friendly, that she can ask to see it, and that the doctor, smiling, will oblige her.

"You need to be very vigilant with this sort of thing," the doctor is saying. "With this skin, bruises are harder to spot, too. You'll have to check him for other signs."

"He still never cries. Not a sound."

"We can't find any reason for it. He's just quiet. You're lucky. A perfect baby."

. . .

She keeps thinking, for some reason, about the professor in her art history class. Going on and on about negative space, how sculpture is about the skin, that edge where substance and absence meet. How the presence of empty space, a void, causes a solid object to reveal itself.

Gabriel stares, pupils floating in near-white irises like flecks trapped in ice. He can be so still, sometimes, as if holding his breath. A statue of a child. When she sees other children she's shocked by the noise, the frenzied motion. One day she sees a neighbor's child squirming in his stroller, bucking against the straps, and thinks he's having a seizure. "Hyperactive," she tells Gabe, whose motions are as slow and deliberate as a chess player's. "Not like you."

. . .

In the middle of the night she reads to him, books she loved as a child. She knows he doesn't understand, but the sound of her voice puts him to sleep.

One night she reads:

The gypsies came and stole the child away in the dead of night. They came all a-creeping, silent and slinking. It used to happen all the time, you know; every family had a story of a dear little lost one. But most peo-

ple don't know that it still goes on. The gypsies take only the naughty, the pretty children. Children are so ugly nowadays.

They carried the children off in great sacks, bouncing against their backs, to the gypsy market, where they were sold to the diamond mines where the shafts are too small for a grown man, or to the factories that need tiny fingers to tighten screws. Or to the circuses to feed the lions and tigers.

We like the circus, the children said. We like lions and tigers.

Oh-ho, the gypsies said, they will like you too.

It's an old book, full of racial stereotypes, grisly violence. She's surprised by how frightening it is. Long after Gabe dozes off she sits up, reading ahead, unable to sleep, afraid to turn the light off. The glowing yellow eyes in the illustrations follow her around after she closes the book.

. . .

"Let's have another baby," Jonas says.

"But not so soon."

"I want to start it now." Pushing her to the bed and bouncing her down. "A little girl? Hunh? As soon as possible. I want to see—"

"You want to see what color the next one is?"

"Let's see if we're capable of producing a normal baby. Don't you want to know?"

"No," she says. "No. Not like this."

Gabe is quiet in the nursery. Jonas pushes her down ungently. He's not rough; he's been much rougher in the past, when they played around at wrestling and manhandling each other. But it scares her now. She goes limp, pictures a rabbit in a dog's mouth, carried so gently the teeth don't break the skin. She imagines she can hear Gabe's breathing.

When he's done he says, "Oh honey, oh sweetie, I'm sorry. I didn't know you were still sore there. It's been months. I thought you were OK by now."

"It's fine," she says mechanically, and totters to the bathroom to wipe herself off. She has her period, but she won't tell him that. Let him think he's hurt her.

The next day he brings her flowers, a recording of the Brahms lullaby, a brick of baker's chocolate, and a bouquet of spinach leaves. The flowers' scent is so strong it nauseates her. The music makes her want to smash something. The spinach is a mystery until she remembers Jonas reading her something about folic acid, conception, healthy embryos in the early stages.

They don't talk about it; it's as though it hadn't happened.

She'd only meant to guilt-trip him a little, but now she realizes she's set a dangerous precedent. Jonas didn't hurt her but he thought he did. And she let him. Now he thinks he can get away with it. Now it will be easier for him to do it again. But it won't be again; it will be the first time.

.   .   .

Gabe glares at Jonas over his high-chair tray, his hairless brows wrinkled.

"He's fussy this morning," she says, though he doesn't look fussy—he looks like a stern Buddha passing judgment. He knows.

"Those eyes," Jonas says and hides behind the tent of his newspaper.

Julia thinks of the storybook gypsy eyes. She keeps thinking she sees them staring out of the shrubbery in the yard. She goes to lift Gabe out of the high chair and realizes she can't; the angle's awkward, but it's more than that. He doesn't look any bigger, but he seems to weigh twice as much, as though there's a magnetic force pulling him toward the earth.

She waits until Jonas leaves for the day, so she can brace herself, heave and strain in private.

. . .

Julia is waiting in the checkout line at the grocery store, Gabe strapped in a pouch against her chest. It's an effort to stand up straight. She's staring at the headlines of the tabloids— MOTHER OF SEPTUPLETS WANTS TO NAME THEM ALL STEVE, LOCAL MAN BURIES FAMILY ALIVE IN BACKYARD THEN PLANTS TULIPS, LOSE TWENTY POUNDS IN THREE DAYS WITH MIRACLE SHAD DIET, IOWA CROP CIRCLES INDICATE LOCATION OF MISS- ING CHILD—when a bejeweled hand enters her line of vision. The hand descends on Gabe's head, fondling his hair in a pro- prietary way.

"His hair's dry," the woman says. "You need to use condi- tioner on him." She's an older black woman with short hair and large earrings and enormous unblinking eyes. She has a bale of Huggies in her cart. So does Julia. Huggies are on sale.

"It always looks like that."

"That's what I'm saying. It's all dry. He needs conditioning. You people don't understand."

"I'll try it." She won't. She likes it this way. She both resents the woman's authoritative handling of Gabe's head and feels strangely grateful. *Take me in*, she wants to say. *Take me home. Tell me what to do.* Gabe's black, she thinks, but he's not *black*. Or is he? Is he old enough to notice these things yet? Maybe he would feel more at home among black people. Why doesn't she have more black friends? Maybe that's what she should do, infiltrate, ingratiate herself. Make friends with women like this one, who seem so sure of the right thing to do.

"You can't have the boy going around looking like Buckwheat. A *blond* Buckwheat. I can't believe you put peroxide on a baby, poor thing."

"He was born like that."

"Listen," the woman says, stepping closer with a confidential air. "I appreciate what you're trying to do and all, but I'm sorry, it's not right. You're hurting more than helping. The child's going to grow up all confused about what he is."

"What do you think I should do?"

"Why couldn't you adopt a nice white child? It's good of you to want to give some child a home, but why not one of your own kind? The boy's going to end up feeling like he doesn't fit in anywhere. There's no lonelier feeling. He needs his black community."

"He's not adopted."

"Oh, really?" The woman takes in Julia's limp colorless hair, the blue veins showing through her pale skin. The kind of pale that prompts strangers to ask if she's just given blood, if she'd like to lie down. "Really? Well, that must have been the blackest black man in the universe! Black-hole black!" The friendly condescension has turned in a second to rancor. There's nowhere to go in the narrow chute between racks of magazines and bubble gum. Heads in other lines are starting to turn. Gabe is struggling, clawing at her.

She tries to comfort him. He fights like he's trying to escape. She looks at Gabe, at the black woman, trying to see kinship. But the woman is about a hundred shades lighter than Gabe, a warm, rich brown. The closest thing to Gabe's color is the black of the checkout conveyor belt.

She feels a foolish grin spreading over her face. Her knees buckling. Jonas had talked about how it would be easier for him if Gabe had some dread disease. She can see what he means. Jonas wants to fight, he wants a distinct enemy. He wants to donate a kidney, argue with doctors, spend nights in a hospital drinking bad coffee, scream at the insurance

agency. He wants heroics, tragedy, not the constant petty battles of the day-to-day.

"He must have been Mister Supernegro, Mister Out-of-
Africa," the woman chortles. "Oh, Lord."

.   .   .

Julia calls Missy and says, "He's getting worse and worse."

"Worse how?"

"All he does now is sleep, eat, and give me these evil-eye
looks."

"Are you thinking about splitting up?"

"No! I could never—"

"But you keep saying you can't stand being around him."

She sighs. "It's terrible, but sometimes I think I'd be happy
if he just—disappeared. It would be so much easier—"

"Then you could get back together with that black guy,"
Missy says. "You never told me his name."

"I keep telling you, there isn't any—wait, what was that?"

"Something at your end."

She knows what it was, the muffled click of a receiver
stealthily put down and, downstairs in the kitchen, the lum-
bering tread of a man trying to tiptoe.

.   .   .

They lie in bed, on their backs, watching reflections of headlights glide across the ceiling. Blank-faced and wide awake,
two paper dolls.

"You're such a hypocrite," Jonas says. "You said it yourself,
I heard you. I don't know why you get so mad at me for wish-
ing it."

"Said what?"

"That it would be nice. If he just. Went away."

. . .

She stops going to the grocery store.

She makes lists for Jonas, and he buys double of everything to minimize shopping trips. Bananas rot in the kitchen, the refrigerator is crammed with fat-free margarine, and there's a wall of Huggies in the corner of the nursery that goes all the way up to the ceiling, like a barricade.

"Why won't you just hold him?" she says.

"I'm afraid I'll break him."

"Don't you want to?"

"I'm afraid of what I might do."

And she's afraid, too, that if he picks up Gabe he'll feel the strange denseness, the rock-solidness of him that is making him harder and harder to bear.

. . .

She lugs Gabe to the pediatrician and is horrified to discover that the doctor has cut off her hair. She now has a mannish crew cut that reveals the irregular bumps of her skull. Julia feels betrayed.

The doctor inspects Gabe.

"There's something strange. About his weight," Julia says.

"I'm not really concerned about that right now," the doctor says. "I'd rather focus on this." She gestures at Gabe's arms, then his chest, then the back of his head.

"What? I don't see anything."

"Bruising. It's common, at this age, when they're first crawling around and bumping into things, but—"

"He doesn't crawl around," Julia says. "He just sits there."

The doctor looks at her probingly. "Are you sure you're not being too rough with him?" she says. "You might be hurting him without realizing it."

"I'd know! He'd tell me!" Julia says hotly, privately wondering how. Write little notes? Use sign language?

The doctor is silent so long they both hear Julia's stomach make a squealing, spiraling sound.

"Just remember to be gentle," the doctor says finally. "Watch the bruises." She makes Julia look closely, pointing out the blacker-than-black marks that she says are sore spots. She talks about the "thumb-shaped" bruises on his chest, and the "finger-sized" ones on his back. "I'd like to do another CAT scan," she says, but just then an unearthly howling arises from another examining room and the doctor dashes out, and Julia grabs Gabe and his clothes and flees.

. . .

"Jonas?"

"What?"

"Nothing."

He looks different. He's shaved something off or let something grow. Why is everyone changing their hair all of a sudden? The difference is that he's clean-shaven, she decides, rather than sporting his usual half-grown stubble. His eyebrows look groomed. And his eyelashes are gone. Has he never had eyelashes? How could she not notice something like that? The absence of hair ought to reveal more of him, but somehow it has the opposite effect: his face seems harder, smoother, more artificial, a rigid mask.

"Jonas?"

"What?"

She looks at his hands. They're thick, blunt, made for crushing things or wrenching them apart. She should leave. She should just leave, right now. Instead, she runs her finger down his cheek. It's soft as suede.

They make love on the couch. Jonas moves so slowly, so

gently, he doesn't break a sweat. Gabe watches the whole thing from his bouncy-swing. He's so heavy he doesn't bounce, just hangs suspended, the frame buckling under his dead weight.

. . .

The second time Gabe vanishes she knows she shouldn't panic. But she does. She panics more than she did the first time. Again she dashes up and down stairs, wheeling and whirling, her own hysterical breathing drowning out all other sound. Finally she stops, pauses, tries to feel on her skin the tiny air currents stirred up by movement somewhere in the house.

She finds him sitting in the empty bathtub, not crying, not lost in contemplation of his warped reflection in the faucet, as a normal baby would be. He's sitting, hands folded, patient, simply waiting.

She lugs him to his changing table, whips off his playsuit, his diaper, turns on a bright lamp, and inspects him all over. She thinks she sees a new bruise on his ankle, then one on his groin. Then a ring of small ones flowering on his shoulder like a bitemark. Then one on his cheek. Then she's seeing them everywhere, his whole hide is mottled with them, coated with them.

"I give up," she says.

She hears Jonas slam the front door. "Baby," he calls. "Baby, darling, mother dear, shoogums, sweetheart, honeypie, sugarlips, babycakes, cinnamon roll—" reciting the litany of eons ago, back when he was always kidding but meant it all and she didn't believe a word of it. She feels a frantic desire to hide—hide herself, hide Gabe, fold up the entire house and hide it in her pocket. She crouches over the changing table and hears Jonas's footsteps on the stairs. She is acutely conscious of her exposed back, the vulnerability of her nape and skull.

She tells herself there is a masked intruder coming down the hall. That fantasy is preferable to the truth.

"Honey," he says, "I'm home."

. . .

She wakes feeling that something is wrong. She wakes to vertigo every morning, but today is different.

She trudges to the nursery, rotating her sore shoulders, cracking her back. The rocking chair nods gently, as if someone has just vacated it. The astronauts and cowboys and lion tamers on the wallpaper wink at her. Jonas picked the paper; she had been skeptical. The astronauts have what are unquestionably codpieces attached to their space suits, and the lion tamers seem a little too fey. For the hundredth time she resolves to repaper the room. She leans over the crib.

A pink-skinned, black-haired green-eyed baby looks back at her. She screams. The baby screams. It's so loud; she's never heard anything so loud; it's like the walls are screaming.

Jonas comes running. He comes just a little too quickly, as if he'd been waiting a few steps down the hall; his surprise is a bit too theatrical.

"Where is Gabe?" she screams. "Where is he?"

Jonas's face shifts from blankness to surprise to ecstatic realization in a metamorphosis that has clearly been rehearsed for hours before the bathroom mirror. "But this *is* Gabe. He's changed. He's cured."

"This is not Gabe! Have you lost your mind? Where did this baby come from?"

"It's a miracle. He finally changed. I knew he would. He's healed."

"He wasn't sick! He was fine before!"

"He's normal now. We can be a normal family. Isn't that what you wanted?"

"What *you* wanted."

The baby's eyes flick back and forth; fists wave in the air; legs kick. A new sound comes out of its mouth. Not a scream. Something else. The audible language of babies is so foreign to her she doesn't understand what's happening. Jonas lifts the baby and holds it against his shoulder, and the noise stops.

"What is going on?"

A loud burp mocks her. Jonas? Or the baby?

"Why can't you just be happy?" Jonas says.

And that's what everyone tells her: the doctors, the policemen when she insists on calling them, her parents, their friends. It's a miracle, people say. You should consider yourselves lucky. Just one of those things. Even the doctors say this.

"Don't put a gift horse in your mouth, right?" Jonas says. "Count your blessings, right? Didn't you say that?" The new baby vomits great lumpy gouts on her shoulder. He has mushy features, a fat chin—nothing like Gabe's. He's light, flabby, insubstantial. She could toss him out the window if she wanted to. She might. He screams and screams. His face turns red when he screams, when he burps, when the slightest flicker of emotion or indigestion ripples through him.

"Like you," Jonas says. Which is true; when Julia gets embarrassed or excited, red splotches appear on her throat and chest, as if she were being throttled by an invisible strangler. She's splotchy now.

"Why can't you accept a good thing?" Jonas asks. "I can understand being in denial about a tragedy, but not this. Why do you have to question it?"

"This is not my baby," she says. No one listens.

But she knows. A mother knows. Her breasts ache. Her longing for Gabe is intensely physical, a barbed fishhook tugging.

The strange baby sucks at her, eating her up. That's not yours, she wants to tell him. It's on loan, it belongs to someone else. When he comes back, you'll have to repay the debt somehow.

She tells herself she is a wet nurse, as in medieval times, suckling the queen's child. It's a job, that's all.

"It was just a phase," Jonas says. "He outgrew it." He's full of authority, all of a sudden. Doesn't he ever go to work anymore? Seems like he's always here, changing diapers, wiping everything down with antiseptic cleaners, plying the baby with soft goggle-eyed toys.

She surreptitiously rifles the house, every baby-sized space she can think of. She peers into the clothes dryer with a flashlight before using it.

With the baby on her shoulder, she searches the backyard for spots of freshly turned-up earth. She's being morbid, she knows.

She finds a soft patch and begins digging at it with the toe of her sneaker. The dirt comes away easily. It would be quicker with a shovel, but she doesn't want to put the baby down and go get one. She can't leave the baby in the house, she needs him here, she needs him to see, bear witness. She must maintain balance, at all costs. Whatever hole she finds Gabe in, she will take him out and leave this strange baby in his place.

She's still kicking and scooping with her foot when Jonas comes home. Headlights. Door slamming. Lights go on in rooms, she hears his voice faintly calling. She sees the light go on in the nursery, now she sees his flitting panicked shadow. She should call to him. But not yet, not yet, she'll watch the show a minute longer. That must be what I looked like, she thinks, when I found Gabe missing.

Something catches his eye, her white shirt, probably, moving against the darkening hedges. He comes racing outside, little loose bits of him—hair, shirt collar, glasses, jowls—jiggling and fluttering.

He looks at her, the baby, the breadbox-sized hole. "What are you doing?"

"I thought . . . I thought . . ."

"I know what you thought. Can't you see how silly you're being?"

Yes, she thinks, I underestimated you. Of course you wouldn't hide him here, right under our noses.

"What do we have to do," he says, "to make you happy?"

"You know."

"Listen." He sighs. "What if I stop trying to convince you this is Gabe? Why don't we pretend this is another kid, who's just dropped in our laps, and we have to take care of him. Would that make it easier?"

"No," she says, staring at his teeth, which are blue in the twilight. She rubs the baby's back. He burrows his way into her neck and glues himself there with drool. Jonas is right; it'll be far easier to be charitable and love a strange child than to surrender her convictions and concede that he's really hers.

.   .   .

But she finds that the former begins gradually to lead her to the latter, in a slow and insidious way. As days and weeks pass, she relaxes into routines, takes pleasure in the baby's burps and crows and crawlings, and forgets for long traitorous periods about her real son. And then it's not a forgetting; she begins to suspect that everyone is right and she is wrong, that this is Gabe after all.

Am I going to react this violently every time he changes? she asks herself. Am I going to be one of those mothers who can't bear for their children to grow up, even a little bit?

She begins to think she sees him, her Gabe, in this baby.

Truly *in* him; she glimpses the shimmer of Gabe's pale eyes behind the baby's greenish ones, the glint of gold beneath the scalp, like hairs trapped beneath stockings.

Impossible, she thinks. But she can't shake the idea.

How clever of Jonas, she thinks, to hide him in plain sight. Impossible.

But they smell the same, don't they, this baby and Gabe? She searches her library of sense memories. And the teeth, the teeth are exactly the same. Jonas never even knew about the teeth. He couldn't have known to find a replacement baby with the exact same—

Gabe's *in* there, she thinks, he's been inside there all along. Trapped. Trying to signal to her, calling silently. She puts an ear to the baby's chest.

She tries to put the thoughts aside but they bounce back up like balloons. What does it matter? she thinks. If Gabe *is* in there, she should be glad to have him, in any form. But she wants proof. She wants to be sure.

A strange line of thought arises, which she tries to erase, but can't. She has sudden urges, imagines smashing the baby like a vase to see what's inside, imagines unscrewing his head like the top of a perfume bottle. Changing his diaper, she pulls his legs apart to clean him and imagines pulling, and pulling, and pulling.

She has to lay her suspicions to rest, once and for all. If she could just lift up a bit of skin and see—

This pale skin that has grown up over him like a crust, a chrysalis—

Just peel back a corner, like getting a peek at the old wallpaper—

Just a peek—then she will be at peace. Then she will lay down her arms, she will concede everything. She will be the best mother the world has ever seen.

Just a little bit. She'll be so gentle, he won't even feel it.

Quick, now, before she loses her nerve. Gabe darling, if that's you in there, just lie still, Mommy's coming—

Jonas has left work early—no reason, just felt something was wrong at home, first stirrings of the parent's sixth sense. He checks the yard, then clatters through the house, vaults up the stairs. Now he pauses in the doorway of the nursery and sees a woman he doesn't recognize, a woman with only the vaguest resemblance to his wife, hunched over the baby on the changing table. The baby is silent, as if curious, waiting. The changeling mother bends studiously to her work, moments away from discovery, revelation, reunion. The baby holds his breath.

My brother puts the new one in the pen out back with the other salesmen. "They just don't ever learn, do they," he says mournfully, as he yanks home the latch and notches up one more on the gatepost.

I like to go down there after breakfast and throw my toast crusts over the top. You can hear them scrambling around, you can see them between the slats. Only a narrow glimpse; none of them are skinny enough yet to be seen fully. But the gaps are wide enough to observe their choice of tie, their sweat-stained button-down shirts, their pinstripe and seersucker and gabardine suits. You can see their priorities at a glance: Some have filthy ties and spotlessly shined shoes; others let the dust build up on their toes and keep their ties and pocket squares clean. Sometimes you can see an eye, sometimes two.

My brother tells me not to, but I like to walk past and hear their voices hooting out to me. I like to pretend they're calling out for my hot body.

"Set of seventeen knives for the price of twelve! And I'll throw in a free melon baller!"

"Ma'am, you look like you could use a handy household—"

"And that's just what I'm here to tell you—"

"Just try to look me in the eye and tell me you don't need a—"

"Seven easy payments. Just seven easy payments. That's less than—"

"Hold it in your hand. Lighter than air, I tell you. Just think what—"

"Per day, that's less than the cost of a cup of coffee."

If you squint your ears, you can make it sound like love.

Hands pop out between the slats, holding limp water-stained catalogs, order forms, metal gadgets shaped like squashed dragonflies. They jostle for the spots closest to the fence. I like to keep moving, give them all a chance. They stir up such a cloud of dust you can see it rising above the ten-foot walls. Inside they get hoarse on the grit but never think to close their mouths.

"Last chance—"

"Just between us, I'm willing to make you a special deal—"

"Limited offer—"

"Practically giving it away, don't tell my supervisor—"

"Don't you *want* to cook fast easy low-fat meals for your family? You could be saving lives with this—"

If they all got together and cooperated, stacked up their sample cases in one column, they would be able to climb out. But they are too competitive to think of that. They are sales-men to the core. Occasionally you will see one digging at the base of the fence with an eggbeater or a corkscrew decorated with poodles, but he always stops early on for fear of damaging the merchandise.

"If only they used their jaws for digging," my brother always says. He says he'd like to use them to clear the fields. "Grab one by the heels, get him started, and just push him along, wheelbarrow-style. Better than a lawn mower." Back in the beginning, crows gathered on the top of the fence, attracted as they are by anything that glitters. But soon even they got tired of the noise.

The newest one has little triangular eyes deep in pockets of skin, and a mouth that's purplish and fleshy and caved in like a spoiled fruit. He gets up and brushes off the knees of his pants, first thing, like they all do. Then he looks behind him, taking in the fact that yet another door has been slammed on him. And then he looks around at the others, sizes up the competition, hitches up his trousers. He's got one of those malnourished paunches that hang low and hard against the belt. The others circle him, eyeing his sample case. They're hunched over, defensive postures, ready to spring.

He'll make his pitch, first thing. That's their territory marker, their plumage, their bellering mating call. If there are two selling competing brands of the same orange juicer/ showerhead adapter, there will be trouble.

"Get away from there," my sister-in-law calls. "Makes you look cheap and easy."

My sister-in-law likes to stand in windows naked, feeling the sun on the freckled space between her breasts. That is why so many salesmen stop by.

"Why cheap and easy?" I ask her later, when we're sitting on the front veranda in sunglasses and head scarves, watching the afternoon dust storms roll past. Today the waves are tight, dense, low to the ground. They form tubes that last for several minutes before breaking. Far in the distance, you can see teenage surfers riding them. They wear rubber suits and gas masks. The surfers paint their surfboards the colors of the ocean: green, orange, gold, black. I can see two bobbing up and down on choppy waves. A third has just wiped out; he's skidding across the ground on his knees, getting knocked this way and that by stray gusts as the big ones crash over his head.

His knees are probably torn up pretty bad by now. We see his surfboard get ripped out of his hands. He lunges for it but it flaps away. Gone. A moment later the wind whips it around behind him and he gets whacked on the head. I bet he's cute.

"You make them think they can score with you," she says.

"But I'm not going to buy anything," I say.

"I mean *emotionally*," Janice says. "They're manipulative because they're insecure. They need to feel loved. It all has to do with their mothers."

"But they don't have mothers," I say.

"Exactly!" she says. Then she talks some more about emotional needs. She always says she doesn't mean to do it, she just happens to walk past the window every day, on her way to getting dressed, and feels like lingering. It's the salesmen who are looking for attention, she says, looking for love, who come to the door longing for some give-and-take. That's where my brother waits for them.

She says the sun will give us wrinkles, but the dry wind will tighten our pores, so the one cancels out the other. Janice is younger than I am but acts older because she's married and has read two books about how your mind works and is very in touch with her feelings. Her face is not pretty in the grand scheme of things, but relative to those around her she's a standout. My brother calls her a hottie at least seven times a day.

Each time I want to tell him—or her—that *hot* is not such great praise around here. *Hot, isn't it?* gets more play than *hello*. *Hot* is common as dirt. The salesmen, no matter how hot it gets, keep their jackets on, their ties knotted. By the end of the day all their suits have turned a new darker color from the sweat. I want someone to call me *hot*.

Janice. Her nose is the perfect shape but three sizes too large for her face. Her hair is long and pretty but grows more from one side than the other, like a wig that's slipped sideways. I could go on. But her neck is like the stalk of a flower, I think, always bending toward you. I don't remember a flower, but I remember that long pliant curve.

The house is set far back from the road. I don't know how the salesmen can see Janice in the window from so far away, but they can. They have a long walk, from the road to the door. They walk with their shoulders back and chests out, even the puny ones: They know they are being watched; the approach is important. The balding ones wear straw boaters, felt fedoras for an old-timey feel. Some let the baldness show and polish their heads; they think it makes them look more reliable. The word for their walk is *brisk*. Everything is brisk: arms, legs, hair if they have it. Hair parted in the middle, flapping in two brisk wings with every step. The briskness extends down to their fingers and toes, flicking away dust, pinching mustache tips. I know they think about her as they climb the steps: bored lady-of-the-house, alone and in need of company, coming to the door in a hastily thrown-on bathrobe.

It is such a long walk from road to house. If I were more fleet of foot, I'd run out to intercept them, tell them to move on, nothing to see here. My brother tells me to stay out of the way.

"Don't yell at her," Janice says. She says I am to be pitied. Janice says I am sick, I have arrested development. It is very sad; I will be a little child forever and will never taste the illicit fruits of womanhood. I ask her how she knows this. She says she read it in her book.

"Hello? You don't have any of *these*," she says, sticking out her chest. "It means you never will. You'll be an old woman in the body of a little child."

But I'm as tall as she is. I think it's just that I'm built along the lines of my mother, who in the picture I have is as flat as a washboard, the effect heightened perhaps by the armor she's wearing, horizontal metal strips stitched together to shield her from the evils in the atmosphere. That's what people thought back then.

Janice just smiles sweetly and says, "You'll see."

I don't believe her. But the more she says it, the more I start to.

I ask my brother if she's right and if I'll never grow up. He doesn't say yes and doesn't say no.

My brother says I should be grateful, that I don't have it half as bad as some. He says he's seen them in town, those born with their eyelids stitched together and nothing underneath, or with their faces coming out of their stomachs like a kid's drawing, or our neighbor with fleshy nubbins growing from his gums in place of teeth.

"You should smile more," Janice says. "World of difference." She says I am lucky I have family who love me no matter what I look like.

It's easy for them to say. They've got no visible defects and are happily married. Except my brother gets sunburned bad sometimes when he works outside, to the point of blisters like white worms on his skin. Most of his hair has been burned off his skull by now; there's only a pale corona of fuzz around his head like a dandelion. But that's nothing. They've got each other. They'll bang out some children soon. In the middle of the night I hear them in their room, the furniture getting pushed around by the force of their love and my brother telling Janice all the things he's going to do to her.

People get married now much younger than they used to, or so I'm told. It's because of impatience, I suppose, because of the rules against fornication before marriage, to contain the spread of diseases. Maybe it's turned out to be more than Janice bargained for, but how can she complain? Big empty house, lots of room, fine view of the dust storms, parents gone, only the old-maid sister to get rid of. And my brother's going places, got big plans. Who wouldn't jump at the chance?

At first I thought she did her standing at the window to needle him. But now I wonder if he asked her to do it, right from the start; if it was all a plan. Salesman bait. I can't remember which started first, him building the pen or her doing the standing. By now they have it like clockwork: she's in the window right at the hour of midmorning when the air is clearest, and within minutes there's a jaunty step on the veranda, a knock at the door.

Now there are nearly two dozen jawing back in the pen. They'll be kept there until the season cools off. My brother doesn't like to exert himself in the heat.

The newest one—I *am* sorry about him. I was up in my room and saw him coming up the path and thought, Oh no. Maybe because he looked less swaggery than the rest. He came up in a tentative way, scanning the front of the house as if it were a face, as if it had something to tell. He had a clump of brown sticks in his hand—there's a weed here that has round leaves ringed with spikes; people call them flowers but I know the truth—he was carrying them like a present. And he is tall and bony and paunchy, but there is something childish about his face. Developmentally arrested? Maybe we have something in common, something we can talk about, given the opportunity.

So I am sorry he is in there with the rest. I go down there in the evening, after the storms, to see how he's faring. It's dark enough that they don't see me and start their pitching. The others are crouched in little huddles, sheltering behind hats and sleeves and sample cases raised above their heads. The new one stands alone. Each time he tries to join a group, they turn their backs and shut him out. I wonder what he's got in his case. Either it's something so junky the others are snubbing him as an amateur, or else it's so wonderful they feel threatened and are plotting against him.

None of the others are friends, but there are alliances,

business arrangements. They're discussing sales strategy. Intense trading is going on. The toast crusts I tossed this morning have changed hands several times.

The new one doesn't want to dirty up his suit by sitting, so he's leaning up against the fence. I slink up behind him and look at the slice I can see between the slats: hair, neck, collar, seam up the middle of the jacket's back. The boards groan. If he pressed hard, probably, he could break through. But none of them think that way. The salesmen all think they can talk their way out of anything.

I warned them once about what was coming, I even told them where the nails were loose and the wood rotten. I pulled back a flap and stuck my head through. They were insulted. Have you no faith in our persuasive powers? they all said. We don't need to stoop to base physicality, they said. Won't dirty ourselves with the sweat of manual labor. We will escape by power of elocution alone. And then they tried to sell me skin-brightening cream, hair pomade, chewing gum that cleanses the obscenities from your speech.

A flabby bit of his back pokes between the boards. It wants to be touched. It will be sweaty and gritty, my fingers will taste like salt afterward. He will turn around and see at most half of my face—my face is wide. He will not, I think, see much of my body.

I don't do it. Instead, I go back to the house. Janice is mending stockings that have been mended so many times before that now they are all seam. She is using thread I took from one of the salesmen. He said it was a free sample. He said once we tried it we'd want to buy out his whole supply. It is supposed to be invisible. The stockings are supposed to be nude. I can see everything but Janice says it's just the light in here.

"Janice," I say. "Will I ever—"

"Of course you won't, baby," she says, biting off thread

with a nasty clicking of teeth. "No man will ever want you, not the way you look. Men like *mature* women. But don't worry. We'll still love you."

"That wasn't even what I was going to ask."

"Yes, it was."

"How do you know?"

"By the lascivious look in your eye," she says. She's sitting on the kitchen table in her underwear, posing and sewing. Apparently she can't get dressed until she repairs the stockings. "I'd just have to take everything off again when I put these back on, so why bother?" she says. I don't know whether she's hoping for another salesman or for my brother to come home. Salesmen eyes on her make her happy. She's not allowed to go near the pen at all.

Her underpants are covered with red kisses. I can't tell whether they're printed on or were made by a mouth and lipstick. I can't see my brother doing that, but who else would? Maybe she made them herself.

"There's nothing wrong with me," I say.

"Denial," she says, smiling sadly.

"You're lying," I say. "Trying to make me feel bad."

"Defense mechanism," she says, with the same pitying smile. "Whatever makes you feel better."

I wish she hadn't read that book. It makes her hard to argue with.

"Honey, we need to work on your self-esteem. Then you'll be better able to cope with this problem of yours."

"How do we do that?"

"A makeover," she says, in a determinedly cheerful way, which means I should leave her alone. She's given me makeovers before. They hurt.

I go up to my room. I have many rooms that I can call mine; it's a big house; there's plenty of space no one wants. Janice is a busy girl. Woman, I should say. She does her busyness downstairs, except when she stands in the window with her nipples close to the glass. There's one room where my brother does his dreaming. The walls are dirty brown but he's painted a white patch on the ceiling. He lies on the floor and falls asleep there, hoping he'll see answers written out on the white cloud.

He's gone most days, but not so far that we can't see him from the veranda. He's flattening the ground, he's building rickety wooden towers. He has a picture from a book, a drawing of a windmill connected to a speedy-looking train on rails. He wants so badly to build it, he has grand plans, but he has no idea how. Even I can see that his towers are no good; each time, before he even gets around to making the fan blades, the windstorms have knocked them to pieces.

I don't know where he thinks he wants to go. What else is there? No one moves except the salesmen, and they keep moving because no one will let them stay anywhere. They are pariahs; no one wants them. That is why they are so belligerent, so full of themselves. Janice says that's a defense mechanism too. Sometimes they come carrying things we need, but most of the time not. They carry diseases; you're not even supposed to touch them. There are signs all along the road, red warning signs with a silhouette of a man with a suitcase and hat, and a big annihilating line through him. My brother says we're doing them a favor by rounding them up.

It's hard to sleep nights with the salesmen yammering. They are out there calling to my brother, making offers he can't refuse. They are bargaining with the night clouds, begging them to part and give us a glimpse of the moon they know is still up there. Now or never, no money down, first come first served. My brother doesn't hear; he's busy telling Janice what she can do with her big mouth even though I haven't heard her say a word.

Maybe they dream about selling. Maybe they're talking in their sleep.

.   .   .

Next day the dust storms come in tall swells and plumes. The surfers are having a blast, rocketing up and down on the mountains of air. One lags behind; he's wearing a helmet and knee pads, as if those will help him.

Janice says she can see their sexy bods in the rubber suits, even at this distance. "It's all about body language," she says. "But then, you wouldn't know about that."

"I do too."

"You're too young to understand. And always will be, baby."

"You're just saying that. You like to think you're the only real woman on the place. Just give me a few months and I'll catch up."

She pats my hand. "Rationalizing. Bargaining. You're going through the seven stages of grief, honey."

Down in the pen my salesman is looking a bit worse for the wear. Yesterday his hair was doing a poufy pompadour thing, now it's lying in sweaty tangles down to his eyebrows. He's streaming, his white-and-blue-striped suit is soaked, sticking wetly to the belly I'm beginning to love so much. His mouth still has a punched-in look. The others rush to the fence and start lipping the minute they see me, but I have yet to hear his voice.

I wait until night, wait till I hear my brother and Janice start up again, then slip back down to the pen. Night is just as hot as day, dark heat like an iron pot. But I know that this means the heat will break soon; it's like a fever that peaks, then disappears. And when that happens my brother will go out to the pen and start counting heads. And later the three of us will go through all the sample cases. And fight over them. If there's something that Janice and I both want, all I have to do is talk about our parents and make the sad doggy face, and my brother will let me have it.

My salesman—I wonder what's in his case, he guards it so closely. The others open theirs up, flash them around, show off the red plush linings and the custom-made compartments. Everything is tattered now, but they don't see it, and they think they can convince you that you don't either.

There is enough dull reflected light from the clouds for me to see that my salesman is right where I left him, next to the fence. He's trying to sleep curled up on his case, to save his suit, but he's much too big, overflowing on all sides. I stick my arm through and poke him in the leg. The others are murmuring all around. He's quiet but his head comes up. His mouth is a darker bruise in his dark face. I pry off a few boards; it's even easier than I thought. He doesn't help me, but the minute there's an opening he wedges himself into it. He gets stuck, I'm tugging at him and he's puffing in my face. He has that salesman smell of shoe polish and overworked salivaries. I'm afraid of his skin so I yank on his sleeves, his hair.

Finally we get him through, and he unfolds himself. He slides his case out and we take a walk in a casual fashion. I tell him he is my favorite of all the salesmen, which is not much of a compliment, but maybe he won't think so. It's still fairly dark. I am wearing a baggy nightdress, and I hope he can't see me too well with his little hooded eyes. I am out to prove something, I am not sure what, but it has something to do with Janice.

He opens his mouth for the first time and says, "Are you perchance interested in a little taste of the illicit?"

At first I think this is his way of telling me he wants my body, and I feel all hot-excited and cold-scared at the same time, like fever chills. But then he pats his sample case, and I realize "The Illicit" is the name of some kind of foot powder or floor wax or magazine subscription that will never arrive. And I don't know if I am disappointed or relieved.

I ask to see what's in the case. He holds it away from me and asks if I'm going to tell my brother about him taking his leave. I begin to realize that he's just like the others, making bargains and once-in-a-lifetime deals.

"I might," I say, in a mincy way. I sound like Janice. "What's in the case?"

"Something good," he says. And doesn't say anything else, which is highly unusual for a salesman. We're walking through the fields and he starts picking the brown weeds, the ones with spiky round suns at their tips. And he gives them to me in a bunch.

Which makes me want to talk him up more. I ask him about his line of work, and where he's been, and what he thinks of the weather. He doesn't say much, but the mushy soft mouth opens and closes and I see the little teeth glittering inside like treasure.

I sashay my hips around. Just a little bit. He gave me flowers, after all.

He puts a hand on my shoulder. It is as warm and moist and gritty as I imagined. Just by chance he touches a sort of funny-bone place there. Nerves shoot off it, and I flinch. But still. He touched me. According to Janice, this is how it begins. We'll touch each other in various places and then lie down on the ground somewhere. I look ahead for a patch clear of stones. The sky is turning pink, a sliver of sun is poking up.

I am trying to decide what to touch, his paunchy belly or his squashy face.

"Show me what's in the case," I say again, in the Janice voice.

"Let's make a trade," he says, all salesmanlike. "I'll show you if you show *me* something."

This is the moment I've been waiting for. "Deal," I say and pull my nightdress over my head so that I feel the hot night wind all over.

"Jumping Jehoshaphat!" he says. "What are you doing? Put that back on!" His eyes are goggly, face frozen. Janice was right. I'm not hot. I'm off-putting. Downright disgusting. He's horrified, hand to his mouth like he might yark. I drop the nightdress on the ground. He snatches it up and yanks it back down over my head.

"Are you trying to get me killed?" he says, looking at me, then back at the house, me then the house. "Did you hear something?"

I start to cry. I didn't know it was possible to be so ugly people could die just from looking at you.

In these dry climes crying is a noise in your throat. I've never seen a tear. I've heard of people's eyes exploding when they try to squeeze one out.

"Would you be quiet?" he hisses. "Please?"

"You said you wanted me to show you something," I say.

"I wanted you to show me the way to the next town," he says.

"Can I come with you?"

"Of course not." He snorts. "That man will have my head."

I look down at the flowers in my hand, and they remind me to feel special. Then suddenly I don't feel special anymore. I remember when I'd seen him do that before.

"You brought some of these for Janice," I say. "When you saw her in the window. You came up to the house looking for *her*."

"She looked . . . lonely," he says. "A mere gesture," he says. "It didn't mean anything," he says and touches my shoulder again, but all I can think about is that I'm not Janice and never will be, I'll never have kisses on my underpants, and the only time a man favors me with flowers is when he's bartering for street directions so he can head up the road and plague more people with his sorry sales pitches.

I know he wishes Janice were here right now. And I wish I

were with one of the other salesmen, who might at least try to
ornament things with words, paint some sugar fantasies, lie to
me, tell me I'm beautiful.

"Which is the way out?"

"That way," I say, pointing the wrong way, not toward the
safety of the road but toward the horizon where the dust
storms are just stirring themselves from sleep. He heads off
without another look at me.

"You never even gave me a peek in the case," I say.

He doesn't look back. He must know what a slow runner I
am. With that head start, I'll never catch up.

"Don't you want to . . . ?" I call.

"No," he calls back. "Thanks," he says, over his shoulder.
He keeps going, fast, not brisk, beyond brisk, sloppily running. He's following the line of my finger, heading for the
surfers' favorite spot. He should reach it right about the time
the swells are highest. With any luck he'll get pounded to
pieces.

·   ·   ·

"Why so glum?" Janice says. She steams my face with a hot
towel, and we practice deep cleansing breaths.

"Some of the stock busted out last night," my brother says.
He doesn't even look at me, he looks at Janice. "They'll be
back," he says.

The dust storms are vicious today, solid masses of brown
and gray. We can feel the thickness of the air as we watch. Bits
of sand scratch against our sunglasses.

"Exfoliating," Janice says.

Later that night some surfers bring my salesman back.
Two carry him up to the house laid out on one of their
surfboards.

"Don't know what he was thinking," one says.

"Got pretty pounded," says the other.

"Didn't have the right gear or nothing," says a third who's tagging along. He's wearing knee pads. I think he's the one I like to watch.

"We figured he was one of yours," the first says.

"Got the marks and all."

"Bring him around back," my brother says.

Janice is blatantly checking out the smallest surfer, from his greenish dreadlocks to his claw-toed surf booties. How dare she? He's *my* surfer. He's *mine*. "He *is* cute," she says, nudging me.

"Yes," I say. I'm *pretty* sure he is, although it's a little hard to tell since he's still wearing his gas mask. And I can't stop looking at my salesman, the one I tried to help, then tried to hurt by sending him the wrong way. His skin is blasted raw, his hair glittering with silica like diamonds, his nostrils plugged with sand. The eyes are all exposed, the folds of skin completely sheared away.

.   .   .

The weather breaks a few days later. We have a few clear cool days before the rains start. My brother assembles his equipment, puts on his faceplate and gloves, and heads out to the pen to make a profit. The salesmen see him coming and their voices rise higher than ever. Each year it's like this; the last day is the worst. Like a few dozen auctioneers in the throes of a bidding climax, or a bunch of tone-deaf opera singers shrieking out their deathbed arias. Usually Janice and I go in the house and stick our heads under pillows.

This year she has other ideas. She holds a needle in a candle flame and then pierces my ears with it. Then I add some holes to her lobes, though they're already so perforated it's hard to find a clear space. She likes to wear all her earrings at once. Then, when I do find a clear space, I strike some kind of nerve or something and she starts screaming and bleeding sort of badly. "You've got to apply pressure," she keeps saying, but every time I get within three feet of her she starts yowling all over again. We're so distracted we don't hear the voices outside.

You don't even feel sorry for the salesmen anymore, just annoyed. My brother never bothered to patch the gaping hole I made in the fence. I guess they all felt it would be beneath them to use it to escape. Except *my* salesman, who might have used it but was too sand-blind to find it.

Afterward we divvy up the sample cases like we always do. My brother takes the knife kits, the ones the salesmen like to demonstrate by cutting pennies or tin cans in half. Janice has dibs on the dried-out cosmetics and hosiery. Also the lint brushes and stain removers and superpowerful glues. Also she has this thing for cheese. I take the books and lawn ornaments. And when we get to my salesman's case, I say I want it.

"What's in it?" Janice says.

"Illicit," I say.

My brother gives me a look. He forces it open. It's empty.

"Oh my God," Janice says.

"I don't believe it," my brother says.

"Big oops," Janice says. "We made a mistake."

"What?" I say. "What does it mean?"

"He wasn't the real thing," my brother says.

"A weekend dabbler," Janice says, "A dilettante."

"You mean he was just doing it for fun? But he wasn't even any good at it," I say.

I picture him walking toward the house, empty case in his hand, Janice's breasts winking at him from the window.

"Just doing it for the love of it, I guess," Janice says. And smiles.

"For the love of it?" my brother says.

"See new places, meet new people," Janice says.

My brother grunts. He hates salesmen, hates being made to want something, the way the salesmen try to make you. "I want to want what I want," he says. "Don't make me want something I didn't even know I wanted till you dangled it in front of me like a carrot."

"What's a carrot?" I say. I vaguely recall that it's something yellow and sharp, maybe a sort of shrew with a pointed nose and golden fur.

"Are you feeling better?" Janice says kindly, patting my back. "Have you made it through all the seven stages on the road to acceptance?"

"I think so," I say.

But the truth is I haven't accepted anything, particularly Janice's answers, so the next day I go searching for my own. In an old sample case I find a bunch of books about teenage development: *Am I Normal?* and *Growing Up Great!* and *Fun with Puberty*. I sit in my brother's room beneath the white cloud and read them all. Then I read them again to be sure. The books say there's not a darn thing wrong with me. Janice has been lying the whole time. Misinformation. Disinformation. She ought to be arrested for that. Not that there's anyone around to do it.

I lie a long time looking up at the white cloud, listening to the wind filling in the spaces where salesman voices used to be. Out in the field my brother curses as pieces of his tower rain down all around him.

When the next season's salesmen start coming around, he and Janice start it up again, Janice in the window, my brother behind the door. But no one comes. See, there are the salesmen, out on the road; they pause and glance up at the house. But they don't come in—they scurry past, nearly running. The pen stays empty. My brother can't understand it. Janice studies herself in the mirror for hours, wondering, picking at her skin till she bleeds. She thinks she's turning ugly, scaring them away.

But she's wrong. What's happened is I've had enough. I'm fed up with the whole process, Janice prancing around thinking she's hot stuff, the yappy salesmen howling in the yard refusing to save themselves.

It's me making it happen. I've been scratching warnings into the roadside. I've been spreading prickly wire and broken glass across the drive. My brother and Janice have no idea how fast I can run when I want to. I crouch in the dry grass at the roadside and leap out to chase the salesmen away, every one. The salesmen don't know I'm trying to help them, they yell at me that I'm ruining business, standing in the way of the normal flow of commerce. *The customer is always right!* they scream, loud enough to flatten my hair to my head.

There is nothing sadder than an elephant boy without his elephant.

.   .   .

"There is nothing sadder than an elephant boy without his elephant," writes the benevolent foreign lady.

"There is nothing sadder than an elephant boy without his elephant," the benevolent foreign lady reads aloud.

"There is nothing sadder than . . . Wouldn't that make a perfect epigraph for my book!" she says. "Oh, dear . . . Do you think *elephant boy* should be hyphenated?"

"There is nothing sadder than an *elephant* without his *boy.*" She reads and writes simultaneously, huffing as she bends over the notebook pressed to her thigh. "That sounds better, doesn't it? It has more of a . . . a *poemic flow.*" She rereads it, frowning. "Though it's not exactly true, is it? I'm not sure I believe all this balderdash about elephants having feelings. Long memories and all that."

She resumes her strolling. "Or," she bursts out, stooping and scribbling, "what about . . . nothing more *melancholy* than an elephant boy without his elephant? Nothing more desolate? More dreary? More darkling?" The man trailing her and fanning her with an enormous palm-leaf fan rolls his eyes and does not reply. She does not expect him to—she knows he cannot understand her language—but she persists in speaking to him nevertheless; she wants to assure him that despite his dark skin she considers him a *human being,* not a piece of furniture. An equal.

. . .

In truth, the man with the fan understands English perfectly well; he does not respond because he's afraid that if he opens his mouth he might vomit. He has read enough poetry to find hers inexcusable. If he knew she considered him an equal, he would be deeply insulted.

. . .

"I'm afraid that's not it. Let's go back to the way it was before. There is nothing *sadder* than an elephant boy without his elephant. There is *nothing* sadder than an elephant boy without his *elephant.*"

. . .

The elephant boy weeps, inconsolable.

. . .

The benevolent foreign lady picks her way across the road and stands over the elephant boy. He doesn't acknowledge her. His shoulders heave with sobs. She angles her parasol to shield him from the sun. Within seconds she feels her hair start to wilt. She returns the sunshade to her own shoulder.

He squats on a rock, knees drawn up to his armpits. His cheeks are swollen and dusty where he has slapped himself.

He weeps. "My black pearl, my queen of Sheba," he cries.

"Here, dear, have a hankie," she says.

He glares at her shoes, hands poised to slap himself again.

"What was her name?" she asks kindly.

"Black Pearl, Queen of Sheba!" he says impatiently. "You met her yourself."

"Perhaps she just went for a walk. I do that myself sometimes. You may find her yet."

"I found her collar. And the piece of her ear where her name was tattooed. Only poachers do that. So the elephant can't be identified when they sell her . . . parts."

"Goodness!" she says. "Such a fuss over an elephant. One would think you had lost your mother."

She stands over him but is at a loss for what to say as he continues to weep. She has chosen the elephant boy to be her Special Project, but he is making things difficult. She walks back to the hotel, thinking, What that boy needs is some schooling. A good bath. Some friends to play with. A shirt and some shoes. She remembers the gift she ordered for him. It should be arriving soon.

.   .   .

He presses his chin between his knees and remembers her smile. She had the most beautiful smile. A slight upward shift of the skin around her right eye, a twitch of her lashes. Not ostentatious, not like the others. Subtle. Just for him.

. . .

The benevolent foreign lady walks back and forth in the cool of the hotel gallery. Every few steps she jumps and says "My," or "Exactly," or "Yes, that's good" and writes down a few words. A watching mosquito hopes she is doing something constructive, like composing a shopping list or revising a nice poem. But no, she is making a list of ways to improve the world, initiate change for the better, light up the uncivilized corners, et cetera, et cetera. Her husband, the beneficent dead industrialist, has instructed her thus in his will. Only so long as she is administering his charitable funds will she continue to receive a personal income.

She has already written *malaria, cholera, leprosy, oral hygiene.* "Of course!" she exclaims and adds *dark glasses for all the blind.* "Of course it's no help to them," she reflects, "but with those eyes they *are* so unpleasant to look at for those around them."

. . .

He and Queen of Sheba were both orphans. They chose each other on the first day of school (she bashful and shy, shuffling her feet, he spotting her across the yard and instantly smitten), and they had been together every day for seven years. He handled her feeding, her grooming, her living quarters, her checkups and tusk trimmings. They were meticulously attuned to each other; she responded promptly to the slightest pressure of his knees or a tap on the head, and he in turn could read the shifts of her shoulders, the curves of her trunk, her dreamboat eyes.

. . .

She writes: *Must stop them swimming in that filthy river.*

.   .   .

He is bowlegged as any gunslinger from straddling her great neck. At his cleanest, he smells distinctly of elephant. When he is alone, people avoid him. When he was with Queen of Sheba, people didn't see him, they saw only Queen in all her magnificence; he was merely a part of her, a bump behind her head, a small extension of her brain.

.   .   .

She decides she must have inspiration; she puts on her outdoor things and paces the dusty street in front of the hotel. A porter from the hotel accompanies her; his job is to slap the beggars away from her skirts.

She writes: *All these cows wandering around.*

.   .   .

He seeks out the other elephant boys, hoping for sympathy. But they regard him with suspicion. He's jealous. They are afraid he will try to seduce their elephants away from them; they eye his pockets for treats.

He would never do such a thing as steal another boy's elephant. Even if he wanted to, it would be impossible. Mature elephants cannot bond properly with secondhand boys. Everyone knows that. With elephants the first love is the only love. For every elephant there can be only one boy. His training was specific. Without his partner, he's obsolete.

.   .   .

She writes: *Must do something about this heat.*

. . .

In his heart of hearts he dreamed of them growing old together, lying in the sun, splashing water on each other's faces, Queen with her ears gone ragged and her tusks gone blunt, him with a potbelly and perhaps a long beard; Queen liked to play with hair. Look at my wrinkles, he'd say, and she would snort derisively: How dare you talk to *me* about wrinkles.

A sentimental dream, he knew. But he treasured it. It was the only future he desired, the only one he could imagine. Now it is gone.

. . .

The biggest problem, she writes, *is that these people have no imagination.* She doesn't understand it, the way they cling to their old ways of doing things. Their lives could be a hundred times more pleasant if they would just shut their mouths and open their ears.

. . .

The two fingers at the end of her trunk were more sensitive than his. He closes his eyes and remembers the touch of them on his cheek.

. . .

The fever-bearing mosquito has been following her; he senses the hot self-righteous blood rising to the benevolent foreign lady's cheek. He circles and dives. With any luck, he thinks, he will sink his proboscis into her and end this foolishness. But try as he might he can find no point of entry. She is dressed like a battleship from top to toe: high-laced shoes with extra-thick soles to carry her over the muck, stockings that fasten to her knickers with a row of buttons, lisle gloves that button to her elbows, three petticoats beneath her dress, a dense double-layered beekeeper's veil to keep everything out, a corset with whalebone stays to keep all of her in, the whole topped by a wide-brimmed hat trimmed with dried flowers, wax cherries, and a small stuffed songbird.

The mosquito, with unusual determination, lingers about her, dive-bombing and searching. If he could speak, he would issue this warning: Mend your prideful ways, or you will come back in your next life like me. He follows her to her hotel room and continues to wait for his chance, the slightest baring of skin, but exhausts his brief life span without success.

· · ·

Vigilance. It is the elephant boy's fundamental responsibility. When an elephant disappears in this city, she does not return. She is too conspicuous to hide or to wander off without caus- ing a furor. When an elephant disappears, it is because some- one made her disappear. Ivory hunters have no scruples, and they are magicians who specialize in making large objects van- ish. She's been taken. She won't be back.

The elephant boy is a disgrace to his profession.

· · ·

The foreign lady had been watching him for weeks. He and the elephant were always together, strolling through the deserted streets or heading down to the river. Sometimes the elephant had an elaborate saddle and canopy on her back for passengers. She wore no halter or restraint of any kind. When they had clients the boy was formal, shouting commands and using a light stick to direct her. When they were off duty they strolled side by side, the elephant's trunk draped over his shoulder.

One day they were passing the hotel with the elephant decked out in sequins and bells and jingling anklets and tassels on her tusks and meticulous designs painted on her sides and around her eyes. The benevolent foreign lady was enchanted. "Ask him what the occasion is," she called to the doorman.

"A wedding," the boy called down, before the doorman could translate.

"An elephant wedding?" she cried. The doorman snickered.

"A people wedding," the elephant boy replied politely.

"Would you mind"—she couldn't help shouting, he seemed so high and far away perching behind the elephant's elaborate headdress—"if I asked you a few questions? For my book."

.   .   .

The benevolent foreign lady is hovering over him again. Like a vulture, he thinks, crouching over an animal not quite dead. "You should try to see this in a positive light," she begins, her voice careful and rehearsed. "You've been liberated. No longer bound to a lifetime of servitude. You are now free to do whatever you want with your life. You can go to school, have a family. You should think about the future." He stares at her as if he has not understood a word. She squats, trying to meet his eyes, and puts on her young-children voice. "Now, instead of *one* path, you have *many* paths in front of you to choose from."

Many paths, he thinks. He can see only one. Or two. Neither is very long. One path leads to him bashing his head in with a rock. The other leads to him bashing *her* head in with a rock.

. . .

To her credit, the benevolent foreign lady is no dilettante, dabbling in charities to soothe the nudgings of her conscience. She cares. She believes. In her student days she was a suffragette, a crusader: She marched in the streets, served soup in the poorhouses, taught calisthenics in the orphanages, and read poetry to prison inmates. She married a hard-nosed businessman forty years her senior because, she says, she was seduced by his power, his position, his potential. She was dazzled, she says, by the vision of the good they could do the world if they joined forces. She will not admit, even to herself, that she did it for the money.

He married *her*, as he freely admitted, for her nice plump calves. After several whiskeys, he would pull her onto his lap and tell his cronies, "First time I saw her, I wanted to take a bite. I said, give me some of *that*, served up medium rare with gravy and roast potatoes, and you won't see a happier man."

When sober he was as relentlessly stern and glowering as the portrait that hung in the front hall. And like the portrait's eyes, which followed one around the room, his eyes seemed always upon her. He liked to indulge her with gifts, then frown upon her frivolity. He was a man who always gave the impression of wearing a top hat, even when he was not.

His new wife threw away her soup kitchen apron and talked brightly of reform on a grander scale, but the truth was that long before she met her husband, the life of a female crusader had lost its glamour; it was no longer an adventure, a charade. It felt too real—she had spent all her inheritance and was beginning to look as haggard as the factory workers and fallen women she was trying so hard to help. She'd been trying to raise them up to her level, but it seemed she had sunk to theirs.

. . .

The elephant boy squats on the bank of the river, tossing in stones. The bones of his back stand out like beads on a string. His skin is golden brown; it looks like it would have the texture of suede. In a week he has gone from thin to bony, his face caved in with grief.

. . .

The first time she saw him he was in the river, his back arched, his arms windmilling as he and the elephant splashed each other. His ragged white pants had gone translucent and clung soddenly to his legs. Each muscle stood out in sharp relief like an anatomy lesson. His mouth hung wide open as if he were perpetually on the verge of a laugh, making him look both blissful and foolish. The elephant stretched out her trunk and gently fondled his hair. Then, without warning, she knocked him off his feet. He sank underwater for a few seconds, then bounced back up with a whoop.

The benevolent foreign lady watched him pulling the elephant close, lifting up the massive flapping ear to whisper behind it. *And the saddest thing about it,* she wrote, *is that he doesn't even realize what he's missing.*

. . .

The most charitable act of her charitable career? Without a doubt, the answer would be those taxing and trying nights spent with her husband. She dreaded nothing more than the rare summons to leave her room and join him in his. She was resigned to the gasping and grasping and clutching, the sticky suffocations, the smell of his feet beneath the covers; what she could *not* bear were his strange prying questions and his perplexing deep disappointment at her answers. What did he expect from her, properly brought-up girl that she was? What on earth did he want her to say?

.   .   .

The benevolent foreign lady visits a local school. They say it is the best primary school in the neighborhood. She wants to use her husband's money to subsidize a whole network of schools in the most impoverished areas of the city, and she has been advised to model them on this one.

The students rise and greet her in unison. She tries to smile politely but is horrified by what she sees. This is a model school? Seventy students are crowded into one room, all ages mixed together. They sit on the floor. There is one book and it belongs to the teacher. The walls are bare. The children fidget and slap at flies. They are not punished when they make mistakes; they are simply ignored.

She withholds her fury until the children have been dismissed. Then she explodes at the teacher, at the two obsequious local officials accompanying her, at anyone in the vicinity. How can children learn in this environment, she rants, with no discipline, no structure, no *chairs*? Where is the globe? Where is the plaque commemorating the beneficent dead industrialist? She accuses them of squandering all the money her husband had so generously provided. She insists that the school be shut down until she can arrange for proper desks, chalkboards, portraits of famous men for the walls, hair ribbons for the girls.

The officials and teacher try to placate her but she refuses to be placated until she sees the door barred, the sign posted announcing the school closed until further notice.

Hours later, she suddenly realizes her mistake. The school she'd visited had not been *her* school. *Her* schools have not yet been built, they exist only in her head. In the hot classroom her mind had made some sort of associative leap and forgotten to jump back. The school she'd seen had nothing to do with her husband's money; she'd had no authority to close it.

She sits in the tub, rubbing at the pink marks her corset has left on her abdomen, wondering how to retract her mistake, to apologize. Where to begin? It's too embarrassing. Of course! She'll send them a gift. Reparation. Desks, books, a chalkboard, the newest educational games, all of it. They'll be so dazzled by her generosity that they'll forgive her outburst. The children will write her thank-you notes. They'll rename the school after her. No, it should be an anonymous gift! A simple, tasteful note, signed: *Your Anonymous Benefactor.*

She wants to write all this down, the list of school supplies, the anonymous note, but she's forbidden herself to take her notebook to the tub—she's dropped it in the water far too many times. She resolves to remember, and retains the idea as far as toweling off and putting on her robe, but then she discovers a scorpion in her slipper and in the ensuing chaos the plan slips from her mind forever.

The confused teacher and the local officials keep the school closed, waiting for something, some signal, some sort of permission, perhaps a reappearance of the intimidating benevolent foreign lady who turns red and bares her teeth like a monkey about to bite. They will wait a month, and then another month, and then another.

.   .   .

His office door ajar. She heard a wet choking sound, a thud. An attack, a fit of some kind? So soon? She rushed forward to help, feeling a surge of something that might have been fear or joy.

And then she heard his voice. She almost didn't recognize it, it was so mellow and full of tenderness and groaning. "Nadine," he said. "Oh, Nadine." She could see, through the cracked door, fingers digging deep into a dress as if groping for money hidden in a mattress.

Then a whisper. "Stop it, you awful man."

She had suspected but never witnessed such a scene before. She knew she should open the door wide, put an end to it all right then, spare the girl any further misery.

But then it occurred to her: The more energy he expends on *her*, the less he'll have for *me*. The thought made her pause for a long and selfish moment.

And in that silence she heard again, "You *awful* man," the words riding on a low chortle, followed by eager complicit breaths. She saw small hands on top of the large ones, pressing them more firmly in place. She heard her husband saying *thank you* a dozen times.

She listened a long time, angry, relieved, envious, mystified.

·   ·   ·

"What do you want to do when you grow up?" she had asked the elephant boy.

"Do?"

"As a profession."

"Do? This," he said, with a gesture that took in his bare feet, the dusty ground, and the elephant pulling leaves off a nearly denuded tree. "I am her boy until she dies."

"Hmmm," she said, and thought: How terrible. "How long do elephants live?"

"They can live a very long time. Like people."

Eternal servitude, she wrote. *And he doesn't even seem to mind. Because he doesn't know anything different.* "But don't you want a wife? A family?"

He smiled. "Elephants get very jealous. I can never have a wife."

"Surely someone else could care for your elephant. Surely it's not so hard."

"She would be very sad. I can never leave her. She would pine away and maybe die. Or she would turn wild, go on a rampage."

Worse than slavery, she wrote. *A slave to an animal.*

"But wouldn't you like to go to a real school?" she persisted. "Travel, learn about the rest of the world? Study history and science and music?"

"Music," he mused. "I like music."

"You could learn to play an instrument. How would you like to go to school back in my country?" She drew herself up importantly. "That could be arranged."

"No, thank you," he said. "I would not like that at all."

. . .

Before he died, her husband summoned her to discuss the terms of his will. He was enthroned on his bed, sitting stiffly upright, and as she entered the bedroom she had the usual fleeting impression that he was wearing a top hat with his nightshirt.

He told her of his wish that his fortune be used to fund charitable institutions in distant parts of the world, particularly the parts that were "unenlightened," "pre-industrial." He was a firm believer in technology. He expressed his wish that she be the one to dispense this largesse.

She felt her stomach fall. She had been formulating her own plans for years. It's not that she was looking forward to his death, of course not. But when one had an elderly husband and was set to inherit a vast amount of money, who could resist a little speculation now and then?

"Why can't I stay here?" she said. "Plenty of nice labor reform to be done right here." She didn't say: Right here in your own factories. "The shorter workday issue. Decent ventilation. Give those sweatshop girls some face powder, get those children out of the coal mines, save the canaries. That sort of thing."

"It's too late," said her husband thoughtfully. "We've made a bit of a mess of things here. Best to get out now. Move on to fresh territory. Take the money and go where it will be appreciated. Dazzle them with new technologies. Cure diseases. Enlighten the masses. Work from the bottom up. If they don't like it, cut your losses, get out. Move on. Someone will eventually pick up the pieces."

When he started in on the generalities he was liable to go on for hours; she wasn't listening. She had already decided to use her share of the inheritance to pursue her own dreams while paying someone else to save the world in her stead. He had not told her about the conditions of the will.

She wondered, then and afterward, what had sparked his late-blooming philanthropy. During his lifetime he was dutifully generous, purely for the sake of appearances. He took no interest. "That's your department," he used to tell her. He had never been a beneficent living industrialist, only a dead one. Perhaps after a lifetime of atheism, he began to fear for his soul and wanted to make amends. In one of his factories a man had been sliced clean in half. Others had been burnt, mutilated, poisoned, crushed, electrocuted. He had plenty to atone for.

· · ·

She's beginning to feel the slightest twinge of guilt. She didn't expect the elephant boy to be quite so miserable; children's memories, she'd thought, were fleeting.

Then the boy's present arrives and her guilt evaporates. "It's perfect," she says, waltzing around it. If anything can cheer up a moping elephant boy, this will. "There's nothing gladder than an elephant boy. . . . Oh, but I *do* think *elephant boy* should be hyphenated, don't you?"

.   .   .

He blames her for Queen's disappearance. He should blame himself. It is easier to blame her.

She had been asking more of her questions. The slightest thing he said provoked a grand reaction: "Really?" "No! Yes?" "Goodness!" He was flattered, despite himself. No one had ever taken an interest in him before, never someone as strange and important as the benevolent foreign lady who was rumored to be richer than ten rich men put together. Most people had eyes only for Queen of Sheba.

Her attention flagged; he was running out of things to say. He had to give her something precious, something to make her eyes go big again and her voice breathy. "I know where the elephant graveyard is," he said. "It's not a myth. I can show you." This was a deep dark secret. Only the elephants knew of it. Queen had taken him there. He had never told a soul.

"Really? Oh!"

He felt a gust lift his hair. Queen had shuffled up behind him and was eyeing him reproachfully. "That sounds *fascinating*," the benevolent foreign lady said. "Would you show me? Would you?"

"I don't know," he said, Queen breathing down his neck.

"Oh, please," she said, and pressed his hand with her white fat lace-gloved one.

Queen's attention had shifted; now she was stretching her trunk toward the intriguing and possibly edible salad of objects decorating the lady's hat. At Queen's touch, the lady snatched her hand from his and screamed theatrically. "My gracious," she gasped, panting, and unbuttoned three buttons on her dress. "She gave me a scare." He saw the flushed base of her throat and, farther down her chest, the beginning of a crease. Something stirred in him he had never felt before.

This was the part he regretted the most. He scolded Queen, scolded her for the first time in years, since she was a calf, and sent her to stand at a distance.

"Do you think we could go somewhere *private* to talk?" she said. "Your elephant—she *stares* so."

He shouted at Queen, and she obediently turned her back to them. A moment later she lifted her tail and released a substantial pile.

"Why don't you come inside the hotel?" the lady said. "Have you ever been inside?"

He hadn't. He'd always wanted to. "I can't leave her."

"It's just across the road."

He could hardly bear to look at Queen's drooping head. He told himself she was just sulking childishly, but deep down he knew that she was grieving. Elephants are sensitive.

At the same time he was embarrassed by her behavior; there is nothing more shameful than a spoilt elephant. A spoilt elephant means an indulgent, undisciplined boy. No one wants to hire a sulky elephant. And in spite of himself he was tempted by the hotel, full of rich and bizarre foreigners. He'd often tried to get a peek. The doorman usually chased him away from the steps and made a great show of sweeping away his footprints.

"Will I be able to keep an eye on her from the window?"

"Certainly."

Of course he couldn't. The windows were too thickly swathed in lace to see anything but dark vague shapes.

The next hour was excruciating. He was too wracked with anxiety to take in his surroundings. The benevolent foreign lady took him to her room and thrust books and pictures at him, but he could not bring his eyes to focus. She handed him objects whose function he could not begin to comprehend and did not try. He interrupted her monologue to blurt his good-byes and blundered into the vast and mystifying bathroom before escaping.

The hotel doorman gave him a mocking bow as he sped past, but he did not notice. Queen had disappeared. She was gone. Gone. And his last words to her had been a scolding.

. . .

She sets out a white shirt, trousers, shoes, a belt. More gifts for the boy. A silver-plated brush-and-comb set. A necktie. She will have to teach him how to knot it. She imagines brushing his thick black hair. She will teach him how to dance.

The beneficent dead industrialist glares at her from the photograph beside the bed. "Oh, shut up, you," she says, turning the picture around. "I'm only carrying out your wishes. Lifting up the downtrodden and all that." Who is he to glare at her anyway? Him and his string of factory girls: red-haired Filing, plump Shipping, dimpled Clamping Station No. 3, eagle-eyed Quality Inspector 12, shy pigtailed Second-floor Sweep-up, broad-beamed Sorting Table 16.

"He's a boy, half my age," she tells the reversed picture, imagining golden velvety skin. "It's absurd."

. . .

An aside: The factory girls speak up and request that their proper names be given. They are: Anna, Susie, Carrie, Janey, Mary, and Nadine. Susie, Carrie, and Nadine have children with incongruously somber, jowly faces; Nadine's baby son in particular looks like a supreme court justice in diapers. The strangest thing, Nadine says, is if you glance at him, sitting sternly in his high chair, clenching his spoon and glaring at his strained peas, if you just happen to glance at him out of the corner of your eye, you'd swear he was wearing a top hat.

. . .

One of the bellhops from the hotel comes looking for him. "That idiotic foreign woman wants you again. She says she has something to give you," the bellhop says, then makes an obscene gesture with his hand.

The elephant boy goes, reluctantly. He hesitates at her doorway, expecting the room to trigger painful memories of his act of betrayal.

But he barely recognizes the room. He's not sure it *is* the same room. He had been oblivious, nearly blind with worry the last time. He looks around. And then he hears it. He must be imagining it. But no, there it is again, faint but distinct: the voice of an elephant.

The benevolent foreign lady totters over to take his arm. "Done sullening, I hope?" Her touch gives him chills. Her hands are bare and cool, fat and white. She is wearing a rustling green dress that drapes loosely around her shoulders and squeezes her so tightly around the middle that he can see her breathe. A thick band of jewels hugs the base of her throat.

She notices him looking. "Do you like it?"

He thinks it is very ugly.

"Come and see your present." She pulls him to a large piece of furniture with three legs and a sort of wooden sail on the top. He touches the varnished wood. The voice of the elephant returns. It is very strong here. He peers inside and sees hundreds of wires drawn taut. He presses his cheek to the wood and listens. He can't tell if the voice is greeting him or talking to itself; the language of elephants is fundamentally rhetorical.

. . .

Look at him, thinks the benevolent foreign lady. Fascinated. Absolutely entranced. Finally, she thinks. A breakthrough. In her notebook she will write: *His eyes have been opened. His mind takes its first free breath.* She can't restrain herself any longer: *"Voilà!"* she cries, and with a sweeping gesture lifts the lid to reveal the white expanse of the keyboard.

. . .

The elephant boy lets out a scream. The phantom voice is suddenly overwhelming, deafening. The keyboard grins hideously at him. He feels a jolt of recognition; he knows with horrible certainty what it is. "Go on, don't be afraid. You can touch it." She presses a key. *Plink.* But he can't. The mere thought makes his hands shake; it would be blasphemous, like juggling the bones of dead relatives.

. . .

"I'll show you, then." She sits on the bench, fluffs her skirts, and begins to play. She longs to be a virtuoso but lacks the talent. "My ears are bigger than my stomach," she likes to say. She tilts her head, undulates her arms, lifts her wrists daintily. Her playing is solidly mediocre. But, she thinks, certainly far beyond anything the elephant boy has ever been exposed to. When she finishes, she folds her hands at her breast and looks up at him searchingly. He looks shaken, devastated. She wants to weep with joy. "Did you hear it?" she whispers. "Really, really *hear* it, not just with your ears but with your heart?"

"I did," he says, "before you started making all that racket."

. . .

The elephant boy flees; he cannot bear the piano. And yet in his idle hours it is all he can think about. He goes back and scratches at her door. She has ink on her face, curling papers in her hair, but she drags him inside. The voice of the elephant swirls around him; if he concentrates he can shut out the incessant twitter of the benevolent foreign lady.

She tries to teach him the rudiments: notes, scales. He says he wants to learn in his own way. His own way involves staring at the keys for hours without so much as touching them.

He comes to her room every day. She convinces him to try on the shirt and trousers and shoes, though when he sees himself in the mirror he grunts and immediately takes them off again. He lets her trim his hair.

She reads to him, hugs him, strokes his shoulders. He does not seem to mind. He does not seem to mind anything, as long as he is within sight of the piano. *Physical contact,* she writes in her notebook. *Likely the first he's ever had.*

. . .

The voice from the piano is like an old senile woman talking to herself in the marketplace. It recalls the best feeding places, the best trees for shade, the best wallows in the river, the faces of other elephants, a string of children. And then it runs through the list again.

He wonders if the voice can hear him. The conversation is one-sided, the voice not at all like Queen's, yet it is comforting.

He cannot understand it. Elephant boys can communicate with no elephants but their own. And yet now it seems he can hear dead elephants.

He wonders if this is some kind of gift, a small comfort granted to grieving elephant boys like himself. Perhaps Queen's death has opened some kind of channel of communication. He decides to test the theory.

. . .

He doesn't know why he brought her. She has to stop and examine and exclaim over everything. She wheezes and chatters. He wants silence. He wants solitude. They are going to a holy place.

Perhaps he brought her because he is a little afraid of what he might find.

Hidden in a cleft between two high rock plateaus lies the elephant dying ground. As he leads the benevolent foreign lady down the final passage, he can already hear the murmur of voices. They reach the entrance and he catches his breath. The sight is frightening, humbling. The massive weathered bones lie everywhere. The giant skulls lie in attitudes of rest and contentment. Elephants come here when they know their time has come and stand until they gently kneel and fall. The voices here are calm, not assaulting him, simply soothing him like the gentle embrace of a familiar trunk.

The benevolent foreign lady is stunned to silence momentarily. "Just look at it all!" she breathes. "There must be a fortune in ivory here! What Captain Henderson Henshaw wouldn't give to get his hands on this!"

She stops suddenly. She has just blurted out the name of the most notorious of ivory poachers. He looks at her, into her small frightened eyes, and knows. He has suspected it all along. She stares back and knows that he knows.

"I did it for your own good! Your own good!" she screams.

Her voice rebounds against the stone walls: *own good . . . good . . . good.*

He recalls how she kept him ensnared in her hotel room while Queen of Sheba waited outside, alone and vulnerable, conspicuous and contrite. He remembers her relentless chatter, the way she kept tugging him back to his chair every time he tried to leave. It had all been a diversion, it had all been arranged. Henshaw is famous for making elephants disappear as if by magic. He thinks of the piano. Perhaps it had been as simple as that: a trade, this for that.

"You ruined my life," he says, more wonder than anger in his voice.

"I gave you a life!" she screams. The way she's cowering makes him want to hurt her. He stares at her hat, the same gaudy treat that had piqued Queen's curiosity. The two females in his life have the same taste.

His hand gropes instinctively for a weapon and falls on a good heavy club. He raises it and aims for her head. He's been wanting to do this for so long. Then he sees that it's an elephant bone in his hand. Blasphemy, he thinks, and lowers his arm. There is nothing in the ravine but bones, bones, not a stick of wood or loose stone. He raises his arm again.

A voice rises from the bone, saying, What are you doing?

He does not know how to explain. Revenge, he says, but elephants have no word for it, no conception of revenge.

What are you doing?

It is too hard to explain. He should be like the elephants, for whom violence is instinct, self-preservation, never a matter of malice or forethought. But he is not an elephant.

He places the bone carefully on the ground. He lifts the benevolent foreign lady from her knees. "I'm sorry, I'm sorry," she weeps. He can almost forgive her. "But it was for your own good," she adds. No, he can't.

. . .

Threatening a benevolent foreigner with an elephant bone, particularly a female, is a serious offense. She could make trouble for him but doesn't. She apologizes profusely, offers to buy him an elephant or three, offers to lay out money for him to start his own elephant school.

But he wants none of it. He does not want just any elephant.

. . .

Victory, she thinks. He had been on the verge of giving in to his primitive uncultured instincts, and then he had changed his mind.

What had made him stop? Her civilizing influence, of course. Thus far it had been minimal, but it was enough to stay his hand.

Such progress! After a matter of weeks! Just think what she could do to him—*for* him, that is—if she could hang on to him for another six months, a year. Just think what it would mean. For him. For her. For the book.

. . .

For the first time, he depresses a key. A shiver runs through him. "Good, good," cries the benevolent foreign lady. She takes hold of his fingers, matching each one to a key. "C, D, E, F," she says jubilantly. He ignores her. He has the idea of playing every piano he can find, every piano in the world, until he finds the one with Queen of Sheba's voice in it.

He lets her shampoo his hair, he wears the clothes she gave him. He shares her meals with him, her strange foreign food. He eats like an elephant. Elephants, given the opportunity, will strip every tree, pull up every blade of grass in sight. Within weeks he is positively portly. The new weight hangs on him awkwardly, he looks bloated, pop-eyed and ready to burst.

. . .

He sees her clearly now and pities her; she has never known the joy of being one half of a perfect whole. She is an unfinished piece of a person, crippled, blind, fundamentally deficient without even realizing it. All the groping, grasping, flailing—it is because she has never had an elephant of her own.

It would take an elephant the size of a mastodon, he thinks, to satisfy her.

She is a thing to be pitied. So when she comes to him, pressing up close, butting him with her head like an elephant calf begging for attention, he tells himself to be kind, to be charitable, to be generous of spirit.

She crushes him in her prickly embrace. She is so covered in jewels it is like being eaten by a geode. He thinks of Queen, only of Queen, and lets himself go.

. . .

It is utterly, utterly inappropriate. And yet—she *has* to, doesn't she? The boy is wretched, clearly starved for affection, for a mother's touch. The touch of a sister, a friend, anyone. How can she ignore it? The boy is abysmally lonely. She does not want to, heavens, no, but there is no one else to do it. She tells herself she must, it is her mission, to submit, and submit again, to the needs of others. To be charitable, after all.

"Oh, utterly," she sighs, stretching her arms luxuriously. "Utterly, utterly!"

.   .   .

"Of course!" cries the benevolent foreign lady. She's had an inspiration: a distraction for the elephant boy, a growth experience. A way to broaden the scope of her experiment.

She's heard tales of them. The legendary wolf girls. Stolen from their beds in infancy by a wolf grieving the deaths of her own pups and seeking replacements. Raised by wolves, as wolves. People claim to have seen them flitting through the woods on all fours, peering through windows at night, their eyes shining. Rubbing themselves against trees. Absolutely wild.

Perfect cases. Blank slates. And she'll have the elephant boy help her. They can be his special project. If he can control an animal fifty times larger than himself, surely he can handle two little girls.

She is already imagining taking the girls out to shop for dresses and ribbons, picturing the four of them sitting around a table, having dinner. A family. We owe our lives to you, the girls will say, weeping with gratitude into their embroidered lace handkerchiefs.

If they even exist. She'll hire hunters, trackers, spare no expense.

And then, too, there are the stories about the South American Bird Boy. Heavens! She has to do something. A child should not be allowed to live in the treetops. A child should not be allowed to fly.

.   .   .

She writes: *There is nothing gladder than an elephant boy without his elephant.*

. . .

The other elephant boys pass him in the street. He calls out to them but they do not answer. He is invisible. He has no name.

We live in a small town a train ride away from the big city. Our
father works there. We've never gone there, not even to visit.
Our mother says the city is full of infections and diseases
waiting to pounce, waiting particularly for children, particularly in the summers. People out here get sick too, my sister Lily says. But not like in the city, where everybody's packed
in on top of each other, our mother says. Out here, maybe
things are a bit old-fashioned, but at least there's room to
breathe.

. . .

Breathing in the germs is what makes you sick. Or if you lick a
doorknob a sick person has touched. Germs like liquids; they
can swim around in them. Lily can fit an entire doorknob in
her mouth, which is unusual. I have to keep her from trying to
impress people with her trick in public places. You can also
get diseases from kissing, which is something we don't have to
worry about yet. The diseases you get in the city can leave you

dead or in a wheelchair or inside a big metal machine that pumps you in and out like an accordion. Cripple fevers, people call them. Brain swellers. Infantile paralysis. The other problem with Lily's trick is that it is not ladylike.

.   .   .

It is not ladylike to pull at the collar of your Sunday dress but sometimes it is unavoidable, especially when the collar is lacy and itchy and too tight, especially when it's a hot day and not even a Sunday. Especially on the first day of summer.

.   .   .

On the first day of summer the pool opens, and if the lifeguard's any good he'll go through the proper rituals of opening the gates and letting everyone line up on the concrete ledges with their toes hanging over, letting them get good and hot, maybe tossing a silver dollar in the water for a prize, waiting till the proper minute to blow his whistle and break the spell and officially open the pool. At that moment we all jump in screaming, every single one of us wanting to be the first to hit the pure, untouched turquoise water.

.   .   .

We're not in the water; we're pulling at our collars (in Lily's case, purely out of solidarity) in the heat of the train station. We've got our bathing suits on under our dresses. Vain hope; train late. We're here to pick up our cousin Mattie. We have to make her feel welcome, our mother says.

.   .   .

Cousin Mattie—not really a cousin at all; she's the orphaned daughter of an old friend of our father's. She lives in the city but is coming to spend the summer with us to escape the heat and contagion and the boredom that is like a disease for a girl that age. So they say. We suspect there are other reasons. She's older than us. Older girls have needs. One of these needs is privacy. For this reason, she gets our room and we are banished to the sleeping porch for the rest of the summer.

.   .   .

The beds on the sleeping porch are always dewy-damp. We hate sleeping there. All the nighttime clicks and twitters sound like they are right there in the bed with you. Moths come and cling to the screen and sleep there all night. Every now and then an extra big one will crash into the screen with a soft heavy sound like a big paw tapping. It's enough to make you scream.

.   .   .

Lily screams when the train comes. She can't help it; any time there's noise she has to add to it. She's a copycat to the bottom of her soul. The train crashes and hisses to a stop. They unload Cousin Mattie off it. It's our first time seeing her. She's a thick column of a girl, a stout log, a dense cylinder from head to toe. Her thick legs are too short to negotiate the train steps; they have to lift her and set her down on the platform. Beside her they set a fat bulging suitcase that looks like another section of the same log she's been cut from. She stands there, waiting for us to come to her.

.   .   .

Welcome, Mattie. We're so glad to have you. This is Catherine. And this is Lily.

Hello, Cousin Mattie.

Hello, Cousin Mattie.

Hi.

. . .

She has highfalutin city ways, you can tell. We hate her right away. She keeps scrunching up her nose to keep her glasses from slipping, newfangled glasses with sparkles in the frames. She ends each sentence with a little grunt like she's out of breath. What's there to do around here? she says, looking around (*our* bedroom) and putting away her folded clothes (in *our* bureau). The swimming pool, Lily says. Cousin Mattie looks at me, knowing Lily cannot be trusted. It's not so great, I say. Cousin Mattie says, I like to swim. I like pools.

. . .

Why don't you like the pool anymore? Lily asks, when we're lying in our soggy beds on the sleeping porch. She's all ready to change her opinion the second I do. I don't want to have to take *her*, I say. Lily does lying-down jumping jacks in her bed. Sometimes a bat will come slamming into the screen, grabbing at the moths and devouring them. The bats have squashed snouts and pointed ears exactly like Satan. There's a lot of clicking and squeaking, flapping and snapping.

. . .

Cousin Mattie's red plastic sandals flap and slap against the pavement. Lily and I are barefoot. Cousin Mattie's body in her bathing suit is a solid block; it doesn't go in or out at all.

. . .

Kids are already jumping in and out of the water when we get there. Everything's in place; it's all exactly the way it is every summer: turquoise water, grown-ups on deck chairs sitting in the sun, the lifeguard on his high stand with his sunglasses and whistle and white beak of zinc oxide. The stammer of the diving board and kids yelling, nonstop, shrill, like the puppies at the pound who don't know you but want you to take them home.

. . .

We try to pretend we don't know Cousin Mattie. The first jump is always the best, cold bracing plunge and bubbles up your nose. Simon and Knobby and the Creavey twins are playing Alligator in the deep end, and we go to join them. There's a clumsy splash and Cousin Mattie's right there with us. She's wearing a nose clip that pinches her nostrils together. It's held by a strap around her head. Her bathing suit fastens around the neck and is yellow with ruffles that make her big behind look even bigger.

. . .

The older kids sit at the far end of the pool near the snack bar. She should be with them. She's too big to be with us. We dive down deep, swim like spies underwater, taking lots of turns and doublebacks. We come up for air and she's right behind us. It's nice, right? she says, with a little grunt. Then she points to the fence and says, Who are those kids?

. . .

Those kids are Cheryl and Melinda and Marcus and Brick and some others. They stand behind the fence watching us the way they do every summer. This is a public pool, but only white kids swim here. The black kids watch from behind the fence. They do it every summer. They watch for a little bit and then go away. They look hot, Cousin Mattie says. I don't say anything. I recognize a lot of them from school. I make my face seem like I don't. They do the same. That's manners.

.   .   .

Their faces are shiny with sweat. They probably don't know how to swim, I say. They are watching Lily jump up and down, bright spangles of water flying off her. I don't know what they're thinking. Soon enough they'll let go of the fence and go away.

.   .   .

Come in, Cousin Mattie calls. She paddles over to them and says again, Why don't you come in? She invites them by raising her arm. A sudden silence descends, so complete that the lifeguard looks around to see who drowned.

.   .   .

I'm holding my breath even though I'm not underwater. The black kids let go of the fence. They're going away. No, they're not. They're walking around to the gate. Everyone watches them but they don't move slow or fast. They walk across the concrete and right up to the edge of the pool. The smallest kid crouches down and very gently puts his fingertips on the surface of the water. Brick takes off his shirt. We all stare at his chest, his nipples, his belly button. Hey, Phil, one of the grown-ups yells to the lifeguard. The lifeguard says to Brick, You kids have to have proper bathing suits to swim here.

. . .

Brick acts like he doesn't hear. He takes off his pants. Underneath he's wearing blue bathing trunks covered with red stars. The others get undressed too and they pile their clothes neatly together. Marcus has a green bathing suit. As he jumps in he lets out a yell so loud it makes my teeth rattle in my head. The others slip in quietly, cautiously, as if the water might bite them. They slip in one by one.

. . .

As one, we all move to the ladders, to the sides of the pool. What are you doing? Cousin Mattie says. We're getting out, I say. Come on, Lily says, hurry.

. . .

The black kids are unhurriedly spreading out through the pool, dispersing themselves, stretching their arms and legs, bobbing up and down the way Lily does so the water flies sparkling in all directions.

. . .

Mattie doesn't seem to know how to follow directions. Come on, we say, but she lingers by the ladder. She watches the other kids climbing out of the water, heaving dramatic sighs of relief as they flop down on the grass. She looks longingly at the black kids, at Melinda doing a handstand in the water with her toes perfectly pointed. Why . . . ? Cousin Mattie says. You can never be too careful, says Lily in our mother's voice.

. . .

There's not a sound but the voices and splashings of the black kids. The rest of us sit and watch them. They play the same games we always play, Alligator and Marco Polo and Go Fish. If you close your eyes you'd think the pool was the same as always. I look over at Simon, whose hair is sticking up in orange spikes. He has an old tennis ball in his hand. When the lifeguard looks away, Simon sends the ball whipping low across the pool, missing Cheryl's head by inches.

. . .

The adults are inching over to the lifeguard's stand, whispering at him. He's shrugging and shaking his head. He's a new lifeguard. Hard to tell what he's thinking behind the sunglasses.

. . .

Clouds slide in front of the sun, but the black kids stay all day, until six when the pool closes. We all stay to watch. When the lifeguard blows the closing whistle, the black kids climb out, dress hurriedly, and disperse. The grown-ups cluster around the lifeguard. There's nothing I can do, he keeps saying. They're allowed to come here. Well, I hope you *scrub* this pool tonight is all I can say, one of the mothers announces, and the bunch of them murmur in agreement. It's like they can't stop talking, even for a second; they make a constant bubbling babble.

. . .

We walk home not talking. I don't have the swollen content feeling I usually have after a day at the pool. I feel hot, crumpled, scratchy like I've been starched. Cousin Mattie limps, her red sandals cutting into her heels. Why did we have to get out? she says. Because, Lily replies firmly. Then doesn't know what to say next. Mattie looks perplexed. Lily looks perplexed that a big girl like Mattie doesn't understand something so obvious it defies explanation. I know that in my thinking I am somewhere between the two of them but don't feel like trying to bridge the gap.

. . .

Next day, I'm showing Lily how I can spit water through the gap where I lost one of my dogteeth. We've been in the water about ten minutes when the black kids show up. They've brought friends. There's at least a dozen of them. They come in briskly, take off their clothes, and jump in. We jump out. Cousin Mattie is the last to come. But why? she keeps saying. Lily and I pretend we don't know her.

. . .

I don't know what the lifeguard's thinking. He sits impassive on his chair, occasionally twirling his whistle on its string around his finger. I wonder if he's blind behind those sunglasses. We sit, sweating in the sun, and watch them play in our pool all day. Not one of us leaves, for the whole entire day. No one goes home for lunch, even. We don't talk. The lifeguard looks at his watch and blows the closing whistle. Only then do we grab our towels and head home, our bathing suits absolutely dry.

. . .

The next day they stay dry too. The same thing happens. The black kids come first thing in the morning. We all watch in silent protest.

. . .

I don't care, Cousin Mattie protests. I'm hot, I'm getting in. Don't you dare, I say. What are you gonna do? she says. You can't, Lily says, you're one of us. I'm not one of *you,* Cousin Mattie says disdainfully. We'll tell our dad, I say. He won't like it one bit.

. . .

Bit by bit, strange things can start to feel normal. We now have a new summer routine: put on our bathing suits and go to the pool and watch the black kids play and bring in friends and more friends so they can occupy the pool in shifts so that it is never empty. Even on cloudy days, rainy days, they come. One morning they're late, and we all pour into the pool. Maybe it's dirty and tainted from the day before; we don't care. Then the black kids show up, just a few minutes behind schedule, and we retreat to dry land. They ignore us.

. . .

We watch their games so intently we feel like we're the ones playing. Each of us has a counterpart that we secretly root for. Mine is Cheryl. She's missing a dogtooth too. *Yes!* I catch myself whispering, when Cheryl races and beats all the boys by an arm's length.

. . .

This is too boring, Cousin Mattie says, stretching her fat legs out in front of her on the grass. Let's do something else, she says. No! Lily says. We can't! Why not? says Cousin Mattie. *Why not?* mimics one of the Creavey twins, who are sitting behind us. Fatty wants to know why not, says the other twin in a nasty voice. Both twins pinch their noses with two fingers, like Mattie's nose clip, and give nasal laughs. We can't just give in, Lily says incredulously. We watch Cousin Mattie's face go red and hot.

. . .

It's a lot cooler out here, Mattie says that night, stepping out onto the sleeping porch in her nightgown. Her nightgown looks like a lampshade on her. It's a lot cooler than the house, she says, maybe I'll join you. There's no room, Lily says. We are all quiet. The insects shrill and scream and grind stuff in their tiny jaws. Have you ever been night swimming? Cousin Mattie says suddenly. It's wonderful. Like flying. I say no. She says, We could sneak into that place, easy. Just climb over the chain-link fence. Lily is quiet, waiting to hear what I will say.

. . .

We wait, hot, dry, staring at the cool water, day after day. It's a standoff. Neither side will budge. The summer grows hotter. Our skins burn and peel and burn and blister and turn a deep burnished brown. All of us except Cousin Mattie, who just gets pink and pinker. I'm almost as dark as *them*, Lily says, admiring her brown arms. You'll never be as dark as them, I say. I'm watching Cheryl. She can swim, all right. She can go

the whole length of the pool underwater without a breath. It's
not fair.

. . .

It's not fair, we tell our father. We've never been to the city.
She's been there her whole life; why does *she* get to go? Cousin
Mattie's homesick, she misses her friends, our father says. I'm
taking her back for a quick visit so she can see them. We don't
believe it. Cousin Mattie couldn't possibly have any friends.
Our mother packs the special overnight case and tries to curl
Cousin Mattie's limp hair. We watch everything and say nothing and make hate blare out of our eyes in flashes like signal
lights. We've been doing it all summer; we're pretty good at it
by now. Our father goes on the train with her to the city. We
hope he leaves her there.

. . .

Here's Cousin Mattie, back already. Can we swim yet? she asks
with her little grunt. Not yet, we say. Eventually they'll get tired
of the pool and go away, Lily says hopefully. There's no hope of
that. The black kids show no signs of getting tired. Now it's a
matter of principle, a battle of wills. When will the lifeguard do
something? Either kick out the black kids or shove us in the
water with them. Either would be preferable to what he's doing,
which is: sitting there, uninvolved, impassive, sunglassed, blind.

. . .

Cousin Mattie stumbles out to the sleeping porch without her
glasses. Her body glows in the dark, round, luminous, like
a giant moon, a mutant firefly. I imagine an enormous bat
swooping down and biting off the top half of her. Wormy bits

of intestines would pop out. There's something tired and bat-
tered and saggy about her face. You can tell what she'll look
like as an old lady. Let's go, she says. Take a swim. I really
need a swim tonight. No, I say, though I'm dying to do it. I
don't want to give her the satisfaction.

. . .

This is the summer of denial. The days trickle away. The
vision of the pool floats before our eyes like a mirage, distant,
untouchable. We dream of the soothing balm of chlorinated
water with Band-Aids floating in it. Cousin Mattie grunts and
mutters her discontent. I don't say a word; Lily whines enough
for the two of us. The past few weeks have been an eternity.
The weeks ahead stretch out interminably.

. . .

I've had it, Cousin Mattie says. I'm getting in, I'm *so* hot. She's
awfully red in the face. There's a whistle in her breath, in
addition to the usual grunt. I hold one wrist and Lily holds the
other. We keep her sitting on the grass without too much trouble. No one notices a thing. On the way home she keeps rubbing her wrists and sniffling. Aw, don't be a baby, I say, we
didn't hurt you. Cousin Mattie tries to catch her breath. Her
face is very red, splotches popping out on her temples and the
sides of her neck. I feel a little afraid of her. After all, she has
seen Death and we haven't. That gives her power over us. Our
mother told us all about it before Mattie arrived. How Mattie
left the dinner table to answer the phone and came back to
find her father slumped over facedown in the mashed potatoes, stark dead. So remember that and be kind to her, our
mother said. Remember that she's looked into the Face of
Death. You have no idea what that's like. Lily was listening,

rapt and horrified. I wanted to say that *technically* that wasn't true, if her father had been facedown in his dinner. She probably only saw the back of his head. I'd forgotten about Death, but now, looking at Mattie's red face, I remember and get a chill. I look at her glasses and small pinkish eyes and wonder how Death felt, looking back at her.

. . .

The next day Mattie won't go back to the pool with us. I don't feel good, she says, and lies back down in *(our)* bed. She's making too much of the wrist-twisting. We barely touched her. We go to the pool without her and stare at the black kids hard enough to count as three people. Maybe even four.

. . .

When we go home at six Mattie is still in bed. She stays in bed the next day too. On the third day our mother calls the doctor. You know what *this* means, I tell Lily. Yeah, she says wisely. A second later she says, What does it mean? She's got *it,* I say, one of those diseases, those summer fevers that eat up your nerve endings; she probably got the germs when she went to the city to visit, probably from one of her friends. I say this just to scare Lily, but then our mother says, I want you two to stay away from her. What she has is very serious and I don't want you to catch it. She could die or end up in a wheelchair. You hear? And don't tell anyone, our mother says. I don't want people thinking I don't keep a clean house.

. . .

That night, as soon as the house is quiet and asleep, I wake Lily and say, It's time. She says, For what? Get your bathing

suit, I say. I go to *our* bedroom, where Cousin Mattie is muffled up under the covers though it is stifling. Our room smells
funny, Lily whispers. It does. It smells like it isn't ours. Come
on, I tell Cousin Mattie. Time for a swim. She looks up at us,
eyes all unmoored without her glasses. All right, she says.

.　.　.

Cousin Mattie says night swimming is like flying. I don't know
if she's lying or not. I'm watching her and it doesn't *look* like
flying. But maybe it *feels* different. Maybe the way the dark
falls into the water makes you feel like you don't know where
one ends and the other begins. Maybe the way the stars are
reflected in the water's surface makes you feel like you're surrounded by stars rather than beneath them. I'm just guessing.
One day I'll find out for sure.

.　.　.

I'm not sure about this, I have to guess, because right now I
am *not* night swimming. I'm standing on the concrete ledge
next to Lily, watching Cousin Mattie night-swim in the dark
deserted pool. We watch her dive and swoop and float on her
back. She throws her arms wide, she seems to grow and stretch,
stroking from one end to the other, spreading herself everywhere. Why can't we get in? Lily whines. We got our bathing
suits on and everything. It's part of the plan, I whisper. What
plan? Lily says. Secret plan, can't tell you, I say. Come on in,
Mattie calls, fly with me. I'm too cold, I answer, it's colder
than I thought, I changed my mind. Scaredy-cat, Cousin Mattie yells. It's all I can do to keep my mouth shut.

.　.　.

The waters open, swallow, recede, buoy her up like a mattress. Dark shadows swim beneath her, around her, over her. She laughs in an enticing, frightening way. A grown-up laugh. Beside me, Lily quivers with longing. She'll never get in without me. I hate her, Lily moans, and I hate you too. Cousin Mattie climbs out of the water, and we take her home, shivering and shaking, and put her to bed.

.   .   .

She stays in bed, still sick. We go to the pool every day, grim and defiant. We will not move, we will not leave, we will not say a word.

.   .   .

Nothing happens. For a while.

.   .   .

One day I notice that the red-and-blue starry shorts are missing. Brick's not there. I've been watching the black kids all summer, I know them like I know my own family, and I notice immediately that Brick and two of the younger boys, regulars, aren't there. Three missing.

.   .   .

The next day the three have become five.

.   .   .

And then the five become eight.

. . .

And then the kids trickle away steadily, none of the missing ones reappearing; they dwindle and dwindle until only Cheryl and two boys dart nervously about in the water, looking anxiously behind them as if they're being chased. And then only one holdout is left, one forlorn little boy, the same boy who first touched the water with one tentative hand. He stands shivering in the shallow end for a full day, not knowing what to do with himself but not wanting to give up. The next day he too is gone.

. . .

They're all gone. They're out. It's time for us, finally, to get back in. We come to the pool early, expectant. We find the lifeguard chaining the gates shut. There's an outbreak of fever spreading through the community, the lifeguard says. He can't allow kids to congregate and pass germs around. He pins up a notice that declares the pool closed for the rest of the summer.

. . .

Maybe it's closed, but we still won. We held out to the end, didn't we? Now we don't get to use the pool, but neither do they. So now we're even. Fair and square.

. . .

We hear lots of stories. We hear about lots of kids getting sick, white and black both. We're not allowed to leave the yard, or play with anybody, or even go in to see Mattie. As if we'd want to! Our mother puts smelly stuff in little cloth bags that Lily and I have to wear next to our skin, on strings hanging around our necks and dangling down inside our shirts. I don't see how it can help. The stuff doesn't even keep away mosquitoes. They're calling it an epidemic, health department workers pinning warning signs on everybody's doors. I don't know if it's as bad as all that.

. . .

We've heard that lots of kids are dying or ending up in wheel-chairs, just as our mother always said. We know some of them. I wonder if this counts as looking Death in the face. We hear that a lot of black kids have died, more than half of the ones that came to the pool—Brick and Melinda and a bunch of others.

. . .

Nobody's saying it, but I know they're thinking it: Those kids got what they deserved; justice has been dealt. Just like in the Bible. They shouldn't have come in, they should have stayed behind the fence, same as always. When you break rules, even unspoken ones, there are always consequences. Nobody will admit they're glad some kids are dead, but I know they're thinking it; deep down secretly they *are*.

. . .

Not that I'm claiming credit, or anything. Not me. I didn't have anything to do with it. It was all Mattie. Mattie did it. Maybe I had a plan, but *I* didn't go to the city and then spread myself all over the pool. It's Mattie's fault. Mattie's guilty. Mattie's the one to bring an end to everything.

. . .

Which is fitting, since Mattie is the one who started the whole thing in the first place, Mattie with her invitation to come in, her little wave. Which is why I am glad she is sick too.

. . .

When people talk about the sickness, they talk about dying, about the wheelchairs and the iron breathing machines. They never seem to talk about the fourth possibility: getting better. Which is what Mattie seems to be doing. Has Cousin Mattie said something to my mother about me? About the plan? But what could she possibly say without incriminating herself? Nothing. And yet . . . and yet. . . . Just a little while ago my mother looked at me, studying, and for a split second her face did a strange thing, scrunching up and smoothing out again but with the imprint of the crumple still there, like when you squeeze a paper bag in your fist. Then she looked away.

. . .

We're lying in the backyard, Lily and I, trying to catch a little of the breeze that blows through the pine trees. We're wondering when Cousin Mattie's going to leave. We want our room back. Lily is very quiet. I'm thinking about the classroom at school, guessing how many seats will be empty. We won't have to share readers anymore. Lily's lying flat on her back, staring up at the cloudy sky. Her face is flushed. Doing jumping jacks again? I say. No, dummy, she says scornfully. I can't remember her ever disagreeing with me before. What are you doing, then? I say. I'm just . . . *remembering*, Lily says, and closes her eyes. Remembering what? Night swimming, she says. It really *is* like flying. How do you know? I say, looking at the red flush blooming along her neck and around her ears. From *personal experience*, Lily says loftily. Lily, you didn't, I

say, sitting up. You wouldn't, you couldn't, not without *me*.
Her pupils are huge and her breath smells strange and even
before I touch her I know her face will feel scorching hot.
When? How? Lily, you didn't, I say. And Lily says, I *did*, and
it *is*.

The journal begins with his arrival at the makeshift hospital. "A church pressed into service, men laid out on the narrow pews, most of them strapped down to prevent their rolling off," he writes. The stained-glass windows shed candy-colored light on faces, hands, bedclothes, the viscous oily surface of the puddles on the floor. I'm paraphrasing here. The nurse who greets him has one crimson cheek, one green one, and a yellow stripe across her mouth. Voices bound and rebound in the empty space above their heads in rhythmic waves. The sound, he writes, is "that of an enormous barrel filled with children rolling down an endless flight of stairs." He is not particularly gifted with metaphor.

The nurse's lips form a question. He shouts that he would like to wash his hands. She leads him between rows of benches. Hands reach out at her from all sides, sleeve-tugging, skirt-clutching. She brushes them away with brisk swipes, then swivels and holds a bucket out to him. He dunks his hands in the soapy solution and looks around for a towel. She offers the front of her uniform. Her whole body is hard, furious, like a clenched fist. "Even her breasts," he writes, "feel angry."

He understands her fury soon enough. "It is like trying to move an ocean a teaspoonful at a time," he writes. Every day more men are brought in on wagons and stretchers. They wait in the cemetery behind the church, lying on the ground, leaning against the stones, until their turn comes to be sorted and seated in a pew. Not enough anesthesia, not enough instruments, not enough bandages, not enough hands. "I have never in my life been made to feel so impotent," he writes. Perhaps he is wiggling his eyebrows suggestively as he writes this, perhaps not. Men in our family consider themselves wits but are not known for their sense of humor.

Not enough water to go around. The well has run dry. The stream behind the church is a dusty crease in the ground, an empty palm. They are hoping it will snow soon. "Cold," he writes, "equals numbness. Poor man's anesthesia." Not enough light, not enough air.

The journal has been passed down in my family for generations, hand to hand, usually from mothers to daughters or daughters-in-law. The women of my family seem to be the ones concerned with lineage; the men are at most ghostly presences. We have a tendency to disappear or fade away while our women cling on tenaciously. My wife sometimes eyes me speculatively, sadly, as if wondering when I will follow family tradition. Sometimes in the night, when she thinks I'm asleep, she takes my hand and holds it tightly, tightly. The journal's cover is cracked leather, the pages crumbling. The handwriting, irritatingly neat, lies in precise rows on the unlined paper, with no breaks or blots. He is a man who today would do a crossword puzzle in ink. Only near the end do you see a change in the script; it softens, as if someone is tugging at a loose thread somewhere and all the knotted words begin to unravel. The last words trail off the page.

The writer is Solomon, Sol, an immigrant, the first of my family to come to this country, who has newly completed his studies as a doctor. He has been trained in the most delicate of surgeries, knitting up the body's most sensitive tissues, ladies'-embroidery work. He comes from generations of tailors who all turned blind before the age of forty but continued to stitch away for their remaining years by touch alone, calling for their wives or daughters to choose colors and patterns. In his new home he has already gained a reputation, in spite of his youth and the reek of the foreigner about him, for his gift for weaving torn flesh together, for sewing up a wound with curlicues and rosettes.

It is this reputation that has landed him here, in the midst of a civil war he has only the vaguest understanding of. All blood is the same color; he doesn't notice if the uniform soaking it up is blue or gray. Certainly he believes that slavery is wrong, that all human beings should be allowed to live freely. But by that logic, should not the rebellious states be allowed to go free as well, if they desire it so badly? It seems hypocritical to him. He keeps these thoughts to himself. He arrives at the military hospital with his delicate hands and his case of clamps and sutures and curved needles no bigger than an eyelash. He is handed a surgical saw and told to begin his new work: separating gangrenous limbs from their owners.

"I have heard that such work has a dehumanizing effect on a man's mind," he writes, "so I am keeping this journal to make a record of the descent." He dissects his own behavior as dispassionately as he would a cadaver.

"First day: vomited three times. Dizziness and weakness in the legs. Clearly due to physical exertion rather than circumstances. Second day: vomited once. Man screaming uncontrollably. Watched the blue patch of light on his tongue until he fell unconscious. Third day: no physical effects. Man says he would rather die than lose his leg. They all say this. I would like to tell him that he will most likely die anyway, but I do not. Am learning tact. When there is a pause in the screaming, one can hear artillery booming in the distance. Everyone pretends not to hear it. This place is a charm school. Fourth day: all clear. Ate a sandwich at the operating table. All the others do it. Benita holds it for me and catches the crumbs in her cupped palm."

He reports that he has successfully made what he calls in his mind "the divide," so that he can perform his work dispassionately without thinking of the life lying vulnerable in his hands. He teaches himself a kind of tunnel vision, so that in the operating room he sees mere objects in need of repair. Only afterward, in the recovery wards, does he allow himself to think of them as people.

He speaks of "the divide" in reference to his patients and does not seem to realize how it applies to himself as well.

The legs and arms pile up at his feet. He ignores them (or he reports that he ignores them: a contradiction here). Even the screaming ceases to bother him. "The acoustics of the room round out the tones," he writes, "so that it all becomes a dull roar." He believes he is doing good work, even improving these people by trimming away their excesses, these messy fringes, these frayed ends. The colored light gives everything a carnival air. It is necessary, on heavy days, to wear wading boots and raincoats. The drainage is not good.

One day he records a lovely sight. He turns and sees that the sun has struck the stained-glass windows at such an angle that a blue-gold-white angel is perfectly projected on the white sheet of a bed. He points it out to the patient beneath the sheet, who looks, begins to scream, and tries frantically to brush the image away, thinking it is a heavenly portent.

His sense of humor surfaces now as he grows more comfortable in his surroundings. He writes, "A man today was screaming that if I took his leg, he'd be half a man. I disagreed, but said that I could certainly take care of that if he would like, and I gestured with the saw. No one laughs, they are all prigs here. But I think I saw Benita smile."

He writes, "When I am off duty I go to the recovery area, to remind myself of whom I am saving. These are men, with names and families and histories. They seem whole and healthy when they are lying in their beds with blankets up to their chins. I love them dearly. I give them affectionate nicknames. Shorty, Stumpy. Hoppy, Skippy, and Jumpy. Their eyes light up when they see me. I call them a pegleg pirate band, and one of them gets in the spirit of things by trying to put my eye out. It does me good to see some feistiness."

The sign above the church door reads GOD WELCOMES HIS CHILDREN HOME. And Sol, too, thinks of them as his boys, his children. He likes to see them bobbing on crutches or dragging themselves along by their arms. "Like toddlers learning to walk for the first time. Oopsy-daisy." He has his favorites; how could he not? "There's a soldier with black hair and a red raw face who says, 'Doctor, my ankle. It hurts so bad.' 'Soldier, you can see for yourself there's nothing there.' 'But I can feel it exactly.' 'Phantom limb. A common effect. The nerve damage. Patience.' 'Doc, my phantom leg is kicking you so hard in the teeth right now; if you only knew . . . ' " He likes this spirited imagination and returns several times, but the boy always feigns sleep, a stained-glass Noah's rainbow striping his face. He has tunneled out an empty ridge under the blanket where his leg should be. Sol smooths out the blanket each time. There is no need to foster fantasies. At a certain point he knows from the smell that the boy will die soon. The next time he visits, as expected, the boy is gone and a truculent one-armer has taken his place.

"Must do something about all the screaming," he writes. "My boys need their sleep. Open the windows and let it out? Hang flypaper from the ceiling to trap it?"

Benita appears in the journal more and more, she of the stubborn chin and unflinching front. He has never heard her voice. He had assumed, that first meeting, that the cacophony drowned her out, but no. Even during their brief walks in the stunted wood behind the church, he has to read her lips. He wonders if she is mute. Her tongue, he reports, "seems functional, the sublingual thread intact." Her eyebrows and arms are so declarative that there is never any doubt as to her meaning. She swabs, stitches, cauterizes. He likes the way her tiny nostrils twitch. He likes to watch her move; she shoots off sparks, exclamation marks. "Her legs," he writes, "are well-formed and exceptionally fine. Except that sometimes, when she is running quickly—her legs almost a blur—there somehow seem to be too many of them."

He writes of the other nurses as a collective horde. "They adore me from afar," he writes. "They stand amazed, like chickens in a solar eclipse. I keep them at arm's length, though I could have any I choose." The narrative has been scrupulously honest throughout, so there is no reason to doubt it here. One might, however, take into consideration the fact that, as one of the only whole men among hundreds of splintered ones, Sol would have seemed much more attractive than he otherwise might. In fact, to judge from his descendants, he must have had very little to recommend him. And as he himself writes of his family, "We are a breed impressive in neither length nor breadth, with hair inclining to the greasy, eyes tending to goggle, features unpleasing in symmetry but betraying a great intelligence."

Come to bed, my wife says at night, when the children are asleep. Soon, I say, batting her hands away. Her fingers will soil the pages.

When my wife frowns, the flesh creases and bunches between her brows. I would like to pinch it off like clay, that bit of flesh. I remember when her brow was as smooth and pure as a young girl's.

There is a soldier who grabs Sol by the jacket after an amputation and says he wants his leg back. "I can't put it back on," Sol says. "Get it," the soldier says. "I want to be buried whole." The voice is rising, booming through the sanctuary, the fingers are digging into Sol's skin. He feels his nipple pinched and winces. Benita's eyebrows jump at him from across the table: Do something, they say, or all the others will start demanding theirs back too. So Sol tells the man, Yes, yes, you'll have your leg, and the fingers loosen their grip. Sol's already thinking logistics: how to contain, conceal, preserve. How long need the leg last? How long will this one live? A day or a week at most, he thinks.

But when he looks below the table for the leg, it's already been cleared away with the others. He spots, follows the orderly with the cart. "I want, I need—" he calls, but his voice is lost in the hubbub. He shadows the cart outside, follows the trail of flies past the stunted wood and over a ridge and sees the pit where the old man is dumping his cargo.

"Wait," he says but the cart is already tipped, its load falling. He peers over the lip and sees the tangled mass of hundreds of arms, legs, unnamable pieces. Each has lost its individuality and become part of a texture, a monstrous many-limbed slumbering creature. The smell is combative and ugly, nastily familiar. Now the orderly is sprinkling lime.

"I need," Sol says, "a leg." "Take your pick," says the orderly, mouth and nose muffled in a handkerchief. If only there was a distinguishing mark, Sol thinks. Would he recognize his own leg if it were taken from him? He looks down. Probably not. He knows others' bodies much more thoroughly than his own. He cannot remember the last time he looked in a mirror.

"Tell you what we'll do," the orderly says, pulling him back from the edge. "I've got a lot of shoes." Together they piece together a stick of wood, a soldier's boot, some shreds of uniform, a bundle of rags to approximate muscle. This will never work, Sol thinks, but the old man assures him it will. "I've done this before," he says, "At least I think I have. I can remember fifty years ago clear as day. But yesterday, the day before? Gone. It's a blessing, really."

And sure enough, when Sol gives the soldier the rag doll of a leg, the man is strangely comforted, hugs it like a toy.

The jealous men around him fight over it, toss it from hand to hand. The rightful owner weeps into balled-up fists until it is back in his arms.

After several bites, instances of tripping-by-crutch, and jabs with forks, Sol is learning not to pat them on the head.

Another time he hears a belligerent voice crying, "But I have to do it myself! I have to write my girl!" He turns to see the familiar legs (trapezoidal birthmark on the back of the right calf, shaped like an as-yet-unnamed state of the union) of Benita bending over a boy. She's holding pen and paper, ordering him to dictate to her. The boy refuses, butting her away with his head. Sol sees that the boy has no arms. He writes, "I remember trimming this one himself; he must have been holding something that exploded in his hands, leaving shredded wings."

"They have to be *my* words," the boy keeps screaming, red and writhing, a beached fish. "How can I send her a letter written by another woman?" Benita is firm, insisting, shouting at him with her whole face. Just when Sol expects her to slap him, she instead steps behind the boy, props his body against hers, and threads her arms through the empty sleeves of his bathrobe. She places her chin on his shoulder, lifts pen and paper, and waits. The boy arches away from her in surprise, then looks at the beautiful white hands emerging from his sleeves, poised and obedient as marionette hands. He relaxes into the strange embrace. He raises his knees to provide a writing surface and puts his lips to her ear.

Sol announces in his journal that he has learned to distinguish the exact moment that the life flows out of a half-severed limb. "There is a moment, independent of the cutting of nerves or the drainage of blood, in which the life force flutters and flares before going out. It can be felt on the skin, an electrical charge. The little hairs stand up; there may be a subtle twitch."

He writes that everyone looks eagerly ahead to the snow and cold, for winter will dampen the fighting, lighten the flow of wounded, deaden the smells. But the weather refuses to oblige them. It is the most brilliant autumn he has ever seen, the leaves and the light outdoors make even the stained-glass glow inside the church seem muted. The sky is such a color, he writes, "that it makes the heart hurt."

He writes that Benita is the most beautiful woman he has ever seen.

There is a sketch of her in the margin, analytical, anatomical, unsparing in its scrutiny, neatly labeled, but not lacking in feeling.

My wife suggests that I sell the journal or donate it to a museum. She tells me it should be locked away, kept safe. She says I am destroying it by constant handling, by the exposure to air. She says it is probably worth a lot of money, that there are collectors who would kill for this sort of antique. "You know, the nuts, the ones who live completely in the past, the war buffs who go around reenacting the major battles with their historically accurate guns and boots and long underwear and what-have-you." She talks about our finances, the needs of our children, but I can see in her eyes that she doesn't care about the money; all she wants is to get the book out of my hands. She thinks it is giving me ideas.

Sol writes more and more of the pleasures of pruning, of reducing bodies to their intended purer shapes. "I am excising tumors," he writes. "I am sanding away rough spots, I am creating more perfect beings." He is shaving away corners and

protuberances, revealing graceful curves. He does not understand this intense need to clutch at things, to gather all
the bits of oneself together and let none escape. "Why hold
together that which would rather be separate?" he writes.
"Scientifically, politically, philosophically, it goes against logic.
Cut off the excess, let it rot. Expose the pure core. The natural inclination of matter is toward dispersal, chaos, not unity. I
am merely helping it along. Trimming hair and fingernails is
only the beginning." My illustrious forebear seems unaware
that his anti-unity philosophy goes against that of the blue-
uniformed army he serves. And equally unaware of his pre-
scient grasp of the scientific concept of entropy. He is more
concerned with the lack of gratitude among his patients.

He walks through the recovery hall now and the men pelt
him with bedpans full and empty, wet socks, single shoes.
They call him the butcher and ask what's the special today?
Chops? Flank steaks? Pinches and punches land on his
thighs. Kicks, both real and phantom, are frequent. "My children, my wayward children," he writes. "They don't appreciate
what I've done for them." He looks into their scowling faces
and is nevertheless pleased. They will come around.

"I want Benita to share it," he writes. "I want to feel it
together." He's referring to the electric spark, the life going out
of a marooned limb. He tries to arrange the event without her
knowing; when she's assisting him, he maneuvers her hand
into the precise spot, next to his, at just the right moment.
The first attempts fail amid the confusion of the operating
room—she is needed elsewhere, someone shouts, she moves
her hand at the crucial moment to cauterize a spurting vessel.
Time and again a limb is hanging by a thread, she turns
away, and he absorbs the delicious shock alone. There comes
a time when he thinks he has orchestrated everything to
perfection—she is here beside him; the bough breaks; he
feels "a charge so strong my fingers vibrate against hers." He
checks her reaction; she is blank, her mouth open and per-

fectly circular. He is certain she felt it too. "It was by my estimate ten times stronger than usual. Two receptors must increase the flow."

He's anxious to try again and cannot resist telling her of his exciting findings. He writes that "her face immediately shut up like a suitcase and I could not guess her thoughts." He deduces that she did indeed feel the life force beneath her fingertips, but rejects it due to her "dour Puritan all-work-and-no-play attitude. She sees this as taking pleasure in another's pain."

She stops speaking to him completely. Though she's never said a word aloud, this new silence is a lead weight upon him. "She's an imbecile," he writes. "How could I not see it before? Deaf as a door, dumb as a post. I have nothing more to say to her."

Despite the break in communication, however, their relationship appears to continue. His sketches become more explicit. He details cross sections of her limbs, trunk, nasal cavity. He draws her fingerprints, line by line. One can imagine him holding her hand an inch from his measuring tailor's eyes, studying the whorls, copying the labyrinthian mysteries down ridge by ridge. Would he pause to kiss her palm, or is he too focused on the work?

He seldom washes his body. He has not the time. He is covered day after day in the sticky crust of young men's blood. One crisp evening an insistent Benita sends him down to the sluggish, rejuvenated stream in the woods with a bar of her carefully hoarded soap and a clean shirt. He writes that he is horrified by what lies beneath his clothes. "My legs, wriggling and antic, I had the impression of beetles, centipedes, overturned, millions of legs waving madly in the air. I had the urge to crush, to stamp out." He writes that entering the water made the situation worse. "The reflections. Everything doubled. Four arms. Horrid."

He does not report whether he completes the bath. And

does not mention bathing again for several weeks. One can imagine Benita's beloved nostrils cringing.

"I feel like a frog that has not yet lost his tadpole tail," he writes. "A shameful aberration. Sometimes nature stalls and requires a bit of a nudge, does it not?"

Now there are sketches in the journal of streamlined bodies without fingers or toes. Fishlike neckless stumps with fin-like appendages that barely part from the trunk.

"Benita will no longer assist me at surgery," he writes. "But her heart, her heart is mine." Followed by a detailed and labeled drawing of same. The four chambers, the arching aorta. One can imagine him lying with his head on her belly, his hand on her chest. His eyes are closed. He is feeling, measuring the quivering thing beneath the ribs in the same way that his blind father and grandfather and great-grandfather measured ladies for their dresses and never made a mistake.

He writes of his disgust for his body, how big and ungainly it is, how flabby and awkward. The flakes of skin, the bits of hair.

He writes that he has been warned about this feeling of his. It is not unique. The other doctors have warned him of amputation envy, an urge born out of guilt or envy or a genuine curiosity to experience what his patients so ungratefully endure. Today it is a disease recognized by the medical community, known as Barnesfeltner's syndrome; the men in my family have a genetic predisposition toward it. In most cases, if caught in time, it can be held in check with therapy and antipsychotic drugs. In his time, however, it was considered sacrilege, or a weakness of character.

He does not look down when he walks. He cannot bear to watch his hands at work.

I have not told my wife about the affliction that runs in my family, but she has nevertheless intuited something. In recent years she has begun dieting compulsively, so that she seems to be in a gradual state of disembodiment. It is as if she has removed pieces of herself and hidden them away in some safe invisible place. She swaddles her body from my sight; she seems to feel most comfortable, most secure, in an enormous woolen poncho that hides her arms completely. What is it, what have I done? I ask her. Nothing, she says, smiling, laughing; nothing, she says, as she takes a step back.

The weather turns colder, the days shorten, the sunlight grows pale and milky. The stained-glass windows turn dull and matte, and their projections grow faint. Gone is the magic-lantern show against the bedsheets, which has been the only entertainment for the bedridden men. They had liked to watch the colors shift, place bets on where the pictures would fall. As the sun moved, the lucky ones would get a naked golden Eve spread out across their laps or a welter of Noah's animals sprinkled over their faces. The unlucky ones got a dying Christ's morose face on their chests. Now the show is over. Now they have nothing to contemplate but their own stumps, which nudge and wave to each other and burrow into the pillow with minds of their own.

A patient drags himself from his bed and hangs himself in the night. Others follow his example.

Sol is devastated. How could they destroy his work so carelessly?

A wave of fever rolls through the church, hopping quickly from bed to bed. Bodies are carted out daily. They are buried in a field not far from the resting place of marooned limbs. Local children make temporary crosses of sticks and twine. These will be replaced by real markers soon, everyone says, but no one knows when.

Sol recalls a scene from childhood. A long table set behind a low stone house in a golden field. Distant hills, narrow trails of white smoke from other farms chalked against the brilliant blue sky. Benches around the table, each bench crowded with sunburned men in baggy trousers, bearded elders, old women in kerchiefs, young women in kerchiefs with fat babies in their arms. Sol has been sent to stay with his great-aunt and -uncle for the summer, to keep him out of the cramped tailor shop and away from the deadly summer heat sweeping through the city.

It's a celebration of some kind. Uncles, aunts, cousins, hired field workers. His great-aunt brings platters of food, jugs of wine. The other children run about the field or crawl under the table, bumping people's knees, but Sol stands at his great-uncle's right hand. He holds his great-uncle's wine cup, and in return his great-uncle gives him the best bits from his own plate, offered on the tip of his knife. Sol doesn't know why he is given this place of honor. Perhaps he is the favorite, for some reason. Perhaps he is simply the oldest of the small children, least likely to spill the wine.

He is watching his great-uncle carefully, ready to offer the cup before he is asked, when he sees his great-uncle's face freeze, as if he is about to sneeze. He follows his great-uncle's gaze and sees a dark figure on the hills, a dark rider on a black horse. He sees a second rider cross the hills, then a third.

His great-uncle says nothing and calmly finishes his meal. The other men do the same, lingering over the last of the wine. A silence falls over the table. The women get up and slowly begin to gather the dishes. By now there are a dozen black riders converging on the edges of the field and still more crossing the hills in the distance. They bring the sound of hoofbeats, the smell of torches. Slowly, slowly his great-uncle rises from his bench.

Looking back, Sol doesn't know what to make of it—the calmness, the lingering. Was it pride or stupidity? Did the men know there was no escape, did they know they were going to die, and did they choose to face it this way, with their dignity intact, no scattering, no screaming? Sol fled, Sol hid, he doesn't remember how, but crammed in some tight hiding place with his fingers plugging his ears he managed to escape what happened next, carnage and devastation so great that afterward witnesses swore that even the farm animals wept to see what man had done to man.

Even now, even after all he has seen, he cannot say. What is better, to face death willingly and proudly, to go easily into the dark, or to cling fiercely to life, to go down fighting, enduring the messiest of indignities for the sake of a few more breaths?

The fever claims more and more of the soldiers, two of the doctors. Benita drags Sol down to the stream and forces him to wash, rubs snow into his hair. She is strong, this woman. Smothers him in her arms, shows her teeth. She could chew through the bark of a tree, and the trunk too. He writes of his disgust for his body, how shrunken and withered it looks in the cold.

The wounded keep arriving in a ceaseless flow. The unseen war is in his mind nothing more than a meat factory, grinding them out. He continues to work but stops visiting the recovery hall. All his favorites are gone: the armless letter writer, the cradler of false legs. Buried, most of them. All the men he sees now are faceless, uniform. Their voices are the same. "If I have to listen to one more of them cry about this person, this 'mother' they all seem to miss so much," he writes. He slices, saws, sops, and moves on. It seems to be the same body over and over.

One day Benita stops his hand. He pushes her away angrily, then sees; he has cut into the wrong leg, a healthy leg. He stares at the leg. The leg stares back, innocent, vulnerable, the red gash a seeping mouth. The bumps and tucks of flesh over the knee have a facial aspect. Why have you done this to me? it seems to say.

After this he begins to pay closer attention to his work. To the limbs he is removing. To his surprise he sees astonishing variety and character. The arms with their branching veins ending in the fascinating mechanism of the hand. The legs with their lumps, bulges, their noble weight-bearing sturdiness. Each unique and eloquent. How could he have not noticed before?

He realizes that it is the patients who sicken and die; their limbs are merely innocent bystanders, abused beasts of burden. They do not deserve such irresponsible keepers.

The journal is now filled with page after page of arms, legs, feet, fingers. He feels the need to record each day's "harvest." They are arranged in neat rows, drawn in the moments before stiffness has set in, while there is still some life to them. Benita appears, jarringly, on one of these pages. It is unclear whether the limb specimens were drawn after her, or whether she was drawn on top of them. In contrast to the meticulous detail of the limb drawings, she is a hasty scratch, the lines hairy and jagged. "She has lost that buoyancy, that angry firmness," he writes. "Now her body has a sadness to it, a slackness and sag. It frowns." In the drawing she is bent over, perhaps washing something, her hair falling down, her back a melancholy curve. He rather cruelly emphasizes the knobby bumps of her spine, the baggy ripples on her thighs and arms. The other arms and legs seem to be raining down on her, burying her.

My wife has not read the journal. I should let her read it, as my mother intended. It is her right. Such has been the prescribed route of the book: from mother-in-law to daughter-in-law, through the generations. The journal serves as both explanation and warning to the women marrying into this family. I should let her read it. I will let her read it. But not yet.

Now Sol murmurs comforting words to the limbs as he removes them from their uncaring owners. He rocks them in his arms, briefly, surreptitiously, before handing them over to the old man with his cart. Benita watches him from across the room, says nothing.

She still comes to him at night, and they find private corners and hallways to lie with their arms around each other.

She comes to him night after night all through the winter until the night that she wakes to find his hand on her leg and his surgical saw poised four inches above her right knee. On her skin she sees the faintest of ashy lines, where he has already made the first practice stroke. His expression is stern and tender, the face of the kindly family doctor with a spoonful of cod-liver oil in his hand and a peppermint waiting in his pocket. This will only hurt a minute, his face says; you know it's good for you.

Later, remembering, she can never be entirely sure whether his nurturing gaze was directed at her face or her shin. She will later ask herself, and ask again, which side of the blade was to him the superfluous part, the part that needed to be pared away.

He is sorry, he is glad when she runs away, the beloved birthmark on her calf dancing inside his eyelids for a long time.

Come to bed, my wife says again.

He discovers he cannot sleep without her. He lies awake at night, clenched and staring at nothing with the wide-open painted-on eyes of a china doll.

He discovers he does not really need sleep.

He draws her, inside and out. He draws her in layers, the skin peeled back. There is one mistake in his drawing, something omitted: a pear-shaped swelling cradled within the flaring iliac petals, with a ripening pear seed inside. No one has told him about it yet.

Now he focuses entirely on his work. His cataloging becomes increasingly intricate. "When a man is brought in," he writes, "I want to harvest it all, every piece. It requires all of my self-control to restrict myself to only the damaged part." At the end of his shifts he refuses to rest, instead watches jealously as the other surgeons hack and hew away.

One particularly restless day he approaches the orderly and offers to man the refuse cart for the afternoon. The old fellow eyes him suspiciously but agrees. "I felt such ecstasy. I could feel the powerful energy emanating from the cart; I couldn't escape quickly enough with my precious cargo." Once away from the church, he pauses to admire his booty. He confesses to chatting with his passengers, tweaking toes, though he does not record any affectionate nicknames.

He cannot bear to dispose of them in the pit with the others so he pushes his cart into a neighboring field where the earth has been broken up and furrowed and left to rest until the following spring. The smell of soil seems utterly new to him, after months of breathing human emanations. He kneels, digs a shallow hole, cradles a sinewy and freckled arm in his own for a moment, and then plants the severed end in the ground.

He plants another. And another. The arms are mottled and stiff, raised beseechingly to the sky.

After all, he says to himself, they are not so different, are they? Armlets, leglings, seedlings. The vascular systems. . . .

He plants them all.

And then, like a child exhausted after play, he falls asleep.

He sleeps deeply and dreamlessly, the first time he has been able to sleep without Benita's arms around him.

He wakes at dawn to a gentle shushing sound, like the ocean, like the wind through grain. He is five years old, lying on warm beach sand, scent of brine and grasses in his nostrils, and a hand like his mother's hand caressing his cheek. He opens his eyes to a field of waving arms, the palms turned toward the sunrise and nodding like sunflowers.

He returns to the hospital barely able to contain himself. He works his shift, again requests the cart, and returns to the field. The arms reach out to him in welcome.

He plants, he sleeps, he wakes to gentle fingers tickling his face.

The third day the old man is suspicious and clings to his cart. Sol is heartbroken, watching the load being trundled off to a mass grave. He returns to his field to find that it doesn't matter; the arms have multiplied and spread on their own. They are growing strong and tall. The hands begin to clap and snap as he approaches. The legs kick up their heels. He walks through the field, caressed by hands, they tug at his pant cuffs, they wave for his attention. Clapping, wringing themselves, clutching at each other for comfort. The sound they make as the wind blows through them is like a deep and cleansing sigh, a contented murmur. As an experiment, he uproots an arm. It immediately goes limp in his hands. He feels a vicious pinch on his backside. He won't do it again.

He visits his crop every day. The small patch soon overtakes the whole field. His arms grow tall and healthy; they are burnished brown from the winter sun, grown muscular from fighting the wind. When he walks through the field, they reach up past his waist. He spends many nights here, warmly nestled among the arms.

He does repair work in the field occasionally: stitching, pruning. Scrapes, blisters, calluses, insect bites. Nothing serious. Nails that need trimming. Sunburn.

All this time, Benita watches him. He speaks to no one. He has always been an outsider, tolerated for his skill. Now, at the operating table, he stares into space and lets warm blood flow through his fingers. But times are desperate, doctors are scarce. He cannot be spared. Not enough hands. Benita has news to tell him but wants to wait for the right time. He will be pleased, she thinks, but is not sure.

The day he packs up his instruments and slips his journal into a pocket, she follows him.

She hears the humming roar first, and then she tops a rise and sees it: the field of golden arms, undulating like ocean waves. The boiling motion makes her think of stirring up anthills with a stick, scattering flocks of birds with a stone, angry mobs with torches. She does not understand what she is seeing at first; she thinks it is a mass of soldiers—she is accustomed to seeing masses of soldiers—perhaps they are involved in some sort of complicated crouching calisthenics. Then she sees her lover striding through the field waist-deep in waving arms, and she sees. He brushes his hands lightly over the surface as he walks, a bobbing skin of fingertips. He combs his own fingers through them like hair. He grasps a wrist here and there; he falls and allows himself to be caught.

Now he has reached the far end of the field, and she thinks she will go out to meet him when he returns and tell him her news. She waits. She sees his head dip down and it does not rise again. She begins to run around the perimeter of the field. Barbed wire she has not noticed before keeps the arms from spreading further. He is lying down. She sees his hat. One of the hands has seized it, now it is being tossed up in the air. Don't lie down, she thinks, and wants to shout it: Don't lie down. She thinks of snowbanks, the drowsiness of drowning.

She shreds her hands on barbed wire.

By the time she reaches him most of his body has already sunk softly into the ground, she sees a patch of his brown hair merge with the soil; a scrap of his white shirt, one last moist glimmer of an eye, and then there is nothing to be seen but bare earth and his hands, which she would recognize any-where as his even if they were not adding a few final looping words to the journal before shutting it. She snatches up the journal and stuffs it inside her uniform, then reaches toward his hands, to press her cheek to one palm or both, one last time, to whisper her secret into the earth, but she is borne away almost immediately on a sea of other hands. She gets one last glimpse of his fingers, waving, penitent, raised in benediction or curse, and then his hands are swallowed by others and she is swept away on a wave of grasping claws. They wipe away her tears, jab thumbs in her eyes, tickle her, rend her clothes. She is passed from hand to hand, caressed, manhandled, tossed, pressed, squeezed, spun like a top. She calls his name, for the first time, finds her tongue and lets out a caw. But he will not answer. She will never find him again among this boisterous chorus. She does not know, in these buoyant, drowning minutes, whether she will be raised up to the sky or torn limb from limb.

"So, if it comes to that, we should be prepared for any possibility," the President said.

"Very good, sir."

"Pray for the best but prepare for the worst, as they say."

"Indeed, sir. Very wise."

"We have to be like those bugs in the fable. The ants and the grasshoppers, hey? Mr. Jessman!"

"Sir?" said the youngest aide, who was dating one of the President's daughters.

"Well, which is it?"

"Sir?"

"Are you a grasshopper, Mr. Jessman? Or are you an ant?" Jessman's face lolled blankly. "A grasshopper, Jessman! Write it down."

"I believe it's the ant that the fable instructs us to emulate," an advisor said.

"Don't give me that manure. A grasshopper's twenty times as big as an ant! Things can jump thirty feet! Raise a racket with their little banjos! Don't tell me an ant can do that."

"The fable, sir, favors the long-term planning of the ant over the instant gratification—"

"Flock of hoppers can strip a field bare in thirty seconds. Leave nothing but dirt. Seen it happen. Eat your hat. Chew the hair right off your head. Chirp you to deafness in the process."

"Beg to differ, sir."

"Ants? Pshaw."

The first step toward preparedness was to close the subway systems in every city all across the country and begin converting the tunnels into shelters.

As a result, millions of people grumblingly took the bus to work, or crammed into station wagons with their daughters' car-pool groups, or wobbled on long-neglected in-line skates, or rang up the friends and neighbors they'd ignored for months, saying sheepishly, "I'm in a bit of a jam, mate, help a fellow out?" or took their children's scooters, or hired the horse-and-carriages that provided a smelly scenic view of the city, or borrowed the skis-on-wheels eccentric Uncle Morris used when he wanted to practice during the summers, or commandeered the electric wheelchairs of elderly relatives, or hitched rides with truckers, or even walked.

"What about shelters for the people who don't live in major cities?" an advisor said.

"What about them?" The President snorted. "Self-sufficient country folk, they've got their root cellars and grain silos. They're the lucky ones. Give me a dry creek bed over a stinking concrete tunnel any day. Shoot."

Nevertheless, a concrete fortress was built fifty stories underground for the President and his advisors and security heads and military chiefs and culinary chefs and his wife and their daughters and all the daughters' boyfriends and the presidential dogs, one of which was about to give birth and wanted nothing more than to be left alone to crawl under the

White House and do what was natural to her, rather than being dragged here and there to sniff lead doors and air vents and provide her input.

"No slacking off, Muffins," the President said. "We all have to do our share."

There were television monitors in all the tunnel shelters, so that the President could speak to the people and keep them calm and reassured. And there were cameras so he could keep an eye on them.

"That's the way!" the President said, when all the work was done. "Now let's hunker down and let 'em come!"

"Hold your horses, that's only half the battle," said one of the advisors.

There was a general gasp. The President glared. Only the President was allowed to season his speech with the odd folksy idiom.

"People need to know what to do, where to go," the advisor continued more stiffly. "Otherwise chaos will be our undoing."

A few weeks later a thick packet arrived in mailboxes nationwide. People saw the sunburst shapes and blaring text on the envelope (URGENT! READ IMMEDIATELY!) and ripped the packets open eagerly, expecting to learn that they'd won ten million dollars, or at least a chance to order subscriptions to several dozen colorful and interesting magazines.

Instead, what they found was a handbook informing them of what to do in a wartime emergency. There were instructions, suggestions, and dire warnings of what would happen if any of it was disregarded. It hinted at tortures more fearfully agonizing than they could ever have imagined on their own. Many of the descriptions were accompanied by illustrations. The stylized people in the drawings had bright orange skin, and no hair, faces, or hands; they were meant to look non-gender-specific and non-race-specific but instead looked as if they had suffered hideous disfiguring accidents.

These cartoon figures appeared on television in lengthy public service announcements, pantomiming safety maneuvers and dashing along maps to illustrate escape routes. In a box in one corner of the screen, a bland face narrated instructions, while in another quadrant, a woman echoed his words in frantic sign language. In a third corner the corporations who had expressed special interest in the project ran a continuous stream of helpful promotions.

The consequence of this overload of information was that most people could not make heads or tails of it and assumed several channels had somehow jammed together. They banged their fists on the box or meddled with the antenna, or they simply went to the bathroom or out for a snack or realized they hadn't called their mothers in ages, and their mothers, answering the phone with pleasure and surprise, asked if their televisions were acting up too.

"Now?" the President said eagerly, dandling one of Muffins's puppies on his knee.

"Now we need to test the system," the advisors said. "Dry run. Simulation."

"Like a fire drill?" the President said.

"Like a fire drill," the advisors said soothingly. The President thought of his bunker, fifty stories below the surface, and had a sudden delightful vision of sliding all the way down to it on a fireman's pole. They'd have to build one. "Jessman!"

"Yes, sir?"

A sobering thought struck him: The dogs would never make it down a pole. "Never mind," he said. They'd have to stick with the elevator.

The word went out: a nationwide test of the emergency response system. No one was exempted; provisions were made for the elderly, sick, and immobile. Everyone would head, in a calm and orderly fashion, to their assigned shelters. Registered volunteers would gather at rendezvous points and arm themselves. Communities were encouraged to choose group leaders to conduct sing-alongs and word games in the dark until the all-clear bells rang.

The power grid would be temporarily shut down. There would be fireworks and smoke bombs to make it all very realistic.

"It's foolproof," the President said proudly. "What could possibly go wrong?"

"We'll see," the advisors said testily.

"Can I give them a pep talk the day before?" the President pleaded. "Put a little fire in their bellies?"

"It might compromise the surprise element of the test," an advisor said.

The President glowered. He couldn't tell which advisor had spoken, so he glared at them all.

.   .   .

The next day, at the appointed moment, the alarms began to sound. A deep rhythmic siren, slightly shriller than a foghorn, more like the honking of geese, began to resound through every city and every town. It created a deep tangible hum people felt in their diaphragms. Children felt it buzzing in their braces. The sound was carefully calibrated to arouse and impel to action, but not cause disorientation or panic. They'd been given a taste of the sound on the public service announcements. They'd been told what it meant: the coming of the Calamity, the Big One, the End, the It, and the All.

The President felt a twinge of disorientation and panic as he gathered up his wife and family and headed down the appointed passageway, but it was a pleasurable twinge. He felt the excitement he'd felt as a boy playing cowboys and Apaches with his friends, the thrill of nearly convincing himself that the make-believe was real, the joy of hiding out in a home-made fort with his gun waiting for the vicious and cunning enemy to appear. He'd been the only one with an air rifle, while all his friends had water pistols. *Not fair!* they used to cry, rubbing their welts. The nancies. Was it *his* fault he came better prepared?

He thought again, longingly, of the fireman's pole as the elevator made its slow creeping descent. His daughters had already begun to whine. Perhaps the dogs could be trained to slide, he thought.

His men were already assembling in the command room, sweating and rumpled. Jessman had his head between his knees. "We think he's claustrophobic," the advisors said.

"Somebody get the boy some whiskey," the President said. No one paid any attention. Jessman had been his usual whiskey runner.

"Ready to see how they're doing?" an advisor said, and everyone moved to the banks of video monitors. The technicians set to work tapping into the cameras in the shelters of one city, then another, then another. As the technicians flipped from channel to channel, a silence fell and grew. Even the presidential daughters were quiet.

"What's wrong with the cameras?" the President said finally. "Where the hell *is* everybody?"

For every single shelter was empty.

"They're all dead," one of his daughters moaned and began to sob. "Mikey!"

"Who's Mikey?" said Jessman fiercely.

"Don't be ridiculous," the President said. "No one's dead. It's not real. It's just a stimulation."

"Simulation," an advisor said.

"What I said," he muttered.

"Maybe they got lost," the advisors said. "Maybe they forgot something and had to go back. Maybe they got the address wrong," they said, as if making excuses for friends who were late showing up for a barbecue.

"What in tarnation are they *doing* up there?"

"Maybe they know it's a drill so they're not bothering," an advisor suggested.

.   .   .

The truth was that up on the surface most people *did* believe the end had come, and were behaving accordingly.

At the first sound of sirens, people lifted their heads, friends and strangers alike, and read the dawning panic, realization, and acceptance on one another's faces.

On crowded city streets, people's first instincts were to touch each other: women embraced, strangers clasped hands, men slapped each other on the back and said, "Guess this is it, big guy." Strangers hugged other people's children, and the children uncharacteristically allowed themselves to be hugged.

Highway traffic eased to a stop. People got out of the cars. Everyone kept looking up at the sky.

It was the most beautiful day anyone could remember. The sky was cloudless, intensely blue, and there was just the slightest breeze, the sort that made people feel buoyed up by invisible hands. The softness in the air made even the most jaded garbage collectors and television weathermen pause and look up, spellbound.

On the tenth floor of an office building heads popped up out of cubicles like prairie dogs.

In another building in another city a man called in his secretary and said, "I've dreamed about you ever since you came to work in this office, and if I could just once put my hand up under your hair I think I could die a happy man."

Elsewhere a man was saying, "I think you are a twit and an intellectual goon and I can't believe I've worked here for half of my natural life, and I *quit*."

On a playground a teacher was trying to gather a flock of

children together but they kept wandering away. They wanted one last swing. They wanted one last turn down the slide.

"Last time . . . the last time . . . last time . . . the last time," a girl chanted as she swung back and forth.

"I hate you," a girl named Audrey told her best friend.

"I only let you be my friend because your mother's dead," her friend said.

They stared at each other, shocked and saddened by the truth they had uncovered: that friendship is deception. Without deception we are all alone. They both started to cry.

I could just go off and leave these kids, the teacher thought. No one would ever know. So she did.

Elsewhere a man was saying, "One more time."

And his ex-lover was saying, "Why not?"

A woman weaving her way through the knots of people on the street began to take off her clothes.

A man who had always known he could fly if he just made the proper swimming movements was poised on the railing of his balcony. If I don't try now, I'll never have another chance to find out, he thought, and jumped.

Two strangers looked at each other and began embracing and mashing their faces together.

A woman whose sole companion for twelve years had been her Pekingese kissed him on the mouth as she had always longed to do. The taste was terrible. The dog did not seem to mind.

"The time has come," a man said in a jokey-ominous voice. "Prepare to meet your maker." "How do I do that?" said his friend earnestly. They went together to a church and sat quietly in a pew, thinking.

It's now or never, a woman thought. She crept over to the baby carriage, lifted out the black-haired baby, tucked it under her arm, and ran.

A man dressed in rags jumped up and down, shaking his

fists in the air. "I *knew* this would happen!" He laughed. "I *knew* it! I *knew* it!"

Several million people phoned their parents and said, I love you, Mom! Dad!

And tens of millions of parents said, We know.

I've always wanted to punch a stranger in the face, just to see what would happen, thought a man, and he did it.

A man took twelve hundred dollars out of his wallet and pressed the wad into the hand of a woman just because he liked the fearless way she wore orange with purple.

A policeman in riot gear, whose job was to herd any stragglers to their proper places, clutched his rifle, confused. He found himself thinking of a picture he'd been aroused by as a teenager—a photograph of long-haired bouncy-breasted bra-less girls sticking flowers into a soldier's gun. "Flowers," he cried out hopefully. "Does anyone have a flower?"

In the parks, on benches, on the grass, on bridges, floating on the ponds in stolen paddleboats, in phone booths, on sofas, on the hoods of cars, up against trees and walls, people were making love. Old and young, strangers, couples who'd been together sixty years, all colors and races and religions and kinds, they held each other and made love, some with the conventional pushing intensity and friction, some with butterfly kisses and half-remembered poems, some by playing checkers. *Are you there? Yes, right here.*

And people were singing, tunelessly, abrasively, wholeheartedly. It seemed that singing, more than anything else, was one thing that people secretly longed to do but were normally afraid to.

Few people thought of their instructions, of the concrete tunnels waiting for them underground.

The sirens had done their job. They had filled the people with urgency, impelled people to action. It just wasn't the action the government had intended.

Toward evening the all-clear bells began to sound, like the chiming of church bells. Voices boomed from loudspeakers: *Go home. Resume your normal activities. The simulation is over.*

People looked at one another and yawned and stretched as if awakening from a dream. The normal clatter and babble of the city began to hum to life. Slowly, with a mixture of relief and reluctance, people returned to the lives and homes they thought they might never see again.

. . .

The following evening the President faced the nation in a televised address. He wore his most presidential of red ties. Propped on a table behind him were photographs of his wife, Kitty, and his five daughters: twenty-eight-year-old BettyAnn and his fourteen-year-old quadruplets, Shayna, Dana, Elana, and Rox. Muffins was under the desk. It was her job to lean soothingly against his legs if he needed reassurance, and to be available for kicking if he found he needed to kick something.

In his speech he scolded the nation for their unpreparedness, their disobedience. "What if it had been a real catastrophe? Who're you going to come crying to then?" He appealed to their sense of patriotism, responsibility, reasonableness, and self-preservation. He laid a guilt trip on them a mile wide. "I do all I can to take care of you, and what do I get in return? Nothing. Nothing but a bad attitude and a lot of ingratitude."

The speechwriters let out a collective sigh of relief that he'd made it past the speech's main oratory hurdle.

The President glared at the noise. His eyes began to glitter. "I've just about had it. You're grounded till further notice."

Behind the teleprompter the advisors were gesturing for him to calm down.

"We've got to do better next time. Or else. Now I want you

to turn off the TV right now and go up to your rooms and think about what I've said."

Most people changed the channel but barely noticed what they were watching; they were savoring their memories of the day before, which already seemed like a pleasant but distant dream. Husbands and wives eyed each other warily. Where were you yesterday? they wanted to ask, but were afraid to. Daughters wanted to ask their fathers about those bruises on their knuckles, the caked dirt on their wingtips, but they did not.

"We'll have to have another test," said the advisors. "Keep at it until we get it right."

"Do we have to?" said the President, already tired of the game.

So there was another siren, and this time people at once rose from their desks and tools and left their places of work and began to move about in a calm and orderly fashion. But they were not heading for the tunnels; they were heading for the places they had drifted to before; they were searching for the faces of the people they had met the previous time. Some went hoping for rebuttal, revenge, but most went seeking another embrace, another few hours of groping with utter abandon on a park bench.

Those who could not find their previous partners found new pairings.

And again, at the final bell, they pulled apart from each other reluctantly and made their way home.

During his address the next night, the President was livid. Despite pale preemptive makeup, he turned a boiling scarlet. He spluttered so emphatically that some of his spittle struck the camera lens. A few of the advisors silently cheered and high-fived each other; there had been bets placed on the potential propulsiveness of the President's fricatives.

"How do you think we look to other nations?" he demanded. "Like a bunch of ninnies. A bunch of children. Now they're more likely to attack than ever. You're treating this as a game. It's not a game. The next one could be the real thing."

But the next time the sirens rang, it was much the same. When they parted in the evening, people told one another, "See you at the next drill" or "See you the next time the world ends."

They did not think of it as a game or joke. People enjoyed the sweetness, the intensity, of those hours on the brink, that feeling that every second might be their last. It made everything they did in those moments feel both pointless and terribly, monumentally important.

And the ending of each drill, each resumption of the old life, was becoming more and more difficult, more and more bitter. They dreaded the sound of the all-clear bells. They wished the sound might never come, that the drills would go on and on forever.

People began to ask themselves, If I take such pleasure in these last moments, does that mean I *want* the end to come? Of course I don't, they told themselves. And yet . . . they craved the sound of sirens more and more.

The more pragmatic among them thought, Well, you could say we live on the brink of death every day of our lives. We might die at any moment. It's just that the sirens make us more aware of it than usual. But they too felt the thrill, when the sirens began and they ran to meet their loved ones or take the drugs or indulge in the secret habits they denied themselves during their normal average-life-span lives.

"If you don't start worrying, I'll *give* you something to worry about," the President raged at the camera. "Is anybody listening?"

The advisors were ready to admit defeat. The President insisted on another drill. "Can't we just *herd* those people down there? How hard can it be? Hell, give me a couple good sheepdogs and an electric prod, or a steam shovel, and I'll do it myself."

When the sirens set up their wail, the President couldn't find two of his daughters, but he marched the other three and his wife down the passageway. "When they turn up, they're in for it," he said grimly, as he hustled. He found the advisors clustered at the entrance.

"Generator's down, sir," one said. "The elevator won't work."

"I say we abort," said another.

"Well, thank God and your granny for the fireman's pole," the President said. He'd finally convinced them to build one, though he'd never tested it out. "And you said we'd never need it. You'd better get out the Tabasco and prepare to eat those words, son."

The advisors were now backing away. "After you," the President said, gesturing to the pole. No one moved.

"If we go, we'll be stuck down there. How're we supposed to get back up?" one muttered, and was quickly hushed by the others.

"Anyone not down this pole by the count of three can kiss their careers good-bye," the President said.

"Sir, you can't do that."

"Darn tootin'," the President replied.

No one knew quite how to respond to that.

"One . . . ," the President said. "Two . . ."

Two advisors reluctantly stepped forward, wrapped themselves awkwardly around the pole, and slid out of sight. Then, after threatening looks from Dana, Jessman stepped up to the pole and was gone. Dana skipped forward and slipped after him.

Wait a minute, the President thought, wait one gosh-darn minute. Dana? I thought he was dating BettyAnn. Dana's, what, fourteen last time I checked?

But he had no time to ponder, because his remaining daughters and wife were vanishing below, and then it was his turn. He shot one final glare at the mutineers and then wrapped his arms and legs around the brass pole and slid into blackness.

He had to restrain a whoop. It was almost like flying. His momentum kept building, he had to keep tightening his grip to put on the brakes, and he found his wool-clad legs to be nearly useless; only his hands were sticky enough to create friction. He didn't know how far below his wife was; he could imagine crashing into her head, and her irritated yelp.

The blackness was so complete, the flying sensation so delicious that he should have been able to forget himself for the moment. Instead his fury focused itself, grew and grew. Ingrates, he thought. We'll give them something to worry about, he told himself; we'll show them a thing or two.

Down below, in the command room, was a console that for simplicity's sake had been designed to resemble the President's favorite video game. By moving the joystick and pushing a few buttons he could point-aim-shoot anywhere in the world, and the orders would be carried out by military underlings. For a long time now he'd had his targets chosen, his strategies ready. Next time he played, he'd make it onto the list of top scorers for sure. For far too long he'd been waiting, waiting to achieve a state of preparedness before starting a new game.

But now, as he slid through the darkness, his ears popping, he had a new idea. A different set of targets. Why not aim *inward*? he thought. Hit a couple of home targets, just a few, just to put a little fear into people. Wake them up to the gravity of the situation. A sacrifice of the few to strengthen the whole, that's all. He wouldn't even have to justify it to anyone—it would be easy enough to blame someone else.

Yes, he thought. Yes, that's what we'll do. They'll be scared straight. They'll come crawling back to the fold begging for help, begging for someone to take care of them. . . .

Yes. Now he was impatient to do it. His hands were itching for the joystick. He had to put the plan into action right away, before he forgot it. He had a tendency to do that, that's why he needed Jessman around, to write things down before they evaporated. "Jessman!" Where was the kid, anyway? Oh, yes. Down below. Making out with Dana, probably. Or was it Elana? His teeth began to grind. He'd fire the boy, next time he saw him.

The plan, remember the plan, he thought. It would be easy enough to do, as long as he didn't have a bunch of advisors breathing down his neck. He remembered suddenly that he'd left most of them up on the surface. Plus he'd fired them. So much the better, he thought. His jaw relaxed.

He slid and slid. His momentum kept building, his groin grew numb, his shirt buttons set off sparks when they scraped against the pole. He should be there by now. Not that he was in any hurry to see his wife's reproachful face or hear his daughters' whines, but he wanted to get the game fired up. The darkness was growing denser and more suffocating with each second. Pressure crowded his lungs; he opened his mouth and—"*Eeeeee!*"—let out a little shriek to make sure he was still there.

Then he saw a pinprick of brightness far below, and just as he did the pole ended and he was no longer sliding but falling. And as he zoomed closer the brightness grew and grew until it swallowed him and he was surrounded by the light, clinging to the edge of a hole with his legs dangling in empty air and his eyes squeezed shut.

He smelled spices and bread and leather and the fur of exotic animals and heard voices bargaining shrilly in an alien tongue.

After a moment he cautiously opened one eye, then the other.

He found himself in a strange land, the likes of which he'd never seen before, full of foreign-looking people in odd flowing storybook clothes walking around upside down. He looked down past his wingtips and saw a dusting of stars and a sickle moon hanging in the sky.

I *knew* it! he thought, furiously, exultantly. I *knew* this could happen! For years they've been lying to me, but I never believed them, not for a second. I was right, I always *knew* this would happen if you dug deep enough.

He somehow righted himself, with a gymnastic maneuver that felt as natural as riding a bike. All around him a foreign bazaar was in full swing, fruit and meat and leather bags and paper money changing hands. No one gave him a second glance. He patted down his hair and tucked his pockets back into his pants and looked down into the round dark hole he'd just fallen from. Even as he looked, an old man scuttled past him to spread a cloth across the hole and then began laying out his wares upon it: copper bracelets, intricately carved scissors, silver rings for babies, braided beaded earrings for very-long-necked women.

"But—" the President said.

The old man raised his face and looked at him disinterestedly.

"But—" the President said weakly. What were the proper words? Where were those damn speechwriters when you needed them? "But—that's *mine.*"

Without speaking, the old man made it clear the spot was his. The peddlers on either side of him corroborated with vigorous nods.

"But I have to go *back*," the President said. He thought of the game waiting to be played, the targets he'd chosen, all the people waiting to be taught a lesson, his name topping the list of winning scores. He tried to lift the cloth covering the hole with the tip of his shoe. The jewelry slid and jangled.

The old man responded with quick slaps to both of the

President's cheeks, followed by a shove that sent him sprawling. Purely coincidentally, the President's eyes filled with tears. With great dignity, he picked himself up and dusted off his suit.

He slunk away, weaving among the stalls, wondering what had happened to his wife and Jessman and the others. He was thirsty and tired and needed a bathroom. He wished he'd brought a map, a guidebook, a phrase book in the local language. Some comfortable shoes, some sunblock, some matches, a compass, a bag lunch. He should have come prepared.

On the other side of the world, the emergency drill continued. The advisors, newly fired, went home and took naps. No one thought to sound the all-clear bells. The people remained suspended in the euphoria of the moment, like flies in amber. The cacophony of lovemaking and unself-conscious singing filled the air. Two strangers held hands tightly, tightly, and swore to never let go.

We live on an island of mothers.

Fifteen years ago when the war broke out, all the men left our island. They packed their shirts and went to the mainland, to fight in the army, or hide from the army, or work in the military factories fitting nuts to bolts. Perhaps some of them were secretly grateful for an excuse to escape the stark island and the women who were stiff-necked and intractable. So the women were left behind, with only the wind-warped trees, the bad-tempered dogs without tails, and each other for company.

They grew fiercer during their time alone. Their hair grew long. Their cooking did not improve.

Then our fathers came. They washed up on the beach, they fell from the sky trailing limp petaled parachutes. They came in their tall boots and spiked helmets with guns strapped to their backs and chests and thighs. They were the enemy soldiers; they came to kill all the island men, but they found no men. They found only dogs and women, who stood on the hills and rooftops, silently watching with their arms folded and their skirts ballooning around them in the wind. The men came up from the beaches and fell in love with the women. They lay down together.

They lay down and became our fathers and mothers.

They became our fathers, but then they had to leave. The sirens rang out and messages burned across the sky, and the fathers ran down to the beach with their trousers unfastened, and they leaped into their boats and helicopters. They loved our mothers, but they had no choice. They did love them, they did. They gave our mothers gifts—chocolate bars and cigarettes and packets of foot powder—as tokens of affection.

Then they were gone and the months passed and the women swelled and wondered how to explain their delicate condition to the island men once they returned.

Then there came the morning when our mothers felt the tremors, like an earthquake, and the dishes did a vibrating dance on their shelves before crashing to the floor, and the window glass hummed in the frames. And our mothers rushed outside to see the dark column of cloud rising up on the horizon, and they swore they could feel the heat on their faces.

For days afterward the sunsets were dim and strange, the air thick, all sound muffled. Dead fish washed up on the beaches and the gulls refused to fly. They crowded the beach, flocks of them, standing for days, motionless on one leg, as if waiting for some signal that the skies were safe again.

Our mothers saw that the world was ending. Everything beyond the island had been destroyed. They were the only ones left. They cupped their hands over their bulging bellies and realized that they would be the ones to replenish the human race. It was their duty and their privilege. They began to carry themselves even more proudly, they felt godlike and strong.

It was a long time before they discovered that they were *not* alone in the world, that the rest of the world still existed and was carrying on as usual, that the war was over, and that the land of the fathers had defeated the country of the mothers. But by that time they did not even care because their children had been born. We so occupied their attention that it was as if the rest of the world did not exist.

Those men who had left the island never returned, neither the original island men nor the soldiers who had become fathers. Many, many years later we learned that military reports claimed our island had been obliterated. It was removed from all maps. A clerical error. Our mothers did not care; they said men always made mistakes of this sort. Men were often wrong.

The men had always called the island barren.

So our mothers raised us all by themselves, and they were glad there was no one to interfere. They named us after our fathers, so they would not forget. Even the daughters were named in this way, so that my name is Joe, and my best friend is Michael, and the others are Donny and Richard and John.

John had bright orange hair that did not seem to match her skin, and bright green eyes. She could have been my best friend too, I wanted her to be, Michael and John and I, I wanted us all three to be best friends. But John had said no, best friends meant liking only *one* other person best, which meant it only worked with two people, not three.

John was never very good at sharing.

· · ·

When we were younger we girls all played together, but we were not allowed to play with the boys, though our mothers would not tell us why. Of course we did not *want* to, anyway, but we would have liked to know the reason. Their mothers kept them on the other side of the island; we never saw them except at a distance. Two of them had red hair like John's. We sometimes called to them, and if the wind was right, we could hear them calling back. *Chicken-legs,* they called us. *Blue-faced baboons.*

We had a playhouse on the beach, built of driftwood and a plastic sheet for a roof, which threw a blue light on our faces when we were inside and sagged low when it collected rain. When we were younger we used to play make-believe, and usually we played house. We invented furniture and sketched out a garden in the sand. We all wanted to be the one to play the mother in the game—she got to take care of the baby and give orders—but none of us wanted to be the father, because we did not know exactly what he was supposed to do.

Now that we were older we did not play anymore; we were too old for that. But we had a club, and no boys were allowed, and the playhouse had become a clubhouse where we held meetings and gave speeches and made solemn promises to one another kneeling around a fire.

Our mothers did not mind this. In fact, they approved.

We were not angels. We did not always get along. Sometimes we fought one another, kicked, scratched, held each other's faces underwater, yanked heavy handfuls of hair. The first time I came home spotted with bruises I thought my mother would be angry. But instead she said only, If anyone ever hurts you, I want you to promise me you'll fight back and keep fighting to your last breath.

Never turn the other cheek, she said. Never sit back and take it.

I promised. She looked so angry. I wondered what she was thinking of.

We girls fought less now that we were older. We sometimes climbed up to a high ledge from which we could see the boys running about on their beach. We discussed what it would be like to fight with them. We decided it would not be much fun. The boys kept their hair cut short, and what was the fun in that? It was so *satisfying* to yank on a good thick hank of hair. And the boys looked so bony; we decided they would not make the same kind of good crisp smacking sound that *our* bodies made when we slapped each other. They looked so puny and helpless; it would not be much fun to try to make them scream.

The sea sent us gifts sometimes, strange cargo that had fallen off ships and been washed up on our shores by the waves. A crate of waterlogged lettuce. A huge bale of rough trousers, dozens and dozens of identical pairs and that we wore like uniforms after our mothers pinned and stitched them to fit us. Barrels of doll parts, pink plastic heads and arms and legs, sculpted swirls of hair and sweet puckered lips.

Occasionally we saw airplanes passing overhead, some-times far away, sometimes low enough for us to see the pilot in the cockpit. We would wave to them, and perhaps twice a year they would drop parcels on the beach. Strange things: bottled medicine, shoelaces, nails, twine, pepper, magazines made of flimsy sheeny paper. We never knew if our mothers requested these things somehow or if they were random gifts. We looked at the magazines, admiring the long-legged women in their fancy plumage, but the words were in a language we didn't know.

We watched our mothers to see how to behave, how to form friendships. Some of them had paired up, they were con-stant companions, and we wondered if this was what marriage looked like. Some of the mothers formed cliques and clubs; their shrill gossip was as constant as the surf and the cries of gulls. And some kept to themselves.

My mother was one of the solitary ones. She worked relentlessly in her garden, bending and unbending like a piece of supple wire. She held long mocking conversations with the scarecrow she had set up there, with his outstretched arms and wide straw hat. She gazed out to sea and picked at the dry skin on her elbows.

I did not know if she thought of my father or if she pictured the island men before him, if she thought of her own father or brothers. Our mothers told us very little history. The only thing they spoke of was that one brief burst of passion and romance (like a sunset, like an explosion, like a fireball on the horizon) that had brought us into being.

And even in this their details were sketchy. We wanted particulars: *How* did they fall in love with you? How did you know? At what moment, exactly, did it happen? How did everyone get matched up, were there enough men, were there any extras, and if so were they sad to be left out? How had our fathers managed to be clever enough, or fertile enough, to father so many children in so short a time? Were they particularly talented that way? Did they promise to return? Did they send letters?

Our mothers folded up their lips at these questions, which convinced us that they were still pining for our fathers, after all these years. Our mothers seemed content with their lives except for this one thing, this longing for the men who had fallen from the sky like angels in dirty boots. Sometimes in her sleep my mother was angry; she thrashed and cursed. What was she cursing? The sea, the sirens, the war, whatever it was that had taken my father Joe away from her.

In the mornings she would gaze at me with slitted eyes, I suppose because I reminded her of him. At least my name did.

We girls did not look like our mothers. Our hair, our eyes; we resembled one another much more than we resembled them. For a long time we thought our mothers looked different simply because they were so much older than us.

Since our birthdays all clustered around the same month, we girls celebrated them all at once, a week-long rumpus in the spring. Our mothers granted us complete freedom to eat what we liked, smash what we wanted. One year we were all fascinated with fire, and our mothers let us keep bonfires

burning through the night. They made us earrings and neck-
laces of seashells and streaked our faces black and red with
soot and ancient lipsticks. We screamed and chased the tail-
less dogs and frightened one another with our war paint.

After a week of this, we were ready to settle back into
another year of obedience.

My mother told me the story of those dogs. She said that
once, long ago, all the island dogs had tails. But then one dog
lost her tail in a fight and so mourned the loss of it that when
she saw the other dogs waving their beautiful plumy tails she
became madly jealous and attacked them one by one and
chewed off their tails. This jealousy continued for generations, the bitter old female dogs attacking every proud feath-
ery tail they saw. Some mother dogs chewed off their own
puppies' tails, to spare them the wrath of the older dogs. And
soon puppies were born without tails altogether, to save themselves the trouble of losing them later.

She told me this story to try to explain why we girls had to
wear identical clothes, why we were not allowed to have anything particularly our own.

.   .   .

As we grew older, we grew restless and uneasy. We pestered
our mothers with the same questions. We fought one another,
not physically but with words and cutting looks and secret
alliances. I could not bear John anymore; she was so big and
loud and rough, and the green eyes sunk deep in her face were
always sneering beneath brows that made a perfectly straight
line across her forehead, no curve to them at all. I could not
believe I had once wanted her as a best friend.

"Look at Joe," she would say. "Look at that hair under your
arms, Joe. What happened, did it get lost trying to find its way
to your head? Even your *hair* is stupid."

Michael had hair there too, and so did Tyler, but it was no use arguing with John.

We were all tense, waiting for something. We slept lightly, woke up early in the mornings, paced the beaches, leaving tangles of footprints. We crouched on our ledge and watched the boys. From this distance they looked small enough to crush between a finger and thumb. Tiny, yet we could see how weathered and brown they were.

We were waiting for something. I think we were waiting for our fathers to come back. To come back and embrace our mothers and make them smile, and to look at us and admire us and say, Look how you've grown! Our fathers would pat us on the heads. No, that was not right, we were too old for that. Would they clasp our hands? Touch our cheeks? Maybe they would put their arms around us and embrace us. But not the same way they would embrace our mothers, of course.

We looked to the horizon, waiting for our fathers, and we were also waiting for men of our own, men who would come to us like gifts from the sky and fall in love with us. We thought of these men, and combed our hair in the sun, and rubbed sand on our heels to smooth the rough skin. Our men had vague faces. We could not quite picture them, they were not like the tiny boys running antlike on the beach, and they did not have the stark hawklike faces of our mothers. They were something beautiful and other. They would come, one for each of us, no squabbling, no sharing. And we would not let them get away. We would find a way to keep them.

"Put him in the bottom of a well," Donny said.

"Burn his boat," said John.

"Clip his wings," said Michael, who still did not quite understand about the parachutes our mothers described in their stories.

And the thought of these men who would come to us, *our* men, got confused with the thought of our fathers returning.

Our men, our fathers: the ideas became mixed up in our minds; they meshed and merged until they became one thing, a single man who would arrive and solve everything and ease the restlessness that made us wander in circles at night.

The island now seemed so small.

.   .   .

One night when I couldn't sleep I slipped out of the house and went down to the beach. There was a warm wind blowing, like a giant's breath in my face. The sky was dark and clear, and the water glowed. I saw someone hunched on the sand near me. It was John.

It was too quiet, the night was too smooth and peaceful to argue. I put my hand on her shoulder. She had plaited her hair into four orange braids that stuck out in four different directions and she was chewing on the end of one. We looked at each other and without a word started walking across the island, to the forbidden beach on the other side.

We walked briskly, swinging our arms, our breath loud in the quiet. We panted climbing uphill, then grunted and cursed and whispered warnings to each other as we scrambled down the rocks on the other side.

It was not as far away as it had looked.

Their beach was not so different from ours. It was the same gentle curve. But the wind came from a different direction here, it pushed against our backs rather than blowing in off the sea.

We saw a fire, and we saw two heads, two sets of shoulders, two long narrow backs casting longer shadows across the sand.

We walked toward them. They watched us coming. It seemed to take a long time.

The bigger boy was one of the ones who looked like John,

his hair was the same color, and he had the same strange eye-brows that looked as if they had been drawn with a ruler. The smaller one had dark wet hair. He must have been swimming. He had his shirt off; his nipples looked like raisins. I had no idea what to say.

John marched into the light. "We've been watching you," she said. "Running around on the beach like a bunch of idiots. Don't you have anything better to do?" Her voice was loud, but I could tell she was nervous.

I stepped away from her. I did not want to be associated with her. I tried to pretend I had come from an entirely differ-ent direction, and that I didn't even know who she was.

She folded her arms, planted her feet. The bigger boy looked at her calmly. "We've seen you spying on us," he said. "We don't mind, if it gives you a thrill."

John said, "Don't flatter yourselves. You're not so great to look at."

"Like I said, we know you do it. And we don't mind. If we did, we'd make you stop," the bigger boy said.

"You couldn't make us do anything," John said. "We're not afraid of you."

I bent one knee, stuck my hand in my pocket. I was being casual, not like John.

The smaller one faced me and said, "We go look in your houses sometimes. When you're asleep. We look in the win-dows, just for practice. You know, working on our stealth maneuvers." He had a higher voice than his friend; it was eager and breathy.

"You do not," John said.

"We do too," the tall one said. He had thick hair on his legs. And I liked his feet, they were so big and bony.

"Prove it," I said.

"Well," said the big one and pointed at John, "*she* still sleeps with a kind of doll, a raggedy thing in a sort of red dress. She sleeps *hugging* it, with her thumb in her mouth."

"Liar," John said. Even in the flickering firelight I could see she was blushing. "When we tell our mothers and your mothers that you've been sneaking around, you'll be in trouble."

"We'll tell them you've been here, and then you'll be in just as much trouble," the little one said.

John glared at them. "Come on," she said. "Let's go."

I did not want to leave. I liked that big one, his knobby feet propped dangerously close to the fire, his slow lazy way of talking. And I liked the little one with the sleek dark head and sharp shoulder blades. I gave them half a smile, kicked a little sand at them to show I would have liked to stay. The bigger boy gave me a half wave. I turned and followed John and could feel their eyes on the backs of my legs.

"We'll come back, though, won't we?" I said.

"Maybe," John said.

"I can't wait to tell Michael," I said.

"You can't," John panted. "You can't tell anybody. We have to keep it a secret. You tell one person, and then soon everyone will know and our mothers will find out."

I knew she was right, though I didn't want to admit it.

"Besides, we can't bring anyone else with us. There were only two of them, and there's two of us, see? We *can't* bring more people."

I could not understand what she meant. "But there are lots more boys. We've seen them. Those were just the only ones who happened to be awake tonight."

"Oh, you don't get it," she said, and tossed one of her heavy braids over her shoulder.

"You didn't like them anyway," I said.

We stumbled home in the dark before dawn. We disliked and distrusted each other as much as ever, but the secret was a bond between us. I knew if I told it, she would find a way to inflict a horrible revenge on me. And I knew she would not tell anyone else for the same reason.

.   .   .

It rained for the next three days, a soft drenching rain with no space between the drops. My mother sat at the window, chin in hand, watching the gray shimmering curtain. The fourth night was clear, and after my mother fell asleep I went down to our beach and was not surprised to find John there, staring out to sea.

"I was checking," she said. "For my father. I thought I heard him coming."

"Maybe," I said.

"Although," she said, "I've been thinking . . . when our fathers come, they *might* land on this beach, but don't you think it's just as likely that they would land on the *other* beach? It's equally likely, don't you think?"

"Yes," I said, for it was true: I had no idea in which direction the mainland lay, or where the country of our fathers was. But I did not think she needed to make these excuses.

"I think we should go over to the boys' beach. Not to see those nasty boys. Just to check for our fathers. I have a feeling they might come tonight."

"Fine," I said. She could tell herself whatever reasons she wanted.

We found the two boys sitting at their fire again. They were both wearing the same trousers John and I were, the trousers that had come washing up on the beach in a huge sodden mass like a beached whale the year before. They grinned at us.

John walked right up to them, arms folded, and said, "We didn't come here to see you. We're looking for our fathers. They might be landing here." Her voice was much too loud.

The red-haired boy leaned back on his hands. "You can sit down, if you want," he said. "What makes you think your fathers are coming here?"

"They should be coming back soon. And they might come from that direction."

"Why would your father want to come back?" he said.

"Because he loves me," she said automatically.

He cocked his head at her. "He doesn't even know you exist. How could he love you?"

"When he comes here and sees me, then he will."

He looked at me. "Is your father coming back too?"

"They'll come back for our mothers," I said. "If not for us, then for our mothers. They love our mothers, for sure."

"They do?"

"Yes, they love our mothers, and our mothers still love them; it's all they think about. Your mothers too."

"Who told you that?"

I came closer. "My mother . . . all our mothers. All the mothers say that."

He reached out and grabbed me, fingers tight around my wrist. "I'll tell you something," he said. "Love doesn't have a thing to do with it. Our mothers and fathers didn't even know each other. Our fathers came in here, and our mothers couldn't stop them, the fathers had guns and they came in here and did whatever they wanted, with whoever they wanted, as often as they felt like it. It was war, see, and what were our mothers going to do about it? What could they do? They didn't know who the fathers were, they didn't want to know, they tried not to look when it was happening. The fathers went from house to house, one after the other. They lined up, took turns, all efficient and orderly. Our mothers were glad when the fathers finally left. They hated our fathers and wanted to forget all about them. Then we were born, you and me and the rest, all of us with our fathers' faces. So we remind them of the one thing they'd like to forget."

John stood with her mouth open.

"You're lying," I said, jerking my arm. "My mother loved my father. She named me after him."

He said, "She doesn't even know who he is. He might be any one of ten soldiers. Or twenty."

"She's not making it up. *You* are."

"Why do you think you live on your side of the island and we live on ours? Our mothers don't want us to mix. They're afraid of mixing blood. For all I know, you could be my sister. Or—ugh—*she* could." He waved his arm at John.

I looked at him. I looked at John. I looked again.

"He's right," the little dark-haired one said.

"Haven't you ever caught your mother looking at you strange, like she hates you? She's thinking of what those men did to her," said the other.

"Let go my wrist," I said.

"They don't ever want it to happen again. That's why they watch you so carefully."

"Come on," John said, her voice gravelly. This time I followed her without looking back.

We climbed the hills in the dark. We were both panting, hard. From the exercise, that's all. "He's lying," John told me. "He's a big liar. He was lying the other night too, remember? When he said he peeked in the windows. When he said I still sleep with Bunny. That was a huge lie." She gave a disgusted snort. "We won't go back there anymore."

"He said—"

"Our fathers *are* coming. Don't you believe that? They'll be coming, bringing us presents and stories, and they'll stay and make our mothers happy, and we'll all be able to sleep through the night, and you'll regret that you ever doubted them."

"Maybe that boy was right."

"What would your father think, Joe? He'd be so disappointed to hear you say that."

I had no idea what my father would think. About anything. The next day, when I asked my mother for the hundredth time if he had loved her, she said, "Of course," but she said it mechanically and did not meet my eyes.

When I pestered her she gestured to the top shelf of the whatnot in the corner, the shelf that was almost like a shrine, with the stale package of cigarettes, the dried and mummified chocolate bar in its silver foil, the helmet liner he had left behind. A photograph so old and damaged by his journey on the sea that you could not make out much more than his hands, the buttons on his uniform.

"What more proof do you want?" she said.

"But did he love you?" I persisted. "How did you know?"

"I could tell. By the look in his eyes. Eyes can't lie." I must have looked unconvinced, because she said, "Look at me. Can't you see how I love you?"

I looked into her eyes as they traveled over my face, pausing here and there. I saw something huge and violent in her, something wonderful and terrible, and I could not really say if it was love or something very different.

John and I did not go back to the far beach, and we did not tell anyone about the boys and what they had said. I thought about it, and I know John did too; it festered in us and we were miserable and suspicious, and sometimes I wanted to tell someone, to get the awful weight off my chest. Not Michael. Michael was still my best friend, but she was not very bright and would not understand. Usually this made her a very satisfactory friend, very pliant and agreeable, but now I did not want that.

So John and I brooded and sulked until the other girls noticed and teased us about it, and we thought about telling our mothers or doing something equally drastic. But then, luckily, something happened, something that seemed so wonderful we forgot all about those boys and their midnight stories.

. . .

Donny came running to me one morning, her black hair sticking out in all directions and her face shiny with suppressed excitement. "Don't tell your mother," she said, "but come down to the beach right away."

As soon as I could I slipped away from our garden and climbed over the dunes. The sun was strong, the sky a hard metallic blue. The waves were strong today; they had thrown up big clots and tangles of seaweed on the beach. I saw the other girls grouped in a circle around something near the water's edge. Some stood, some were crouching. Every now and then one of them would lean forward, then recoil with a squeal. I came closer and saw they were prodding it with sticks.

"What is it?" I said.

"It washed up here this morning," Michael whispered.

"*He* washed up this morning," Tyler corrected.

He was much bigger than anyone I had ever seen, taller than the tallest of the mothers. He was curled up on his side, dressed in a sodden uniform of grayish-green, bunched up in some places and torn away in others. There were straps and buckles, flaps and buttons and zippers. The helmet had slipped down low over the face so that all you could see were the tip of a nose and some lips flopping open. No shoes; I saw one gray sock and one long bony fishbelly-white foot, the nails blue. One hand lay outstretched, palm up. The girls were poking that hand, squealing when the fingers twitched.

"He's not dead yet," Donny said proudly.

"How do you know it's a he?" I said. "Let's turn it over and see."

"John said so," Donny said.

"How do you know?" I said. I put my hand on the shoulder and started to push. The other girls were afraid to touch him.

He was heavy, I pushed and pushed until he flopped over on his back. The chest shifted ever so slightly; the briny breath gasped in and out.

"I just *know*," John said. I looked up at her. She had a strange calm look on her face. "I know who it is. Take off his helmet," she said.

I started loosening the chin straps. The other girls backed away. Finally I took out my knife and cut through them, and lifted away the helmet and water poured out. His hair was full of tiny silver fish that writhed and shone in the sun. We could see his face now, the swollen purple eyelids and blood-less lips, the short dark hairs bristling out of the pores on his face.

I looked again at John. The sun was behind her; her hair made a fiery halo around her head. Her eyes were wide and teary; she looked angelic and holy as she held out her arms. "It's my father," she said, in a hushed theatrical voice. "It's my father. You came back." And she dropped to her knees and touched the one bare foot.

Something shifted in my gut when she said that.

I looked at her again and suddenly she did not look holy at all, she looked overdramatic and foolish. Her hair was a mess and her nose was running as she whimpered and cradled that ugly dirty drowned foot in her lap. I put my hands on the man's face, peeling back the closed lids, stroking the wiry eye-brows, putting my fingers inside the hairy tunnels of his nose, the wet cave of his mouth. His stubbled cheeks felt like coarse sand. I put my hand down his throat, to see how far I could reach. He started to gag.

"Get your hands off my father," John said.

I ignored her, and turned his head to the side so that he could vomit salty water onto the sand.

"Don't touch him," she said.

I buried my fingers in his dark slimy hair, and with my

right hand I gripped his jaw. John hung onto the foot and yanked. I pulled back. The eyes popped open all by themselves and stared up at me. They were pretty eyes, I thought: gray, with a ring of yellow around the pupil.

The other girls were watching us. Then all at once they came forward and they all put their hands on him, they each snatched at an arm or leg or a handful of wet uniform and hung on.

"He's *my* father," Donny said, and we all began to pull.

"How do you know? He could be mine!"

"He's mine, he's mine, I know it, I can tell," John shouted.

We pulled and tugged, the body jerking about as if he were having a seizure. The cloth of the uniform was rotten with seawater; it began to fall apart. I looked down at the face in my hands and saw new blood on his mouth. He must have bitten his tongue by mistake in the tussle. I felt a little bad about it.

I hung on, but some of the other girls were losing their grip on the smooth, slimy skin. They were digging in with their fingernails, or reaching and grasping for a better hold. Michael saw a convenient sort of handle protruding from the middle of his body, and she snatched at it. That was when he let out a scream.

The scream startled us, shook us out of the brawl. We let go of him and backed away shamefacedly. Even John. The man lay looking up at us, rocking, then flopped over on his belly. He seemed to be trying to roll back into the sea.

"Where's his boat?" we asked.

"Where's his parachute?"

"Where are the others?"

"Look," Donny said.

A small white package had fallen from one of his pockets. John picked it up. A pack of cigarettes. Crushed and waterlogged but still intact in its plastic wrapper.

"That settles it," John said. "This is just like the ones he gave my mother. She still has them at home. This proves it."

"But my mother has some just like that," Donny said.

"So does mine," the others said.

"We'll have to share him," I said. "Maybe after a while he'll remember whose father he is. He'll have to be the one to tell us. But until then he belongs to *all* of us. All right?" I looked at John. She nodded grudgingly.

So we brought him to our clubhouse, dragging him across the sand. We piled blankets on top of him, built a fire, and watched him shiver and bare his teeth in his sleep. We did not want to tell our mothers. We knew they would be happy to see him, but we wanted to keep him to ourselves for just a little while longer.

Also I wanted to help him recover his strength a little. Because though I knew our mothers would be very glad to see him, overjoyed, I thought they might also be a tiny bit peeved. Just a *little* angry at being neglected for nearly fifteen years. I knew what they were like when they were angry. So I wanted to be sure he was strong enough to withstand both their enthusiastic welcome and their tempers.

I knew he was my father. I could tell, right from the start. It was the way his eyes always lingered on me a little longer than the rest. I could tell. He felt familiar, he looked at me as if he'd known me for years. I did not say anything about it to the others; it would only make them jealous. It would only make them feel sad to know that my father had cared enough to come home and theirs had not.

I was certain, but I kept the knowledge to myself. I was content to sit in our clubhouse and watch him sleep, touch his hair, and count his fingers and toes as if he were a newborn baby.

It was perfectly obvious to me, but from the start John staked her claim. She spent as much time with him as she could without her mother noticing her absence. She hovered over him, always talking, trying to get him to speak to her, give her some sign.

She changed. She became serenely happy; we could not rouse her out of it. She went about with her hands folded and a saintly smile on her face. It was infuriating. I had liked her better when she was loud and rough.

I could not tell whether he did not understand us or whether he simply chose not to speak. Or perhaps he could not really see us; perhaps he thought we were hallucinations. In the beginning his eyes were often bright with fever. Perhaps he thought we were dreams come to life. For surely he had thought about us, about *me,* over the years. Surely he had felt guilty for abandoning his little daughter; surely he thought of me and dreamed of me over the years and now that I was actually here he could hardly believe it. Perhaps he was speechless with disbelief, with happiness. It was understandable. I felt the same way.

We brought him food every day. He smiled at us more and more.

"Yesterday he said his name was Donny," Donny said. "That proves it. He's mine." But nobody believed her.

"He likes me best," Michael whispered to me. "I know it. He holds my hand. I shouldn't tell the other girls, should I? It would only make them feel bad."

"Yes, you're right," I told her, thinking, She is even stupider than I thought.

He did not speak, but he liked to sit in the sun. He could not walk, there was something wrong with his legs, we could not tell what. He watched us curiously. His sweat had its own particular smell, not like ours. The hair on his face grew and grew. We tried to trim it with scissors. He sat still with his hands in his lap and let us do whatever we wanted. His hair was coarse and wavy, chestnut brown.

John insisted it was reddish.

We spent less time with one another, wanting only to be alone, or alone with him.

The tense waiting feeling had not abated with his arrival; it had only gotten stronger. We were waiting for some sign from him, anything. We had so many questions, but he refused to speak.

One afternoon I crept into the clubhouse, hoping to spend some alone time with him. The light that filtered in through the plastic tarpaulin was murky, underwater blue, I could not see clearly at first. Then I saw movement in his usual corner, a dark tangle, a rhythmic rocking, a flash of bare legs. Animal panting.

"Michael!" I said. "What are you doing?"

She glanced over her shoulder, then rolled off him. She pulled up her trousers and ran outside. My father looked at me, sat up stiffly, gave me his usual meaningless smile.

I chased Michael and caught her arm. "What were you doing with him?"

"Nothing," she said. "A game. He likes it."

"You can't do that anymore. Your mother will kill you if she finds out."

"Why? Our mothers did it too."

"But Michael . . . ," I said.

"He loves me," she said. "He told me."

"You're lying."

She tossed her hair. "Maybe he didn't say the words, but he means it. I can tell. He says it with his eyes."

"Michael, no, you can't do it ever again."

"Why not?" she said. "You're just jealous because he didn't pick you."

"I'm not."

"You think you're so smart. But I know more than you do."

Her hair was much longer than mine. I had never noticed

that before. It shone in the sun. And she swayed her hips as she walked. When had she learned to do that? And when had she grown so much taller than me?

She did not talk to me much after that.

Then I discovered the others were doing it too.

"It sort of hurts the first time, but then it feels nice," Anthony explained.

"But why do you do it?" I asked.

"Because we're in love," she said, surprised. "Isn't it obvious?"

I stumbled into Donny late one night as she was coming home from the beach.

"What's it like?" I asked.

"It's a lot like fighting," she said, "except that you're not angry."

"I suppose you think he loves you too?"

She patted my shoulder sympathetically. "Don't feel bad," she said. "Someday one will wash up on the beach for you."

It seemed that almost all of them had tried it. Even Tyler had tried it, Tyler who was afraid of everything: swimming, and the dark, and thunder, and her own mother.

"But what if he's your father?" I asked them all. They shrugged.

Only John, swathed in her own strange saintliness, seemed oblivious to what was happening.

I could hardly bear to spend time with my father now. I still thought of him as my father, but I was terribly disappointed in him. And he had lost his hard edges, his pretty bones. He had grown fat on our food, he had burned pink and crisp from sleeping in the sun all day. Why had he waited so long to come back? Why didn't he open his mouth and explain everything?

I watched storm clouds building. They grumbled in the

distance; the sea turned gray and nudged farther and farther up the beach.

That was the day John went to the clubhouse and discovered Michael playing that game again with my father (or was he really John's after all?). I met her as she came storming up from the beach, her hair wild around her face, her eyes shocked and glassy and the tears running down.

"It's not just Michael," I told her. "It's everyone."

"It has to stop," she said. "I'm telling my mother."

I watched her thrashing her way over the dunes, sobbing and gouging her eyes with her fists.

A moment later Michael came sauntering past. "So I guess she's gone to tell all the mothers?" she said. "Now we'll *really* have to share."

I climbed up to where our houses stood clustered on the hill. I expected to hear sounds of rejoicing, of our mothers preparing to welcome a father home. But I saw no one. The clouds were building, the light was leeching away. I went home.

I found my mother in the yard. "Did you hear?" I said.

"Yes," she said. She was searching for something on the ground.

"Aren't you glad?" I said. "That he's finally come back to you?"

She stared at me.

"Well, he *might* be my father," I said. "Couldn't he be?"

"We'll see," she said. She was searching through the stones piled at the edge of the garden, testing their weight, hefting them in practice arcs through the air. She chose one the size of a round loaf of bread, too heavy to carry in just one hand.

"You stay here," she said. "Don't you dare leave this yard."

"What are you going to do?"

"We're going to do what we should have done years ago," she said.

She headed toward the beach, and I saw that all the other mothers were also leaving their homes and following her with stones in their fists.

I wondered what they were doing. I thought perhaps they were going to build a pen for him as if he were an animal, or a tower with no door, wall him in with their stones so that he would never be able to leave them again.

I waited and waited, and the storm blew in and the rain fell, and she did not return.

I sat all night with the tiny stained photograph cupped in my hand.

The next day he was gone. The little house had been broken to pieces, and the blue tarpaulin was gone.

"You're too old now for a playhouse," my mother said.

Our mothers looked so fierce that we did not ask about him, not for months afterward.

They must not have been happy to see him after all.

.   .   .

In the weeks that followed, the other girls swelled bigger and bigger. Only John and I stayed the same. Our mothers looked at the fat girls and shook their heads, and they watched the beaches like hawks and kept us home at night.

The other girls have changed. They have become dreamy and contented as cows; they sit for hours with their hands folded on their bellies, comparing symptoms, feeling for kicks. John and I can find nothing to say to them anymore.

Perhaps we feel left out, John and I. Because in a few months' time they will all give birth, to a passel, a posse, a litter of children who all look like sisters and brothers. And this island will be more than ever an island of mothers.

Hopefully we will not be here to see it. Because these days, whenever we can, we slip away from the watchful eyes of our mothers and take our tools and go to the other side of the island, where the boys who might or might not be our brothers are building a boat with a mast and a sail, and oars for each of us.

acknowledgments

For assisting in the birth of this book, I would like to express my thanks to the National Endowment for the Arts, the Fine Arts Work Center in Provincetown, Robin Desser and Diana Tejerina at Knopf, Leigh Feldman, Kristin Lang, and Philip Gwyn Jones. Special thanks are due to my incredibly supportive family, and to my husband, Jeff.

a note about the author

Judy Budnitz grew up in Atlanta and attended Harvard University. She was a fellow at the Provincetown Fine Arts Work Center and received her MFA in creative writing from New York University. Her stories have appeard in *The New Yorker, Harper's Magazine, Story, The Paris Review, Glimmer Train, Fence,* and *McSweeney's.* She is the author of *Flying Leap,* a collection of stories, which was a *New York Times* Notable Book in 1998, and the novel *If I Told You Once,* which was short-listed for the Orange Prize in the United Kingdom and won the Edward Lewis Wallant Award in the United States. Budnitz is also the recipient of an O. Henry Award and a National Endowment for the Arts Fellowship. She lives in San Francisco.

a note on the type

This book was set in Fairfield, the first typeface from the hand of the distinguished American artist and engraver Rudolph Ruzicka (1883–1978). In its structure Fairfield displays the sober and sane qualities of the master craftsman whose talent has long been dedicated to clarity. It is this trait that accounts for the trim grace and vigor, the spirited design and sensitive balance, of this original typeface.

Composed by Creative Graphics, Allentown, Pennsylvania

Printed and bound by R. R. Donnelley & Sons, Harrisonburg, Virginia

Designed by Iris Weinstein